Help Thy Neighbor

To Pat Fersch
With thanks for
many things
Linda

"IF I AM NOT FOR MYSELF, WHO IS FOR ME?
BUT IF I AM ONLY FOR MYSELF, WHAT AM I?"

—Hillel
Mishneh: Ethics of the Fathers, I.14

Help thy Neighbor

How Counseling Works and When It Doesn't

Linda Weingarten Scheffler, Ph.D.

Grove Press, Inc./New York

First Hardcover Edition 1984
First Printing 1984
ISBN: 0-394-53504-9
Library of Congress Catalog Card Number: 83-48300

First Evergreen Edition 1984
First Printing 1984
ISBN: 0-394-62495-5
Library of Congress Catalog Card Number: 83-48300

Library of Congress Cataloging in Publication Data

Scheffler, Linda Weingarten.
Help thy neighbor.

1. Counseling 1. Title
BF637.C6S29 1983 158'.3 83-48300
ISBN 0-394-53504-9
ISBN 0-394-62495-5 (pbk.)

Manufactured in the United States of America

GROVE PRESS, INC., 196 West Houston Street, New York, N.Y. 10014

In appreciation of the

BALD EAGLE

Contents

Preface

Help Thy Neighbor is a book for the layman about counseling and psychotherapy, which are usually regarded as exclusive prerogatives of professionals. Psychotherapeutic principles and practices were developed by experts in such fields as medicine, psychology, and social work for treating the mentally ill; they have been largely restricted to those undertaking long and arduous postgraduate training for the mental health specialties. There are good reasons to limit the knowledge and use of therapeutic skills to those qualified to use them, but there are also compelling reasons not to do so.

Psychological distress is not always a consequence of mental illness, as was first imagined. Psychological problems and emotional difficulties are common everyday occurrences. Although essentially "normal" and not indicative of a disease process, these ordinary upheavals are nonetheless painful and alarming; if not adequately resolved, they continue to affect and damage the quality of many lives. Furthermore, people not handicapped by mental illness respond better to psychotherapeutic practices than do the mentally ill for whom many of the methods were originally intended.

Counseling is more efficient and effective, and its results more lasting, for people adapting to developmental and situational crises—trying to decide on binding commitments, coping with the loss of loved ones, and undergoing other stressful but common challenges. The chronically ill are, unfortunately, just that—chronically ill. Since our limited professional resources have never been adequate to cope with the relatively small number of mentally ill, mental health practitioners are—and always will be—hopelessly outnumbered by the "normals" who can also benefit from their practices. Who can help to fill this chasm?

We are all currently witnessing a distressing phenomenon. Narcissism and self-involvement seem pervasive in our society; mental health professionals have become alarmed at many signs of self-absorption and indifference to others. Yet, many current bestsellers, often written by professional therapists, instruct the public in techniques of self-assertion, self-promotion, personal enhancement and gratification, and how to get ahead of others. Are we a people who care nothing for our fellow man, our neighbors, our peers?

Fortunately, there is evidence to the contrary. Most people are grateful for an opportunity to help others. There has been startling growth recently in: peer counseling programs within all our major institutions; "mutual-help" associations (estimated by the National Institute of Mental Health to number 500,000 in the United States) in which people with similar problems help each other in a variety of ways; and community organizations providing advising and counseling services through nonprofessional personnel as in suicide "hot lines," Big Brothers, and rape crisis centers. Still more individuals, on their own and outside of any identifiable group, try to help their employees, or their students, or their colleagues, or their friends with psychological problems. Since they have frequently coped with somewhat similar difficulties, they use their own experiences as the major tools to help others—not as professionals but as individuals who are concerned. In short, many, many people without professional training, titles, or compensation spend hours each week in the service of others, contradicting the assertion that we are a nation of narcissists.

Still, many of these volunteers are handicapped in their efforts because they have no accurate idea of what counseling is and whether they can use it beneficially. Oddly, more has been written for popular consumption by mental health professionals on how to enhance and promote self-interest than on how to help others with personal problems. Ironic as it is that psychotherapists have both encouraged self-involvement and decried it, there are obvious reasons why professionals do not promulgate the principles of psychotherapy for a general audience. They are not just protecting trade secrets; counseling is a powerful relationship which can harm as well as help. To anticipate and avoid all its dangers, extensive training is required. In addition, therapeutic skills are complex and intertwined, and they cannot easily be translated into "how-to-do-it" terms. Professionals have written books for new and future professionals, but since there are ways for laymen to help others short of counseling, these nonprofessionals are expected to confine themselves to constructive acts which require no special training, and refrain from those called counseling or psychotherapy.

But how is this expectation to be fulfilled if all the layman understands about counseling is that it is an activity reserved for the professional? Where does "helping" stop and "counseling" begin? The expectation makes little sense also, in view of the fact that, as identifiable entities, the mental health professions are barely more than a century old. All psychological assistance was rendered by "nonprofessionals" just a century ago. Moreover, the injunction that "only professionals do it" contradicts the experience of anyone who has surmounted a personal crisis with help extended by an interested peer or concerned nonprofessional. Therapeutic talent is not limited to those holding professional credentials; we recognize it in our neighbors and we turn to them more readily than to professionals. If professionals cannot provide training for all those who wish to help their neighbors with psychological problems, they can at least explain the risks and the realities of the counseling role in a way that lay persons can understand.

Help Thy Neighbor, which describes the counseling relationship in all its complexity, is not a textbook. It helps differentiate counseling from other helping acts and investments. Contrary to many popular notions, counseling is not a costly version of friendship or parenting or any other familiar relationship, nor is it the same as advice or information-giving. Because counseling is different from other relationships, some of our natural helping impulses can undermine it. By exploring these confusions, *Help Thy Neighbor* describes the counseling relationship in human rather than technical terms, using simple concepts to explain the demands and dynamics of the therapeutic role. It treats counseling as a serious, demanding, and time-consuming responsibility for which professionals are much better prepared, but it also explains the misconceptions and confusions that spoil the well-intentioned efforts of nonprofessionals and beginners.

Educational materials currently available for laymen who counsel do not address their special needs. More is written for a general audience on how to be a client or how to choose a therapist than on how to be a counselor. Even professional literature written for the novice does not address the issues that concern those who want to counsel but do not yet have or do not expect credentials in counseling. This book is intended to fill the educational gap. Using explanations, examples, and exercises, *Help Thy Neighbor* provides laymen with guidelines and helps them cope with their distinct problems—of identity, of determining their effectiveness and limitations, and of establishing realistic goals and expectations.

Another type of educational material available to students and nonprofessionals is the training manual which dissects the helping process into separate skill components such as eye contact, posture, voice quality, and question phrasing. Readers who master the components are presumed to be able to act "like" good counselors. This approach can sensitize students to certain behaviors which help or hinder communication, but putting these rules into practice can also be distracting and anxiety-provoking: "Am I maintaining good eye contact?" "Did I phrase that question in a nonthreatening tone?" "Is my posture too stiff?" By raising mechanistic questions about an essentially human process, the "skills" manuals focus on the method rather than the meaning of counseling.

Counseling has an emotional significance to its participants. Psychodynamic factors influence interchange and outcome no matter how correctly the skills are performed. The most obvious of these dynamic factors is that while it may be more blessed to give than to receive, it is also a lot more gratifying—psychologically! The role of help recipient or client is one that most of us find distasteful. Counselors who focus primarily on practicing skills correctly are likely to miss the inevitable expressions of resentment and resistance from those needing help. If unrecognized, these feelings will sabotage the human helping alliance.

As a clinical psychologist and instructor of college and community counselors, I have seen impressive therapeutic talent displayed by people with little or no professional training. And I respect the enormous potential of the many nonprofessionals who wish to and can offer help with psychological problems that are beyond the reach of the mental health specialist. But as a professional practicing for twenty years, and still learning, I believe that nonprofessionals need special help. They need a comprehensible guide to the psychological concepts, risks, and rewards in counseling. They may or may not wish to undertake the demanding responsibility of counseling once they understand its dimensions, but they need not be mystified by technical language or reduced to performing component skills like robots.

There are problems in trying to inform the lay counselor. Since helpers vary so much in personal style, in aspiration, in abilities, in motivation for helping, in problems which attract them, and also in the settings in which they work, a written guide which tries to address them all has its limitations. There are problems even in the terms employed: Is the help recipient a client, a patient, a member of a mutual-help group, an interviewee, a peer, a neighbor, or just Mary, my friend? Readers will have to stretch to make terms used here fit their circumstances. But a bigger problem still is that effectiveness in counseling depends on counselors' self-awareness. Self-awareness, the best asset a counselor can have, is enhanced in professional training by case supervision which melds counseling theory with individual application. While no written material can approximate continuous expert supervision of counseling relationships, this guide does ask readers to engage in self- and/or group supervision—to participate in exercises to check the validity of the book's concepts against personal experience. It provides tools, imperfect as they may be, for increasing self-awareness and for examining personal motives and expectations. At relevant points, readers are advised to review their own reactions to helping and to being helped and to measure their efforts against professional standards.

The plan and objectives of this book reflect the philosophy and teaching method of a graduate (Masters) program, College Counseling and Student Development, at Hunter College of the City University of New York. This program admits students who are judged to have good counseling potential on the basis of personal interviews, rather than by more typical academic criteria. Those accepted learn counseling by performing helping functions immediately—they learn by doing. Course work is designed to supplement and supervise their extensive fieldwork. Since their important achievements and failures occur primarily with clients rather than in the classroom, their experiences more closely resemble that of peers, volunteers, paraprofessionals, and other nonprofessionals than those whose education is largely academic. Even though the trainees have professional supervision, not often available to lay counselors, they nonetheless learn their most important lessons while struggling with their own and their clients' problems. In some ways the students of the C.C.S.D. program—and their clients—have written this book, because they taught me how difficult it is to learn to be a counselor. Many case examples in *Help Thy Neighbor* are drawn from the college setting, but since counseling is not a parochial undertaking, they illustrate universal points. As a result of my experience as a therapist and supervisor of counselors—both in and out of the university—I have begun to regard counseling, not as a technical expertise, but as a human alliance of unusual dimensions often misunderstood by the public, by clients, and by would-be counselors.

In summary, *Help Thy Neighbor* is focused less on models of "perfect" counseling than on the obstacles and difficulties with which all counselors—professionals and nonprofessionals—have to struggle. It is a plain and practical primer for nonprofessionals engaged in counseling and helping others as well as for students of counseling and psychotherapy. It is intended for those who engage in peer counseling, mutual-help, and volunteer programs; for high school, college, and graduate students in counseling or community fieldwork courses; for paraprofessionals who, with limited training opportunities, work in overcrowded, understaffed institutions; and for the friends and colleagues who, in counseling their associates, find they have taken on a troublesome responsibility. It is also for those whose jobs, interests, and community activities expose them to people needing helpful human contact—a long list that includes teachers, nurses, administrators, recreation and youth leaders, and many others. It will alert the lay counselor to the special appeal and advantages, as well as the pitfalls and problems, of seeking help with psychological problems from a peer rather than from a professional. And, finally, since no one gets as much out of the process as one who knows how counseling works, it is also intended for those who receive help from counselors and psychotherapists or from their nonprofessional brethren.

One question of public interest is not addressed directly in this book: whether, considering the century's significant advances in the mental health specialties and the excellence of some professionals, nonprofessionals *should* be engaged in individual counseling. Are they good enough to function as counselors? One thing is clear: Nonprofessionals may not and should not charge money for their therapeutic services or pretend to have experience sufficient to equip them for the private practice of psychotherapy. But with that caution aside, there are simply too few professionals to help people to cope with the stressful challenges and psychological upheavals of everyday life. Though their time and their skills may be limited, lay people in great numbers are helping others. Their services are badly needed in every capacity, including that of individual counseling. Sometimes and in some places, there are no practical or professional alternatives. To help nonprofessionals do the best they can as counselors—without the professional education and supervision that might make them better yet—*Help Thy Neighbor* is intended.

Linda W. Scheffler
New York City, N.Y.
April 1983

Help Thy Neighbor

1

Counseling by Nonprofessionals or Peers

Who and Where?

Because professionals are not meeting all the needs of troubled individuals, many who are not trained for the mental health professions, but who are certain of their desire to give comfort and aid, are reaching out to offer their services. Though friends and relatives have often tried to help, now the concept has been extended to others as well. Not as experts but as peers, many people try to make a difference in the lives of others by using their own experiences and natural abilities.

These nonprofessionals work for little or no pay in community or crisis centers, on telephone hot lines, in hospital wards and institutions for the physically and psychologically disabled, and in school systems. Individually or through groups or organizations of which they are members, they work with the young, old, sick, the struggling, the abandoned and neglected. In mutual-help groups, they help others face the same challenges they confront in their own lives. Their motives vary: they may want work experience or school credits, or wish to enrich the quality of their own lives; they may work because of religious or humanistic conviction; or they may work because their own lives have made them aware of the unmet needs of others. Usually they get little or no supervision, critical evaluation or instruction, or public recognition.

Another group of nonprofessionals that try to help others are those whose jobs bring them into contact with people with problems, but whose expertise is in some other area. College department secretaries often have to deal with student problems, as do faculty advisors who may be more familiar with European History. Hospital aides, technicians, and nurses charged primarily with patients' physical well-being may have to deal with psychological distress as well. In the general community, business people, lawyers, accountants, brokers, and others without any training in psychology find themselves asked to help not only clients but also colleagues and employees with emotional problems.

In fact, more counseling of troubled individuals is conducted by people who are not trained mental health workers than by the small group trained in professional skills. Certainly the desire and the ability to be helpful are not restricted to trained professionals. Even when professionals are accessible, lay people reach out to those in trouble and use their concern and their own awareness of personal suffering as guides. In offering themselves and their experiences rather than professional training, they function as peers rather than experts. They volunteer their help and are rarely paid for their efforts as counselors.

Peer counseling makes so much sense and is so appealing that it is being introduced to virtually every segment of our society. Some systems use group meeting exclusively, but typically participants are paired to permit individual counseling, one peer to another. There is little instructional material for this vast and valuable group despite its growing number. Perhaps this is due to the disinclination or inability of professional helpers to share the secrets of the trade, or to their genuine belief that years of college and postgraduate education and training are a basic requirement. But for whatever reasons, the plain fact is that while professionally trained counselors and therapists have been active as consultants to special groups, they have not made information available to all. These limited professional efforts and the limited number of professionals have left many without guidance.

The Appeal of Counseling Peers

Counseling peers is a process of guiding another person like oneself through difficulties one knows from experience. It seems an appealing and gratifying prospect. Saving others from repeating one's errors, dispelling some of the loneliness and terror of an unfamiliar route, reaching out to extend a firm hand—these are appealing to those who feel pride in having negotiated a difficult passage or known similar distress. Who could be more helpful than one who has already been there? Firsthand experience and the inclination to help others seem sufficient qualifications for assisting others with similar problems.

Thus in schools, upper-class students, remembering their first uncertain steps and disappointments, reach out with confidence to protect new students from institutional or self-inflicted wounds. They feel uniquely suited as mentors; not part of the administration of the institution, they need not defend or report to it, and they know the student experience firsthand. The potential of peer counseling is so clearly recognized that most schools and colleges offer not one but a variety of opportunities for students to help peers in educational and personal adjustment. Structured as a learning task, peer counseling can earn credit toward graduation and employment and form the basis for vocational choice. Atypical students—those who have returned to college after years of homemaking and child-rearing, military service, or employment—are in a special position to help others like themselves make the transition of returning to school. For minorities and other special groups—homosexuals, racial, religious, cultural, and sexual minority members, handicapped and foreign-born individuals—support networks and individual relationships developed therein make a vital difference.

Those who have suffered traumatic experiences such as rape, the death of a child or other bereavement, imprisonment, and other personal catastrophes, often find similar comfort in forming support groups, providing contact between members. In the New York City area alone, there are groups for the disabled and for the parents of the disabled, parents of exceptional children and those with learning handicaps, people recovering from emotional illness, those who are incurably ill or who have lost important family members to such disease, people who have undergone surgical trauma, patients with persistent, chronic, and serious illness and their families, and people in difficult circumstances—abused women, mothers of twins, single parents, and remarried parents, to name a few.

Counseling is also provided by people who have overcome addictions to alcohol, drugs, gambling, and overeating. Experienced in the ruses and excuses addicts use, the formerly addicted helper is also available at all hours, in person or by telephone, when most professionals are "off duty." This model of mutual help has spawned many profitable nationwide businesses and attracted funding from government and private sources to develop model projects to treat still other social problems.

There is another group of people, not normally considered peer counselors, but they are: students of counseling and other mental health specialties. At the end of their education and training they will be professionals, but at the beginning, the work they do with clients is based more on their personal experience, their natural inclinations, and their ideas about helping than on the theories and techniques they will master in the course of professional education.

Finally, there is the telephone "hot line." Although initially designed to reach suicidal individuals during the desperate hours of the night, the "hot line" is now in almost universal use. Its anonymity permits counseling on issues considered embarrassing or shameful—sex, birth control, marital problems, or difficulties coping with academic or personal pressures. Its availability and convenience permits contact with those confined to home—housewives, the elderly, schoolchildren, and the disabled. Requiring minimal expense and space, these services also offer an impersonal quality that reassures hesitant and ambivalent help-seekers. The hot line volunteers may be less obviously linked to the caller by common personal experience than is the ex-addict to the addict, but frequently these individuals have had first-hand and disturbing experience with the topic prompting the callers. They may, for instance, have experienced a similar problem or had a family member who did.

The mutual-help movement is large and growing rapidly here and throughout the world. It makes sense to seek help from someone experienced with the problem. Lost in a city or a train station, we look for an experienced traveler for accurate directions. Struggling with personal difficulty, we are reassured to find another who has coped with the same trouble. When family members or friends are insufficient, or unavailable, or seem likely to disapprove, we want counseling from someone like ourselves, a stranger perhaps, but someone who "has been there."

In using peers rather than professional resources, the help-seeker believes he or she will be spared the awesome spectres of financial expense, public exposure, and age, sex, ethnic, or role barriers. The peer or colleague who volunteers is seen as free of dubious motives: financial profit, disapproval, or allegiance to a system or organization which is sometimes perceived by the help-seeker as the source of his or her problem. A peer, another human being, who has experienced the same feelings and problems is likely to sympathize rather than impose a set of values or demands. Furthermore, individuals who are beset by persistent and troubling experiences often endure a sense of isolation from others. They become hesitant to burden family members or friends with the pain that daily disturbs their lives, and they feel, perhaps correctly, that professionals cannot mitigate the distress of a permanent loss or condition. Joining together with others who face, or have faced, similar hardship permits a sense of community and belonging, and shared suffering takes away some of the sting. All these features, as well as the desire to help others, make peer counseling an appealing alternative to traditional forms of treatment for psychological distress.

On the basis of shared experience, persons untrained in counseling skills can do much for one another. They can gather and disseminate information, share personal experiences and express private concerns, provide services and support, meet in social or task-oriented groups, and pool resources to effect political and social change. These are constructive activities, helpful and therapeutic in the broadest sense, and usually without risk to participants. But by design in some groups and in the course of such activity in others, members are often called upon to help others individually with personal and psychological problems. Overwhelmed and floundering, one member will turn for more extensive assistance to another who, despite similar adversity, seems strong, concerned, and sensitive. Many groups assign an "old" member to each new arrival to be a confidant, a buddy, a friend-in-need, an advisor, a counselor. In these one-to-one arrangements, the risk to participants is greater. When on the basis of shared experience, individuals function as counselors or therapists, they are handicapped by their lack of professional training in counseling skills. Wanting to help any way they can, they are often not aware that they have assumed the role of therapist, because it is difficult for anyone but a professional to differentiate the role of counselor from other types of assistance. But the amateur, willing or not, will be entrapped in the same complex demands exerted on a professional therapist. The nonprofessional not only lacks the preparation to perform the role knowledgeably but the guidelines to know where the line should be drawn. *A relationship established to affect or influence the direction of a person's life, behavior, or feelings is a therapeutic relationship, even if it is called by some other name.*

The Troublesome Assumption

In some ways a therapeutic relationship is complicated rather than aided by participants sharing a common problem, illness, or life experience. Peer counseling participants assume what professional therapists know to be false: that shared characteristics and common experience, in and of themselves, form a reliable basis for the recognition, understanding, and response to psychological problems. Shared experiences between client and counselor are often reassuring to both but they can be a source of error in the helping process. Identical experiences are resolved differently by different people, and it is often hard for someone who has chosen one resolution of a problem to accept a different solution for someone else. Close emotional involvement may distort the helper's perceptions and introduce tensions in the helping relationship. Because of these intrusions, doctors are rarely able to treat family members or intimate friends successfully; because of their attachment, they are apt to make errors and to underestimate or overestimate the importance of physical complaints. The same concerns apply in counseling.

An illustration. As a counselor in a college program for disadvantaged students during the strident days of the Black Power movement, I was surprised that some of the black students preferred white counselors. They explained that they avoided blacks in almost any helping capacity because black professionals, having "made it" the hard way, were demanding, unsympathetic, and punitive toward younger blacks who fell short of their expectations. Whether or not their perceptions were accurate, some black clients felt that common group membership would hurt them in the counseling relationship.

Typically, when nonprofessionals experience difficulties as counselors, they blame it on ineptitude or inexperience, but frequently it results from confusion about the helping process and failure to recognize the importance of objectivity. *Counseling is an activity which enables people to help themselves, not get them to do what counselors have done or want them to do.* Yet peers often have a narrow view of client options—blinders provided by their own experiences and their own solutions to personal difficulties.

Amateur counselors tend to equate "objectivity" with the distant and noncaring attitude they attribute to professionals. On the other hand, they cherish their sense of attachment and personal investment. They rarely see that emotional involvement on the part of a helper, or even a strong determination to achieve a particular counseling outcome, robs the client of self-determination and personal control. It hurts rather than enhances the helping relationship. As desperately as we may want the client to change, the will and willingness to do so comes from the client, not the counselor.

In contrast to opting for peer counseling, needing professional help implies that the client's problems are serious or unusual enough to require an expert. If a peer, a former or fellow sufferer, or a student, can provide the help, then the problem appears to be a temporary disturbance which can be resolved by attention and concern. Choosing a peer, then, entails some self-diagnosis, maybe a hope that the problem is simple enough to be alleviated by anyone who really cares. When that self-diagnosis is wrong, the peer, with high hopes for effective intervention, and the help-seeker, looking for a simple human solution, can become profoundly and destructively entrapped. Consider those familiar examples of college cheating scandals in which competent scholars are expelled for their efforts to assist their less-prepared friends.

When peers discover their help is not enough, the simple and often suggested option of referral to another counselor is a painful blow. To the counselor it means failure, to the client rejection, exposure, and disappointment. Furthermore, it is likely to fail. Referral, once the helping relationship is under way, is a difficult process even for professionals; its impact on and implications to the client need to be understood if it is to be done successfully.

Counselor, Yes! Client, No!

It may be obvious by now that there are pitfalls in peer counseling that are concealed in the same features that make it appealing and useful. Commonalities between peers permit easy access but cloud objectivity. The commonalities are often more apparent than real, and equality of status does not facilitate referral when the client's problem is beyond the peer counselor's ability. But there is still another issue. Help-giver and help-seeker have different and often divergent motives in counseling. We think of giving and taking as equivalent: one person gives, the other receives help. But for most people, giving is psychologically easier. The role of helper is gratifying: it makes us feel good; it allows us to forget our moments of vulnerability, anxiety, and difficulty, and we feel strong and useful. Those who need help are generally looked down upon as the charity cases, the welfare recipients, the needy, the "psychos," the incompetents. These are some of the words applied to people requiring help from others; few accept this role in life willingly or without shame. Even admitting a problem to a friend or colleague can be difficult, but it is easier than seeking professional attention. There is real danger that peer counseling can be an *avoidance* rather than an *acceptance* of the need for help, a detour rather than a direct route; and in those instances when peer counseling is inappropriate or insufficient, neither party may be willing or able to recognize it. This can occur when professionals counsel too, but they are alerted to these dangers by their academic training and supervision, and sensitized by their own experiences in therapy, often an additional requirement of the training process. Peer counselors are more naive about possible abuses of the helping relationship and less able to tell whether their efforts are or are not in the client's best interest.

Strange as it may seem, most people do not really want to be helped. Help through counseling often requires a basic and difficult change in ourselves. Lending ourselves to the process requires that we recognize problems beyond our means to solve; that we share our problems and our inability to handle them with another who may judge us; that we lean on another's support and perspective much as we did when we were children; and that we attempt to alter our familiar patterns of behavior. None of these are easy. Society stresses the value of independence and self-sufficiency—the capacity to solve one's problems on one's own. Our favorite hero is the pioneer who carved an existence from an inhospitable land without benefit of expert, specialist, or model. Each of us hopes to do the same. In our age of specialization we are now more accustomed to calling the plumber, glazier, or carpenter to repair objects; but when we have problems in our personal lives and relationships we feel very differently. We somehow expect to bear sorrow and disappointment without public display. We feel shame needing assistance in the conduct of our private lives. We admire strong, self-sufficient people and fear weakness and dependency. However much we want relief from our suffering and help from someone knowledgeable and experienced, we dread putting ourselves in someone else's hands. Many live in isolated misery rather than admit to problems beyond their capacity. The more we need help in daily living, the greater the discrepancy between ourselves and the standard we hold for ourselves. The more unlike ourselves the helper appears in age, experience, or acclaim, the more acute our problem seems—the more incompetent, vulnerable, and childlike we feel. We more willingly consult experts in legal, medical, or educational matters because we do not expect to be competent in technical areas. Even here we may not follow their advice unless it matches our intentions. In asking peers for help, we expect to be spared the awe and fear we feel toward the expert. We imagine ourselves gaining a friend and advisor, or at worst, an older, more experienced sibling.

In contrast to our fears of needing help is our enjoyment in helping others. It is flattering to be consulted and considered capable of assuming not only our burdens but those of others. Passing on what we have learned, sometimes the hard way, lessens the pain we have experienced. Aware of the competitiveness, selfishness, and cruelty of people, we create a different image for ourselves in helping others. Not like "them," we have compassion and concern. We are not just out for ourselves in this "dog-eat-dog" world. Sometimes nagging questions about our own personal worth are silenced by helping others. When we feel effective and appreciated, we think more of ourselves.

Peer counseling offers a great deal to its participants. It can provide understanding support at little or no cost to many not requiring or beyond the reach of the mental health professional. But while averting some problems of traditional counseling such as inaccessibility, expense, and confusion about professional qualifications and motives, it obscures a more fundamental one: the basic resistance to change. Well-meaning peers do not expect their good intentions and helping efforts to be ineffective or rejected, but they often are. They expect quick and dramatic change in their clients and become disappointed when it does not occur. They sometimes conclude they are inadequate and give up, or they try to force change to justify their efforts. Often they blame the client's motivation or attitude. They may try new methods thought to be effective in themselves rather than understanding the complex forces and counterforces in every helping relationship, peer or professional.

These days we seem to thrive on how-to-do-it books. Written guides for peer, nonprofessional, or beginning counselors tend to show how to perform helping behavior as if counseling were a mechanical process. But the human elements in the helping relationship are more troublesome than technical ones.

These psychodynamic forces, discussed in professional literature by such terms as resistance, transference, counter-transference, and the like, are complex phenomena which may seem technical to nonprofessionals. But they are, as we shall see in later chapters, basic and understandable in layman's terms. They operate not only in counseling relationships but in everyday human experience. We identify these forces by looking inside ourselves, by understanding our own motives and feelings and by applying our understanding to the helping process. Whether we understand them or not, they will affect the outcome of our efforts.

I have found a surprising feature in some peer counselors—a disrespect for the person who seeks help. Counselors-in-training sometimes show, in presenting cases for supervision, disdain for or disapproval of their clients. Their disapproval, not always fully conscious but clearly evident in their tone and description, is due simply to the fact *that the client needs help.* They see this as a weakness for which they have more contempt than empathy, especially if they have surmounted without assistance challenges similar to those facing their clients. Obviously this attitude creates problems; disapproval does little to enhance counseling effectiveness. Case supervision is probably the most direct way of helping counselors recognize interference from underlying values and stereotypes, because few of us are aware of our own. But subsequent chapters will provide exercises for self-exploration as well as examples of common attitudes which sabotage helping efforts.

In order to deal with the problems resulting from stereotypical attitudes and inexperience, some peer counseling systems limit the tasks in which peers engage. For instance, they restrict peers to counseling interventions which reflect and restate what clients say, prohibiting any expression of approval or disapproval. Or they limit peers to crude methods of behavior modification; they are trained to reward and reinforce desired behavior and ignore that which is undesirable. Or they screen clients in advance and assign to peers only those whose problems are judged within their competence.

But these methods are suited only to situations where there is professional direction, supervision, and control. These are rarely available. In more typical circumstances, nonprofessionals themselves need to understand the complexity, pitfalls, and confusions in the helping role so they, on their own, can perform the role more effectively.

Cautions for Nonprofessionals

Are there any restrictions that peer counselors should impose on themselves? The answer is yes and no. There are obvious restraints inherent in the *circumstances* and the *role* of the peer counselor. Professionals usually engage in counseling full-time and are located in a more or less permanent place or institution. Nonprofessionals are usually part-time and often temporary helpers, who leave when the course, the project, or their interest ends. Long-term and ambitious objectives are often impractical and unwise. If the inexperienced counselor cannot gauge the effort involved in trying to help a particular person, it may be possible to consult a professional for guidance.

An example. When her cousin was arrested for forging checks, an undergraduate in an abnormal psychology course suspected that the cousin's behavior matched a textbook description of pathology. She consulted her professor who agreed with her "diagnosis," and he helped her arrange a consultation for her cousin with a specialist. With this assurance, the police were willing to drop charges and release the cousin in the student's custody. While acting only as a concerned relative, the student used her knowledge to arrange a helpful and expert intervention.

Although the prospect is awesome, nonprofessionals can and do work with people considered very ill or seriously disturbed. However, they need an institutional structure and supervision to feel secure. Rarely can nonexperts work effectively in frightening circumstances or with people who make them uncomfortable, without having someone around to provide assistance. If foolhardy, they place themselves in situations which may be dangerous. When the assessment of risk is beyond one's competence, caution indicates checking with a professional.

Another caution: nonprofessional helpers, like professionals, must be careful not to undermine therapeutic relationships already established. Individuals in treatment may seek other counselors—sometimes to supplement the help they are getting, sometimes to compare and replace it. When the latter is the client's intent, the peer may be praised and the professional derided by the client. While it is flattering for the peer to be preferred, and tempting to step in, it is usually not in the client's best interest. If the client's complaints seem justified—often a difficult thing to tell—the client should tell them to the original therapist, or if that seems impossible, discuss them with another professional. An example: Volunteers, field placement students, and aides in psychiatric hospitals are often turned to when patients get angry at their assigned therapist. Both flattered by and trusting of the patient's report, they try to help the patient themselves when the problems need to be brought back to the treatment relationship to be worked through or acknowledged. The point is not to circumvent the professional relationship, but to help the patient improve it.

Outside an institution, nonprofessionals have to inquire whether someone seeking their help is or was engaged in treatment. When a client, paying for counseling, is dissatisfied, finding a free source of help may seem both a blessing and relief. When cost is a troublesome problem, it needs to be discussed with the therapist, but sometimes the reasons for turning to a peer are more complex. It is unlikely that money is the only dissatisfaction. Even when the change is from one nonprofessional to another, the counseling issue is the same. Switching or adding helpers to avoid difficulties encountered in the primary relationship may conceal resistance to change; switching lets the client avoid, rather than deal with, and perhaps resolve, problems. Clients' complaints about counselors may indicate dissatisfaction with the process rather than the person and will crop up again with the new helper. Peers can perform helping functions with clients already getting counseling from another counselor, provided the role and function of each helper is clearly defined and not overlapping.

Usually this requires cooperation and communication between helpers.

Other restraints on the activities of peers seem to me a function of individual competencies and situations. Nonprofessionals working within a particular program or system have to observe the guidelines provided or work to change them. Held responsible for the nonprofessionals they supervise, professionals may feel it necessary to minimize danger rather than enhance opportunity. All helpers must be cautious in initiating relationships with clients whose problems or situations require special intervention. Offering help implies a promise that one can be helpful, a promise that should hold possibility of being fulfilled. Someone in serious legal difficulty should have the advice of a lawyer and someone with medical difficulty should see a medical specialist even if the problem is thought to be imagined. Obviously even hypochondriacs get sick sometimes. Peers may find problems beyond their competence or power to handle, especially in the beginning, and should err on the side of caution. If they can identify more appropriate resources and help the client to reach them, they are providing a real service.

Whatever limitations are applied to or inherent in counseling by nonprofessionals, it is still a common and beneficial occurrence. This chapter has presented an overview and we will now proceed to examine the issues more closely.

Hidden Agendas and Pitfalls in Counseling by Nonprofessionals

II

Introduction

Perhaps it is a function of our language or of our hopes, that we think of counseling as a method for solving problems. It is not. Arithmetic is a method for solving problems. *Counseling is a process by which people are helped to solve their own problems.*

Counseling is not a mechanical or programmed process like adding two numbers to get a sum or computing bank interest. It is a human and complex interaction, based on the arithmetic proposition that two heads are better than one, but but having no other resemblance to automatic formulas. Although we can describe many features that contribute to effective counseling and others more or less incompatible with it, the counseling relationship is a complicated and unpredictable interaction between two personalities. There are no automatic solutions to human problems—to the feelings and experiences that determine those problems—and we get in trouble by thinking there are. Counseling relationships are jeopardized when participants think the counselor has the answers.

Although most of us know that no one can live our lives for us or tell us how to feel, we sometimes think that as counselors we can direct others. After all, we know that the solution for the problem drinker is to stop drinking; the solution for an individual unsure of what to do with his life is to choose a career; the solution for a young woman struggling with indecision is to make up her mind. To problems, there are easy solutions. For people with problems, there are no easy solutions; if there were, they would not need the help of counselors.

The Search for Acceptance

For the inexperienced helper, especially one drawn to counseling through personal experience with the same problems others are facing, the focus on solving problems and giving answers is troublesome. Peers feel able to counsel because they know the problem, not from a textbook, but from life experience. But knowing the problem—or even a "solution"—is not the same as knowing the person who has that problem or what kind of help that person needs. With full knowledge of the problem of alcoholism including experience as a problem drinker, comprehensive study of the subject, and contact with hundreds of drinkers, a person may still not be able to help one alcoholic stop drinking. Sometimes thinking of someone as an "alcoholic," rather than a person who has a problem handling alcohol, is, in itself, a counseling mistake. *Treating the problem without treating the person is an error with undesirable consequences.*

One consequence of focusing on the problem, especially a familiar one, is the tendency to assume we know more about the person with the problem than we really do. Having experienced the same problem is much like sharing the same geographical area, religion, occupation, gender, or sexual orientation. There is a common frame of reference and perhaps a common core of experience. But, obviously, not all New Englanders, not all Jews, not all chemical engineers, not all women, and not all homosexuals are alike; nor are all people who share a common problem. Few generalizations prove true for all members of any group, so the problem does not tell much about the person. People seek out others who have had similar problems or experiences in the hope that they will be *understood* and *accepted.* They also assume that a person who has found *a* solution has found *their* solution, but this is rarely true.

Another consequence of focusing on the problem is that the counselor feels responsible for solving the problem. But counselors can rarely solve others' psychological problems. They can help people solve their own problems—help them assess responsibility for their circumstances, help them explore available options, identify their strengths, and support their efforts in understanding and working through their difficulties—all important contributions. *But it is neither the counselor's responsibility nor power to resolve the problem; only the client can do that.*

Few clients understand how much of the effort and responsibility in counseling is really theirs. They come expecting great and impossible things of those who want to help them. Common sense might tell them that long-standing problems, mistaken values, and habits cannot be made to vanish in thin air. They may know, intellectually, that they cannot be told how to feel or what decision to make, but they hope and expect that someone who understands their problem, and does not disapprove, also understands them well enough to tell them what to do. When clients have unrealistic expectations, counselors may feel required to fulfill them.

Many people think counseling consists of information-giving or advising, but it does not. Advising is a part of the counseling function but only within the context of helping an individual use and adapt information to personal needs and problems. To illustrate, we can tell someone where to find the bathroom, but we would not call it counseling. In a discussion of career choice, we can tell someone what job functions and opportunities are likely to be in demand in the future, but that alone is not counseling. Whenever information can be transmitted to a large group of people as effectively as to an individual, that help is better considered advising than counseling. Frequently, clients seem to request information only ("I need information to help me plan my career"). However, brief discussion makes it clear that the request for information only provokes more questions and concerns. ("Yes, I know computer technology is a promising field for jobs, but I want to work with people!")

When we are faced with specific kinds of problems, there *are* people we call counselors who tell us what to do and which procedures to follow. Tax counselors advise us how to prepare I.R.S. forms, lawyers advise us how to make out a will, and school counselors tell us how to apply to college. They cannot tell us how we should feel about paying taxes, how to decide who gets what when we die, or whether or not we want to go to college. We get their advice or opinions about what to do, but the consequences are ours, and, therefore, so are the choices. Counselors for psychological problems also can tell us how to go about doing certain things, but their advice is useful only when we are clear on what we want, or (as in the case of taxes) what we have to do.

Whatever the difficulty, choosing a counselor with whom one has experiences, background, and/or problems in common is attractive. One can approach easily with less fear of being misunderstood or judged. Communication is facilitated by the use of a common language. But this ease and familiarity go to waste if the focus stays on the problem rather than on the person who has the problem. Peers can talk, share experiences and ideas, give advice, and even become buddies, on the basis of shared experience. But if the purpose is to establish a relationship which can help a troubled or confused individual with psychological problems, the counselor has to start exploring not only the problem but its history and its meaning to the client. It's easy to assume knowledge about someone whose problem is familiar. It's tempting to offer advice which reflects more of what *has helped* in the counselor's experience than what *will help* the client. To help someone grow and make personal changes, one has to know who the person is, and then assist him or her in a process of considering and weighing alternatives, leaving the final choice to the client who must live with it.

People often choose to discuss their problems with others like themselves because they feel that *only* someone with similar experience will be able to accept them without prejudice and disapproval. Someone who can "understand" often means more than a person who can comprehend the problem; it means someone who can view the problem sympathetically rather than critically. The search for acceptance is probably the most compelling reason for seeking help from a peer rather than from an expert or professional. We approach the latter with apprehension.

The Desire to be "Normal"

Nonprofessionals need to examine the reasons people avoid professionals because these reasons have implications for and effects on counseling among peers. The problems of cost and inaccessibility are obvious but these are not always sufficient to explain the preference for a peer's help. Another reason is that professionals in the field of mental health provide services for people who are seen as deviant or crazy. To see a professional for treatment suggests something is "wrong"—the client is mentally ill, psychologically or emotionally disturbed, or at least immature. Since few of us think of ourselves in such terms, and none of us want to, we use the fact that we have never been to see a mental health professional as proof of normality. This view is so common that one hears it all the time: "Well, my problems have never been serious enough to require the services of a psychiatrist"; "Yes, I must be crazy talking to myself. Maybe I need professional help"; or "Kathy must really have serious problems. Did you know she was seeing a psychologist?"

Psychological problems and emotional difficulties are not always an indication of mental illness, as many people seem to think; they are common occurrences of everyday life. But we think, if these problems are "normal," they should not require the attention of an expert. We should be able to bear them alone, or at worst, lean on the strength of a loved one or neighbor. Understandable as these feelings are, the logic is questionable. Therapy is necessary and helpful for the few among us who are mentally and chronically ill, but it is also effective, if not more effective, for the normal upheavals that occur all the time: trying to break destructive habits, deciding binding commitments, coping with the loss of loved ones, dealing with developmental and situational crises. If these normal problems are not adequately and satisfactorily resolved, they can leave scars or continue to affect and damage the quality of many lives. An individual may function well in some areas and still have trouble with intimate relationships, drink or eat too much, lack confidence, or be accident-prone. We all have trouble admitting to ourselves that we have habitual, disturbing problems. If we can join with other "normals" who admit to the same problem, or can find a nonexpert who can help us, we don't need to question our sanity and subject ourselves to the scrutiny of those who treat "crazy" people.

It is, of course, a misperception that only those who are mentally ill can use professional help and that therapeutic techniques are suited only for "abnormal" behavior patterns. But we are distressed to find that we have problems that will not go away by themselves or by our own efforts to resolve them. We reassure ourselves every time we find help in the normal course of life, and we get scared every time we don't. When we think we have learned to be assertive through reading a book or attending a class, we are dismayed at finding that we act like "simps" when an important occasion demands assertiveness. We think we have struggled with and learned why we have trouble in intimate relationships and then are horrified if another of our relationships flounders. Again we are left struggling with nagging questions: Are we disturbed? Do we need professional help? Are we, or will we be seen as, "crazy"?

In this context peer counseling is a great relief. Not only are our problems admitted by others so we feel less like freaks or deviants, and not only are we promised help without enormous cost and inconvenience, but we are reassured that we are normal.

These very real fears of not being "normal" prompt many people to avoid professional help, but few of those fears are avoided when nonprofessionals provide counseling. The public's view of professional practices is not an accurate one. It is a distortion of the truth. The judgments and disapproval expected from professionals come from inside us; they reflect our concerns with our normality, our acceptability, our adjustment. We can reassure ourselves in avoiding professional help, but if the results of counseling are not dramatically effective, we are still left pondering the seriousness of our problems—how long will it take us to change, what is wrong with us? And counseling rarely is dramatically effective! When unhappy with our progress and with ourselves, we are likely to see others, even nonprofessional counselors, as disapproving, judgmental, and critical. Or we may blame nonprofessionals for being ineffective, make it their fault that we are so slow to improve. Because psychological problems are not easily banished, and all of us feel shame admitting to them, we are always on the brink of self-condemnation. Whoever the counselor, whatever the qualifications, the same issues arise. Why do I have these problems and what do they mean about me? How effective is the help I'm getting and can someone else do it better?

Said straightforwardly and simply, the fear of professionals is, in many ways, a fear of ourselves and our expectations about what people will think of our being persistently troubled. We think avoiding professional counselors avoids the problem but it does not; the same fears accompany us when counselors are mutual-help group members, students, peers, and other nonprofessionals. We are always afraid of what counseling may reveal to us and to others. Nonprofessionals must expect and deal with these fears in clients as professionals must.

Professionals are also avoided by minority group members who believe their problems will not be understood by anyone who does not share the same background and experiences. Those who hold their background, race, past experience, sexual orientation, religion, gender, or any other characteristic crucial to their integrity—and the determining factor in their troubles—will be inclined to reject help from anyone they judge unable to understand this feature. Many feel that *only* someone like them will understand them. This expectation is often reinforced in our daily personal contacts. We are more comfortable initially with people with experience and attitudes which are similar to ours. Teachers are more knowledgeable and sensitive to the tensions and pressures felt by other teachers. Blacks are acutely aware of the effects of the black experience on others. Homosexuals are reassured by the presence of other homosexuals.

Seeking Others Like Ourselves

We also seek people like ourselves to help us because we

think they will understand and accept us. We will not have to explain ourselves or convince them that our problems are justified; they will already know from their own experience. We will not suffer disapproval, condemnation, or criticism, because anything that applies to us applies to them as well. We trust them to view us fairly and sympathetically—a trust we do not feel initially with those who are strangers to our ways.

Indeed, insensitivity to or ignorance of cultural and religious heritage can present profound problems in counseling. I still shudder remembering a group session in which several students were listening to a newcomer's impressions of college. The recent arrival, Jim, was an attractive and articulate young black man from the rural South. He was enthusiastic about many aspects of college life but he also expressed dislike for two campus buildings. Asked why, he replied casually that the Devil did his work there. His fellow students, first shocked, began to smirk as he explained that biology and other modern science (taught in the buildings he disliked) were the Devil's creations. His earnest justifications were met with giggles, disbelief, and teasing by group members. Suddenly Jim's face showed a look of terror. Luckily I shifted focus and imagined his cultural context—Clarence Darrow . . . the Scopes "monkey" trial . . . the Fundamentalists who believed in a literal interpretation of the Bible. When I asked Jim to tell us about his prior education and religious beliefs, he shared his convictions that modern science contradicted the Bible and represented evil powers at work in the world. His peers did not have backgrounds which enabled them to accept a belief system so contrary to their own, and it was clear that Jim was in for an unsettling time in a northern secular college where Darwin was taken for granted. But at least momentarily we were able to calm the panic he felt facing a group's rejection of beliefs he had held all his life. For a time he must have felt we were in the presence of the Devil.

It is no easy thing, understanding and accepting the variety of human experience. When the beliefs of others challenge and contradict our own we can all change from liberal to bigot, from approving to incredulous or rejecting. We tend to regard our own views as universal, those that differ from ours as "peculiar." All counselors are at some disadvantage because there are no universally accepted definitions of mental health or of "normal" behavior. Few notions about mental illness hold across all cultures and circumstances. We tend to regard hallucinations as "sick"; some cultures have revered them as the voice of God or a mark of special vision. Talking to imaginary people we believe to be strange, but talking to God is prayer. "Normal" people enduring extreme stress will all show signs of mental and emotional disturbance. *We cannot evaluate others on the basis of conformity with, or deviance from the standards we hold for ourselves. But we may also fail, through lack of perspective, with those whose values and experience parallel our own.* We cannot help clients with options we cannot see. The following incident occurred when I, a white middle-class psychologist, was counseling clients who were mainly young, black, academically underprepared college students. Pearl, who had been my client for two semesters, asked if she could switch to a black female counselor, whom she had gotten to know informally. The other counselor, Betty, a black graduate student in psychology, and I agreed that a transfer might be helpful to provide Pearl with a role model she could emulate. To my surprise, the following semester, Pearl asked to transfer back to me. She was not unhappy or disgruntled in either counseling relationship; in fact, she was pleased by both. But her observations were telling. She explained, "Betty was more aware of my problems; I hardly needed to explain them to her. She would sympathize when I complained I had no money to visit Europe over the summer and said she knew how painful it was to be denied things one wanted on the basis of perpetual economic hardship. That was comforting." But Pearl continued, "On the other hand, you saw the world as offering me unlimited opportunities. When I complained to you about the same problem, you said, "Why not try getting a job in Europe? Find a professor taking his children abroad who might need help with them or look for other possibilities in the Personal section of magazines." She summed up the experience: "Betty saw and shared the problems I had; you saw the possibilities. In a way you were both right, but at the moment I want your approach."

This incident and others convinced me that, as counselors, we are both limited and enhanced by our backgrounds, characteristics, and personal experience. A background in common with clients can blind us to possibilities because, enmeshed in the same circumstances, we may not be able to see beyond them. Too great a gap can promote unrealistic expectations, perhaps in both participants. But the establishment of trust across ethnic, sexual, age, or class lines, if it can be achieved, is an enriching and therapeutic experience. People in the minority need to know that they can meet or challenge the expectations held by the "majority" in order to recognize their own strength.

Accepting the idea of cultural variance is sometimes easier than dealing with its manifestations in counseling. We can comprehend the "macho" Latin tradition which affords privileges to men that are denied to women and yet feel outraged when it hurts someone we are trying to help—the young woman who believes herself, and is considered by her family, "unmarriageable," because, as a rape victim, she is no longer the virgin required by a "respectable" and sexually experienced husband. We may think ourselves tolerant of all religious beliefs until a Christian Scientist refuses necessary medical treatment for a sick child.

The behavioral standards of certain cultures are at variance with values inherent in the counseling process. In counseling we expect and hope to help people express their feelings about problems and people in their lives. But such behavior directly conflicts, for example, with old-world Chinese values. Traditionally raised Chinese believe it rude to speak freely in the presence of an elder, or an authority such as a counselor, who is regarded as a superior from whom one learns by listening. To them, discussing parents in less than reverent terms is unthinkable no matter what parents may have done to upset them. And they are shamed, rather than relieved, by emotionality under any conditions.

We are all culture bound and biased to some degree. Given this premise, we can understand client preference for counselors with certain features or characteristics. Sometimes clients want a counselor of like gender to make it easier to discuss certain topics, particularly sexual problems. A woman, recently traumatized by male aggression or rape, might find it difficult to tell her experiences to a male counselor. But at times seeking help from peers with special characteristics severely limits the effectiveness of counseling. People who feel mistreated and misunderstood in the larger society, may hold society responsible for all their problems. As a basis for building support groups or helping networks, this viewpoint is useful and mobilizing, but it is a poor basis for personal counseling. When clients are seen or see themselves as helpless victims of social forces, it puts the focus outside the individual and what the individual can do in coping with and resolving personal problems. Viewing the client as only a representative of a group robs the client of individuality and self-determination. Some minority members avoid professionals and seek help from peers with characteristics in common: Thus, the common characteristic and its consequences will be the likely focus of counseling, and not themselves.

In summary, some clients seek counseling for the wrong reasons, reasons that would undermine counseling no matter what the counselor's qualifications. But counselors also may believe that the acceptance and understanding that come from sharing similar characteristics and experiences are sufficient grounds for counseling peers. Shared backgrounds and outlooks are sufficient for some helping purposes, but as we shall see in this book, these assumptions about commonality miss requirements essential to counseling and to the ability to help others help themselves.

III

Understanding the Ambivalent Quest for Help

Introduction

Robert Burns wrote that the greatest gift would be the ability to "see ourselves as others see us." For the counselor, the greatest gift is to see the world as it is seen by clients and to know how clients feel, including the way they feel about us as counselors. To do that, those of us who seek to help others must recognize the help-seeker within us. That is what this chapter is about.

We tend to think that helping another human being is something we can do naturally. Warmth, interest, and common sense seem the only essentials, and we expect the rest will take care of itself. We tend to believe that help should be from the heart, not from the head, that if we think about it or analyze it, the lack of spontaneity will decrease its worth. We get pleasure from being helpful, and we cherish our natural inclinations to give, to understand, to be sensitive to others. If we try but don't succeed, we prefer to think that the problem lies with the receptiveness of the recipient, the circumstances, or somewhere outside ourselves.

In casual encounters with others, the spontaneous helpful impulse is often unexpected and appreciated, even if off the mark. But effective help in counseling is more than impulsiveness; it is providing the help the client needs. If we are concerned, not just with giving, but with knowing what will help the client, we have to look beyond our immediate inclinations. We have to consider how to make those impulses

Is it possible to teach people how to use themselves effectively as helpers? One can argue that there is really no such thing as counseling but only an infinite variety of counseling relationships, each unique, each made different by the needs of its participants. Generalizing from such diversity may seem foolish. There is certainly no single definition of counseling applicable in all circumstances.

However, even acknowledging the great diversity of counseling relationships, settings, methods, and goals, we can still extract some general principles. Most of us would agree that counseling is a relationship established to foster growth, change, or adaptation in an individual experiencing distress or difficulty. The client is a person who is uncomfortable with life and/or self, who feels out of step with others or unable to achieve some desired goal.

At one time or another we have all felt this way—out of step, ineffective, dissatisfied with where we were and, yet, uncertain where to go. So a good place to start discovering how to help others is to explore what has, in the past, helped us. Here are some exercises to help you identify important elements in the helping process. It is useful to stop here and take some time to answer these questions carefully in terms of your personal experience.

Self-Discovery: Getting and Failing to Get Help

Start with yourself as a help-seeker. Think of times when you needed someone's help with a personal problem. Begin with an instance in which you sought help *but were not satisfied with the help you received.* Take time to recall the feelings and circumstances of that event. Then answer these questions.

Exercise #1

- What made you choose that particular person to help you?
- What were your expectations of the helper?
- How did you feel about asking for help and how was your request responded to?
- What did you feel about the helper?
- What do you think the helper thought of you?

• What was wrong with the help offered, the helper as a person, or the relationship? What went wrong?
• What disappointed you?
• How could the situation have gone better?

Now choose another time, *one in which you got the assistance you needed.*

Exercise #2

• What were the feelings that prompted you to ask?
• What made you choose the particular person to help you?
• What were your expectations of the helper?
• What were your feelings about asking for help and how was your request responded to?
• What did you feel about the helper?
• What do you think the helper thought of you?
• What did the relationship provide that you were unable to get on your own?

It may seem odd to begin a discussion of counseling from the viewpoint of the help-seeker and from personal experience needing, rather than giving, help, but it is the best starting point for evolving principles of counseling. Doing these exercises is important because understanding our need for, fear of, and experience in getting help provides more insight into what others need from us than all the counseling tips in the world. This viewpoint also determines what we will offer as helpers. In contrast, approaching principles of counseling from the standpoint of the counselor inevitably makes the counseling role seem dominant and powerful. But the purpose of counseling is to foster change, growth, development, and adaptation, and these potentials reside in the client, not the counselor. Growth can be encouraged but not coerced. The power to correct, alter, direct, and control behavior is often attributed to the counselor, but, again, it belongs to the client.

People imagine that counselors or therapists are able to make them do things against their will. *Typically, effective helpers act as human mirrors through which individuals can see themselves more clearly and discover their own potential to effect change.* Counseling relationships are human bonds which, at best, enhance the self-fulfillment of the help-seeker. They are cooperative, not coercive, relationships.

Your own recollections may have enabled you to differentiate those helping efforts which recognized and encouraged your autonomy from those that seemed to diminish or discourage it. We seldom view the latter as helpful. As an example, many years ago, when away from my home in Manhattan at a summer camp and without access to newspapers or radio, I wrote a letter home. I asked the question, "What place is Brooklyn in?" From one parent, I received the reply, "The Dodgers are in third place and stand a good chance to win the pennant." The other sent a lengthy and stern answer, indicating that although I did not pay enough attention in school, I really ought to know that Brooklyn was in New York City since I had been born and once lived in that borough. To be sure, this help-seeking example is a trivial and partly semantic problem, but to this day, I remember how I felt. The first reply provided what I wanted, information I needed to follow my team, while the other made me feel stupid and misunderstood. Perhaps you remember similar experiences, asking for help and feeling "put down" in the process.

It is often hard to ask for help at all, and given our hesitancy, few of us are tolerant of responses which seem to threaten our integrity as relatively self-sufficient individuals. Faced with problems, we may need a new perspective, a more accurate sense of ourselves, some understanding of the ground we are attempting to cover, an expression of concern and caring, information or other practical assistance. But we are rarely willing to give up control of our own lives or view ourselves as deficient individuals. Counseling is an "enabling" process, one that helps us go from where we are (and do not wish to be) to where we want to be in achievement and self-esteem.

As counselors, we are often eager for quick change, prompt amelioration of problems, even radical transformation, but this impatience is seldom helpful to those we are trying to help. Even when miserable with things as they are, and impatient with themselves, clients, and many of us, find it hard to change lifelong habits and behavior. To be able to help others we must understand the developmental processes that affect us all, the way we grew up and established independence. Understanding that is the only way to have realistic expectations of clients and the ways they can change.

Principles of Children's Growth and Development: Socialization

As far as we can tell, the infant enters the world with a sense that it is the center of the universe. It expresses discomfort and, sooner or later, the problem is met; hunger is satisfied, pain is quieted, warmth is provided, cuddling and creature comforts supplied, and when the infant tires, sleep arrives. Unable to do anything purposefully on its own, its needs are satisfied nonetheless. The infant experiences its needs and pleasures as all-important and is only concerned with securing gratification. Having limited perceptive powers and reasoning ability, the child has, for some months, little awareness of other people at all; they simply appear or don't appear when needed. The infant, despite its puny size and apparent helplessness, is powerful since it commands others to care for it and cannot comprehend the independent existence or rights of others.

Gradually, the infant makes primitive differentiations. It starts to recognize others, like mothers and fathers, who provide its satisfactions. The infant learns slowly to indicate needs and wishes through sounds and actions and begins a lifelong quest for mastery over the environment and those elements that cause discomfort. The child begins to appreciate the world outside of the self, full of potential pleasures. With increasing competence, it begins to claim anything that intrigues, delights, or satisfies as its own and exclusive possession. This sounds like a description of a tyrant and it is.

Some realities and the needs of others begin to make an uncomfortable impression. The pretty flame hurts, some appealing delights are withdrawn, and "big" people begin to say "No" to some of the child's behavior and desires. The people who say "No" are, in fact, the very same people who grant and provide satisfaction and safety, and so the frustrating process of socialization begins. With considerable ambivalence the child begins to curtail self-indulgent pleasure-seeking and to accommodate the demands of others.

The young child does not delay satisfaction easily or well. Frustration of any wish is painful. But gradually the child does learn because accommodation to others provides more pleasure and less pain and fear. Compliance is also the route to the promise of even more pleasure, the promise of finally becoming an adult, free to do precisely what one wants with no one bigger or more important to say "No." In the young child's version of adulthood, the older one becomes, the fewer limitations on pleasure. With greater experience and independence, the fewer the accommodations and denials one has to make and the more satisfaction one is able and entitled to have. Adulthood, then, is seen as the return to infantile omnipotence and gratification. Meanwhile, socialization or accommodating to others is a frustrating and enraging process, but temporarily necessary.

Once past infancy, one of the most evident and abiding drives in children is for independent mastery. A baby tries to hold the bottle, take the spoon, walk unaided long before the skills are perfected. The young child wants to push the button, pay for the purchase, negotiate the stairs, cross the street alone, and display other "grown-up" capacities. The child is angered if prevented from doing a task for which she/he feels competent, even if childish inefficiency makes the task a long and difficult process. "Let me do it. I can do it myself," is the constant refrain.

Children imitate "grown-ups," take adult roles in play, imagine themselves enjoying the roles and pleasures of adulthood while still in childhood. As kids, we want to be big and enjoy the privileges and pleasures of unrestrained freedom. But we can do that only if we control and direct our own lives. In time, our motives for wanting self-determination alter from simple hedonistic pleasure to more complex goals—we want to be loved, admired, respected; we want to test and prove our competencies; we want to be able to take care of others. But still, like the infant, we want to maximize pleasure and satisfaction, and minimize pain and frustration. There is another side too. While no child is content to stay a child, in times of stress, sickness, fear, or hunger, it wants to be taken care of. To get attention, we sometimes pretend to be younger and more helpless than we are. But once a feeling of security is reestablished, back we go to the pursuit of adult skills and prerogatives. Any child will tell you, especially at bedtime, it's more fun to be an adult than a kid.

We celebrate the milestones which mark our progress: the first step, the birthday, the graduation, the religious confirmation. We relish proofs that we can make it on our own—scout badges, a driver's license, voter registration and credit cards, the trip cross-country, the wilderness expedition. Fear of incapacity and return to dependency colors our image and anticipation of old age. People say, and sometimes mean, that they would rather be dead than dependent on others for basic needs. When we are ill or disabled, we submit to the ministrations of others, but our appreciation is often tinged with resentment. We are no longer our own persons, able to do what we please.

All our lives, it disturbs and frightens us to need others. It arouses the ambivalence of childhood. Potential providers are potential deprivers. Those who give can also take away or demand something in return. We find it difficult to be subject to the will of others, even when it seems in our best interest and by our own choice. We rebel against the will of others as children, as adolescents, as citizens, as minority group members, as students, sometimes even as parents. The urge for self-determination and total satisfaction plagues every relationship we choose to make—whether marriage, friendship, or group affiliation—and we resist some relationships lest they impinge on our freedoms.

Then, again, there is the other side. Life without others is no life at all. We don't want to be left alone and uncared for. It is painful to feel abandoned or bereft. Most of life's pleasures depend on the participation and presence of others. Yet having needs that must be satisfied by others raises fears of childhood dependency: accommodations, limitations, compliance, and denial. Not self-sufficient in childhood, we had to conform to parental expectations when they did not suit us. We had to stop our activities for meals or bedtime, had to submit to the indignities of the bath, had to stop fighting just when we were getting even, had to discipline our own bodily functions on command. We could say "No" too, and did, but our refusals never had the power of the parental "No." Our pleasures were curtailed by the same forces who protected and provided for us and made us feel loved. Our parents, in retrospect, may seem benign despots but they controlled and curtailed our pleasure. They required compliance with a switch, a shout, a word, or a stare. Our innovations, like painting our own design on the all-beige living room couch, were met with punishment and we felt an enraging loss of self-esteem. Who are they to tell us what we could and couldn't do? But what would we do without them? Parents and all their surrogates—schoolteachers, relatives, babysitters, scoutmasters, even Santa Claus—seemed to conspire to direct and correct our drives for satisfaction. No wonder we imagined adulthood as a state free of restraint, a state of constant pleasure.

Few of us can really remember the rage we felt as infants and children when our satisfactions were denied or postponed, but we can observe it in the young: the infant incessantly fretting and crying for food even briefly delayed, the temper tantrum, the dire threats and imprecations ("I'll kill you." "I'll die if you don't let me . . . " "You're a terrible Mommy."). We learned to suppress our anger, not only because at times our parents redeemed themselves, but because we feared jeopardizing the vital link with those who sustained us. Remembering the delight in getting away with something, sneaking the forbidden cupcake, or thwarting the all-knowing powers with courageous misdeeds, is easier than recalling our murderous rage. But in the dawdling, sulking, and messiness of our childhood, we can recognize our resentment of the power once held over us. Young adults, living on their own for the first time, are often amazed at the neatness with which they maintain their living quarters since their rooms at home were always in chaos. As children, we learned to comply grudgingly or we rebelled, but neither was comfortable. We sustained ourselves with future visions of freedom and intentions to raise our children without hateful restrictions.

The painful surprise is how little our childhood view of

adulthood conforms with the reality. With age, we find more freedom but also greater risks and harsher penalties than we could foresee. Now we can have all the ice cream we can eat, but at the risk of having no spending money left for something else. We have freedom to party instead of doing homework, but the fun may not compensate for failure in school. Making our own decisions, we find, can increase momentary pleasures, but it makes us responsible for our mistakes. As we become more self-determining, we are less able to blame others for the things that go wrong.

Another consequence of growing up is finding that others around us have needs and rights too, sometimes in conflict with our own but just as legitimate. In the urgency to satisfy our impulses, we are confronted with others whose wishes interfere with ours. Away from parental restrictions on loud music, we find, instead, that roommates or neighbors demand quiet. We may resist tying ourselves down in a commitment or a love affair only to find that the someone we want will not have us any other way. Or, we can suffer rejection by someone who fears being entrapped by us! The adult world of which we were so envious and for which we were so eager is not the world we imagined as children.

Attaining, finally, some measure of freedom, we discover the limits to our liberation. We find penalties for the privileges of free choice and for the right to seek satisfactions without parental restraint. We experience unanticipated pain and problems. Then we find ourselves, ironically, longing for the comforts of childhood, advantages we never appreciated when we were there. Sometimes we wish we could relinquish some of the freedom we fought to get and return to a world of diminished responsibility. As we struggle with ourselves, with the gaps in our knowledge and experience, and with the challenges we cannot handle, it suddenly seems more appealing to think of being taken care of. Instead of having to provide for ourselves, we would sometimes rather turn to and lean on someone else. Though our parents were sometimes around when we did not want them, they were also there when we needed them.

Although the vision of childhood in the mind's eye differs for each of us, the love and security provided for a cherished child is easy to picture. Even those with miserable or deprived young lives can remember or imagine the "good" times and the loving moments, and we all have an idealized view of what childhood should or could be like. At those moments when the present seems too much for us to handle, we all resort to behavior which belongs to the child in us. Like overtired kids who simply cannot cope, at times we feel we cannot handle the situations, relationships, and responsibilities facing us. Overwhelmed, we retreat to old and familiar patterns of behavior; we act out problems instead of working to solve them, we withdraw and retreat from personal contacts and tasks, we indulge our various appetites as if there were no tomorrow, or we develop rigid and inflexible approaches to deal with the world and our relationships. Sometimes, we become ill and require special attention. The more fragile among us may actually display infantile behavior such as thumb-sucking, bedwetting, outbursts of rage, fetal postures, and the illogical logic of young children. Since few of us ever feel "all grown-up," and probably none of us is, we may not be aware of behaving immaturely. We may not recognize or allow ourselves to tell others that we are in trouble, for there is shame in not being able to cope with responsibility.

This form of behavior is called regression, and it often alerts others that we are overwhelmed. We regress to relieve stress, in reaction to and anticipation of physical and emotional pain, and to evoke caring responses in others. Sometimes a little regression and a little tender loving care is all we need to pull ourselves together again. But should that fail, and we continue to feel alone, we become more willing to forfeit a part of the childhood dream of self-determination. In search of regaining security, we act in ways to make others provide nurturance, control, or support. When our providers tire of taking care of us, we may ask, or be told to ask, for counseling.

Many resist, but some of us do get ourselves to a counselor and manage to express, directly or indirectly, our concerns. We are rarely comfortable even then. Though we may be reassured and gratified to find someone to help, we are, nonetheless, back on the horns of several dilemmas. First, there is the clash between our needs for nurture and the aspirations we hold for our more mature selves; all of us fear displaying weakness and dependence. Second, we view helpers with considerable ambivalence just as we viewed our parents; if they do provide for our needs, we don't know what will be expected of us in return.

When stress and frustration make us regress to earlier and less mature ways of behaving, we want helper responses that are familiar and acceptable to us from past experience. We are fearful of those responses which used to make us feel babyish and deficient as children. For some, an affectionate gesture seems reassuring; for others, it would be humiliating.

Unknowingly, we want to evoke helper behavior which comforted us earlier and prevent those responses that recall parental actions we feared or disliked. Clients sometimes reject helpers on sight because they resemble demanding parents or teachers. By the same token, they are likely to accept counselors initially on the basis of superficial but pleasing similarities. Our parents are not always there, or available, or permitted to provide old modes of comfort. Instead, we seek assurances from others who are unfamiliar with what used to make us comfortable, strangers to the expectations of the child within us. We are so well-armed psychologically that we often distort the helper's behavior to fit what we want or what we fear. We may hear an innocuous question as a rebuke or see a smile as praise.

As counselors, meeting a client for the first time, we expect to be seen as we are and judged on our merits within the context of today. We are seldom prepared for all the yesterdays that mold the client's perception of us.

Reactions to Helpers: Transference

Based on parental models, we have notions, images, expectations of therapists before we actually encounter them. (Sometimes past experience is the reason we avoid seeking help; we think we know what will happen and, on that basis, reject it.) These images continue to color interactions with helpers throughout relationships. One client sees a counselor as too tough and demanding while another sees the same person as too lenient and soft. Often, we are most comfortable with authority figures whose style seems to parallel that of a respected or idealized parent, but rarely can we recognize how much our internal frame of reference determines our perception. Since most helping relationships are not mutual or reciprocal in nature, we as clients do not know the helper as an individual. In counseling the focus is on us. However active and talkative in sessions, the counselor remains an ambiguous figure. We become aware of what we are projecting onto this figure only when the helper fails to act in the way we anticipate or wish. If we report some behavior or desire that used to perturb our parents, we may be amazed to find understanding acceptance. Or, we may be angered if a counselor questions one of our attitudes that a parent would have approved.

Endowing the counselor with these inaccurate expectations, characteristics, and attitudes is called transference. It means that what people have experienced in an earlier situation—childhood—is transferred or applied to a different one, counseling. Many people think transference means "falling in love with the therapist." That is a narrow and partial understanding of a common phenomenon of attributing to an unknown but powerful figure the marvelous or awesome features a child associates with parents during formative years.

Transference is a constant and ongoing process, a part of all helping relationships and a part of our reactions to other authority figures as well. We usually remain unaware of our reactions because we seldom have a chance to compare our view of a person we barely know with what the person is really like. (If we become aware there is discrepancy, we usually attribute it to a faulty first impression.) But it is necessary for all counselors to understand transference phenomena. Even if there is no need to focus on them extensively, they will sometimes trouble and confuse the unsuspecting counselor. Clients may ask counselors to behave in a certain way and fault them if they don't. ("Aren't you going to scold me? You warned me I might fail, and I did!") Or clients may accuse helpers of having thoughts or feelings of which they are unaware. ("I know you say you aren't disappointed with my performance in the play, but I know you are!") Counselors unaware of transference possibilities will fail to explore the origins of these expectations and feelings. Instead, they can become defensive, attempt to match the client's expectations, feel guilty, or question their own personal awareness.

The new counselor who is told by a client, "You sound just like my mother," is immediately on guard and convinced that he or she has made a big mistake. That may or may not be true. Either way, it is necessary to find out what the client's statement means, what parallel is observed between the counselor and the parent. It is possible for the counselor to "sound like Mother" and be offering a useful comment to the client, whether the client accepts it appreciatively or not; it is also possible that the client hears a criticism where none was intended.

Whenever we deal with distant authority figures who can help or harm us, we are on guard. We want to know more about them—whether they are candidates for president, movie stars, teachers, or therapists—but often the purpose or structure of the relationship does not permit our learning much about them. So we fill the gaps in our knowledge by attributing to them the motives and attitudes that are psychologically significant in our lives. We elaborate from the little we know to explain them from our perspective, but not necessarily from theirs, not necessarily accurately. We assume and distort things about counselors without conscious awareness or intention. Why we do this is not easy to answer. It probably makes us feel less vulnerable, as if we could better control the control they have over us by figuring out how "they tick." Perhaps, as a result of the painful process of growing up, of going from omnipotence to accommodation to the dilemma of independence, we wish to know more than we can about the real motivations of those in whom we put our trust and welfare. Our parents had the power of life and death over us. We had to conform with their expectations long before we understood why. We did not know we could be poisoned by some of the things we wanted to drink, but we resented the power that refused us. If we disobeyed, we got sick or punished (the two things seemed equivalent) just for seeking pleasure and satisfying our curiosity. We thought self-determination was the route to greater pleasure and felt as children we were denied that and all it promised. As we got older, we understood more and knew that at least some parental interventions were in our best interest. Still, our conflicts with parents continued, until eventually, and in certain circumstances, we felt ourselves to be more competent than they to make our decisions. Still, our independence was a hard struggle, and we don't surrender it easily.

So when we seek help, even from a person who seems to resemble us more closely than our parents, we want help but on our own terms. We do not wish, nor will we permit, a stranger to have the power of our parents. Sometimes we do things to limit the counselor's impact on us; we withhold information, explain the kind of assistance we desire and the kind we will refuse, miss or "forget" appointments, prepare so well for meetings in advance that little can happen that we are not prepared for, or go but refuse to talk. Some clients are so distrustful they try counseling a brief time, and although nothing happens to change their problems, they insist they have been helped greatly and require no further assistance. They put a toe in the water but refuse to get wet. Others go endlessly but do little work on their own, as if attending were the sole effort they are willing to make. These are a few of the many ways people participate without becoming involved, without trusting the process or the helper.

Transference, usually an unconscious mechanism, also protects us. It acts as a kind of defense—a way of anticipating and fending off, of determining and controlling what may happen to us. Transferences are not all negative; many are positive and facilitative. Clearly, the statement, "You sound just like my mother," can be meant as a compliment or as an insult. In seeking help from strangers, we often see in them qualities we want or do not want rather than what is really there. We respond as if our distortions were reality. It is as though the act of putting ourselves in the hands of a powerful caretaker who may reenact a parental role is so risky, we must try to determine both roles—that of client and counselor. In that way we retain control. We can replay our growing up without experiencing the discomfort and without addressing unresolved conflicts with our once (and, psychologically, still) powerful parents. We imagine we can correct the deficiencies or abuses of the parenting we received—by not permitting the counselor total control over us.

For instance, we may insist that the counselor tell us what to do. We may blame our current problems on our parents' poor guidance. Forcing the counselor to make better decisions for us seems natural and appropriate; parents should advise their children wisely, and if they don't, the counselor should. The counselor is a caretaker, and an expert as well. If the counselor declines to give advice, we may be angry as if deprived of something we had every right to get. We expect direction from the counselor, not because it is the counselor's function, but because it is a common parental act. Inexperienced counselors, afraid of disappointing us, may see our expectations as legitimate without questioning why we assign them that task. They may be frightened of our anger and so eager to satisfy us that they respond to our demands with advice, however little chance it has to be effective. In this way they at least provide what we asked for. Yet, we may never discover what else counseling or the counselor might have done for us.

This is one example of how a psychological set derived from experience with our parents can influence our interactions with a counselor. Unrecognized, such sets can affect the outcome of counseling detrimentally. There are several transferential views of counseling which are commonly held but are still inaccurate stereotypes of the counselor's role. Clients often expect and "hear" approval or disapproval from counselors, although the counselor's primary intent is to understand and then help clients understand their feelings and behavior. Novices can spend much time searching their psyches for their "real" feelings when accused of harboring a certain attitude by a client. Since counselors do have personal reactions to clients, they do not always recognize when clients are projecting their own expectations rather than correctly reading counselors' views. As children, we were sometimes sure our parents "knew" and disapproved even when they were ignorant of our misdeeds. Since assessment is a counseling function, clients often imagine their behavior will be seen as "sick" and may insist that a counselor's observation implies that judgment. Again, this may be a misreading of the counselor's reaction but it can be troubling to the counselor.

The role of disciplinarian is another transferred from parents to counselors. Since we were often corrected by our parents, told right from wrong, and even coerced from one choice to another, we expect similar acts from counselors. If we were made uncomfortable by parental domination, we may view the intervention of a counselor as the act of an authority telling us what to do. And then, we may try to fight the battle for independence over again. Actually, change occurs when clients are ready, not according to any counselor's timetable, but society and individuals often imbue counseling with a transferential corrective capacity. Since counseling can change behavior, it is assumed the counselor effects it, when, in fact, it is the client. But, on the basis of this assumption, lawbreakers, unproductive workers, misbehaving children, and others with undesirable traits are, willing or not, assigned to counselors.

The inexperienced must be careful too, because if they are exclusively concerned with specific behavioral outcomes from counseling, they will play a disciplinary role. If the goal (such as weight loss, scholastic achievement, or making a career choice) is the primary focus, rather than the client's concerns and problems trying to reach the goal, counseling is aimed at behavioral conformity. The pressure clients feel then is like the perception of the kid who says to his father, "You don't care about me. All you care about is my grades!" Counselors certainly want positive outcomes from their efforts but these are not achieved by coercion. Demanding certain outcomes makes clients hide or invent information about themselves. It provides the same elements of a power struggle inherent in childhood socialization. When counseling is used to make people do something they resist or cannot do, it violates the individual's right to self-determination; it also fails to acknowledge that established patterns of behavior are slow to change. Counselors can make suggestions and offer strategies to bring change about, but these must serve as encouragement to try new approaches rather than as injunctions.

The psychological sets clients transfer from childhood can

strike a responsive chord in counselors. Counselors, uncertain of the legitimate dimensions of their role, can try to act in accordance with clients' unrealistic expectations. Counseling does not often require identifying all the unresolved conflicts and unrealistic expectations clients bring with them, but it should differentiate between the transferential and realistic features and possibilities of the helping relationship. Counselors err in thinking they must fulfill every client expectation; they must, instead, help clients see the purpose of the helping relationship and the real intentions of the counselor.

Perhaps the most common transferential expectation of counseling is that it will comfort our hurts, reassure and encourage us, and provide safety and refuge from harsh realities. Providing support is a counseling as well as a parental function, but in both situations, it is the means rather than the end. All of us have needs for attention, comfort, and reassurance that are not always met in everyday life, and in times of trouble, we are relieved to have someone on our side. But that tender loving care can be destructive if it does not enable us to identify and mobilize our own resources to cope with future challenges.

There are people who resist helping relationships for fear of becoming hopelessly dependent on a sympathetic, understanding helper and losing their capacity for self-sufficiency. They fear their wish to be dependent. There are others who, in treatment, use it self-indulgently, constantly complaining about others, exaggerating feelings of weakness and uncertainty, and trying to evoke concern and protectiveness. These individuals seem to expect counseling to attend to and relieve them of every discomfort and failing. The fear of becoming dependent and the willing surrender of independent striving are opposite reactions to one distorted view of counseling—that of a hiding place, a security blanket, a safe haven in which to nurse wounds and be relieved of responsibility.

Effective counselors, understanding the wish for and the consequences of dependency, provide extensive support only until clients can recognize and call upon their own strengths. For people with severe disabilities—some clearly apparent to others, some not—therapy is a lengthy process, one that is necessary and constructive for years, even for a lifetime. But, however long the treatment may last, the purpose is to help clients meet and assume responsibility, not avoid it. The client who uses counseling to complain about others avoids the struggle with the only person who can really change his life—himself.

Of all the transferential expectations, a client's demands for nurturance and support are the most difficult for counselors to handle. They tap the very wellspring that motivates counselors—their wish to help, support, and comfort. It is difficult to resist a request for help even when we know someone is capable of performing without it. This is why the assessment of each client's strengths and abilities, as well as his or her problems, is so important. It is essential that counselors evaluate what their clients can do instead of relying entirely on what clients report. How often are we convinced that we will fail at something, only to find out that we can succeed! Disagreeing with or confronting clients is difficult. But helping clients to differentiate real needs from wishes, to recognize when and how they need us and when they are able to dispense with us, are all essential counseling functions.

These are some of the dimensions of transference, a complex and varied phenomenon. Although the preceding discussion is necessarily oversimplified because transference reactions are so varied, it can alert counselors to the fact that clients start with misconceptions and misperceptions. Some of these are based on childhood experience, some are "carryovers" from encounters with authority figures, and some stem from current wishes and fears. Counselors sometimes need to help clients recognize them.

To recapitulate briefly, the quest for help is an ambivalent one. At every stage of life, we hesitate to admit to ourselves and to others that we have problems we can't handle alone. Striving for independent mastery and self-sufficiency is vital to our integrity and self-esteem. Going for help makes us vulnerable to the power and control of others; it reawakens conflicts with parents and authority figures. When problems are persistent and there seems no other choice, we may—with many reservations—reach out for someone to lean on and guide us, but our misgivings accompany us into the relationship. We are afraid of being told what to do as if we had no judgment of our own. We are afraid of being shamed or scolded as if we were wayward children (which we suspect we are), and we stand poised to receive and reject either punishment or correction. We may want reassurance and support, but coddling will only disguise and undermine our coping capacities. We defend ourselves against counseling before and during the relationship by misperceiving its nature and purpose. If counselors miss these indications of our fears and distortions, they will not enable us to redirect our energies to the work; and we will invalidate the process by using counselor responses as convincing evidence that our misgivings are valid.

Resistance

There is another, but related, source of trouble for counselors—client resistance. Originally a concept from orthodox psychoanalysis, the term resistance gained wider meaning and application as other methods of psychotherapy and counseling evolved. Now it is used not only to refer to the rejection of a psychoanalyst's interpretation, but also to a broad array of patient behavior which reveals the inability to use, profit from, or even engage in the therapeutic relationship. Sometimes it refers to the persistence of behavior which both client and counselor regard as destructive, such as bingeing on food or sweets. Thus, symptoms, clients, or both can exhibit resistance to change.

Resistance is something counselors can understand from the inside. Those new to counseling often expect that clients will be able to do "what is good for them," once it is apparent. But doing what is good for you is not easy! Perhaps the exercises at the beginning of this chapter reminded you of difficulties you had in altering your behavior. If not, you may recall broken New Year's resolutions, other promises you made to yourself and were unable to keep, and "bad" habits which tend to persist despite your intentions to break them. It is important to recognize that we *often* fail to meet our own goals and match our own expectations. If this fact is not clearly understood by counselors, they are likely to blame slow progress in counseling on themselves or on the help-seeker, when it is, in fact, what we should expect.

Although counseling may result in our changing conditions outside ourselves, typically it demands recognition and alteration of our own unproductive or destructive behavior. There are times when a new job, a vacation, or a divorce will reduce the problems we face, but more often the problem lies with us and what we contribute to many situations. Changing a situation doesn't change *us*. We have spent years being and becoming the persons we are. How very hard it is to understand and then alter our basic perceptions, values, habits, defenses, or goals!

Furthermore, we are secure with the familiar even when we are unhappy with it. Predictability gives us a sense of control over things, a feeling of comfort and security. At times we enjoy novelty and variation, but too much strangeness and surprise make us apprehensive. Children believe that the order of their lives is "right." They trust what is certain and prescribed, and they rarely comprehend a world that does not conform with their expectations. Growing older, we gain perspective and tolerance for change and variation. We manage to adapt to new circumstances, new people, new ways of doing things, but not without difficulty. There is a strong sense of self, an identity constructed of our background, our experiences, our abilities, and our values; we find differences and contradictions disturbing. We are accustomed to our logic, our view of the world, our ways of interacting with others, our definitions of friendship and love. Even when we are unhappy with ourselves, we find it very difficult to change our behavior, adapt our beliefs, or set a new course. The characteristics we dislike in ourselves are intertwined with qualities we cherish. We cannot pull out and discard a thread without jeopardizing the fabric of our identity.

Occasionally we may recognize that we engage in behavior that is no longer necessary, as perhaps it once was, in behavior that no longer protects us, as perhaps it once did, but still we find it very difficult to rid ourselves of it. We may hate being shy but find it impossible to be outgoing. We may not like what we are, what we have, and what we do; but it is us, what we are accustomed to.

We all bear some resemblance to the man in the joke who, when asked by his therapist to describe his daily routine, reports his patterns of waking up, washing up, eating breakfast, vomiting, leaving home, getting to work. . . . The therapist interrupts, "Did I understand you to say that you vomit every morning?" "Yes," the patient replies. "Doesn't everybody?" What may strike others as strange about our lives seems commonplace and natural to us; sometimes we are not even aware of other alternatives.

We also "resist" growing up. Growing up means facing and dealing with unpleasant realities, assuming responsibility, postponing or sacrificing pleasures to "make a buck," pass an exam, or meet some pressing practical requirement. Growing up means relying less on others for security and support, having to make and live with difficult choices, and fulfilling or disappointing the expectation of important others. Growing up means performing for ourselves the tasks parents and others used to do for us—or should have done for us. Sometimes we are unwilling or resentful, convinced we never got as much as we were entitled to. Maturity is a more difficult state, and adulthood more arduous and demanding than we imagined. Counseling may seem a way to recoup, a place to receive what is owed to us, and we are surprised to find it not a refuge from maturity. Perhaps our stubborn and sometimes well-concealed refusal to grow up is the basis of resistance to change in counseling. It is common for clients to blame current difficulties on the failings of their parents, only to find, in time, that such attribution alone does little to help them.

But, however well we recognize our own difficulties with personality or behavioral change, it surprises us and frustrates us in our clients. A student doing poorly in school ought to study more. When insufficient time preparing is pinpointed in counseling as the major problem, why doesn't the student just go home and study? With such an obvious solution to the distress school failure brings, it seems inconceivable that the student may show up at the next appointment with no more accomplished than at the last. When simple advice fails, a second explanation may be offered; for example, a lack of motivation. Now, from the counselor's point of view, the student knows *what* he is doing wrong and *why* he is doing it; surely now, change will occur. If the diagnosis is on target and the correction fairly easy, there may be some improvement, but more often than not there is none.

As counselors, our expectations may be out of line. Naming problems and finding reasons for them does not solve them. We actually contribute to client resistance by thinking change is easy. We contribute to resistance when we focus on what the client is doing "wrong." In any given situation, people are likely to keep on doing whatever they did the last time. Our efforts have to be directed toward understanding what the problem behavior means, what satisfaction it brings, and what threatening situations it avoids. To mention just a few possibilities, the student who is "not studying" may be: attending to an ailing parent and be emotionally drained; convinced that he or she would fail even with greater effort and afraid to find this out; convinced that academic success would bring rejection from his peers; or only interested in the school's athletic program or extracurricular activities. In any of these instances, the student is unlikely to study unless his priorities, perceptions, values, or commitments change; and none of these will change readily.

The counselor's task is to understand and explore resistance, not avoid it or oppose it. Resistance needs to be uncovered step by step. Slow progress toward the eventual goal may not indicate deficiencies in either helper or client. Learning new ways of interacting and behaving is a bit like forging a new path in unfamiliar terrain. The underbrush has to be cleared; the map consulted; the destination evaluated; and the progress, already made, acknowledged before we gather strength and confirm our readiness to move ahead. A client's resistance may represent an effort to gain a secure foothold and a clear view of the way ahead before taking the next step. Does the client who is a poor student really want to be a good student? We cannot be sure without exploration, and the real answer may be "No, not at the moment."

It is impossible to enumerate the forms and expressions of resistance, but there are many. Fearful of discussing a particular topic, an individual may miss or come late to the session, come on time but avoid, forget, or deny the importance of an issue, or be unusually quiet. At times the client may be vaguely aware of resistance as in the case of the young woman who talked all the way through her first session so no question could be posed, and repeatedly alluded to things she was *not* discussing. But more often the client is unaware of resistance. The counselor has to be especially alert since resistance may be suggested by what the client does *not* do, or say, or show. A client who spends time in session discussing a friend's unsuccessful counseling experience may be concealing his or her own feelings of apprehension or suspicion. A counselor who suspects there is an unspoken message or a topic being avoided should not immedately label it "resistance" or vigorously attack it. A protective measure, resistance needs to be explored gently lest clients feel their actions need defending, or believe themselves criticized for involuntary behavior, or find themselves overwhelmed by topics they cannot yet confront. When understood, specific forms of resistance often fade away. But resistance is never eliminated; it continues to precede progress and movement throughout therapy.

Sometimes it is difficult to distinguish resistance from failures or problems in the counseling relationship itself. Not all of a client's objections to or criticism of the counselor can be attributed to resistance; some need to be addressed and resolved directly by a shift in procedure. Some new counselors fail to investigate tensions and problems because they either think them unimportant or see themselves at fault. Unfortunately, counselors who are wary about questioning client reactions or hearing criticism of themselves limit their understanding of both transference and resistance, and may discourage real engagement in counseling. They may be mistaking a stumbling block, which can be removed, from an impenetrable wall. There are no simple rules for distinguishing resistance from other problems in the counseling relationship; sensitivity, sharing and articulating observations and impressions, and exploration of "undercurrents" are helpful, despite the risk of discovering something uncomplimentary.

To conclude the discussion of resistance, we are all aware of the persistence and intractability of some of our behavior. Sure that nothing can be done, some of us refuse help, doubting that we will ever be able to handle ourselves or others differently. At various times all of us have tried to change and have failed or sought advice and been unable to use it. We may not recognize that advice is often difficult to follow because it is unsuited to us and our circumstances. When our feelings are involved, when personality or behavioral change is required, when we are advised to discuss a problem with a person we fear or to make a decision between two equally appealing or unpleasant alternatives, advice is more easily given than taken. Few of us can distinguish between failure to change in the face of overwhelming odds and failure where we could have succeeded. In either case we feel remiss in not using the advice we have already sought and not followed. If we are still willing to attempt counseling, we may come with only a thin hope superimposed on a deeper conviction of the permanence of our problems. That conviction is part of resistance. Counselors can understand client resistance by recognizing it in themselves. As helpers, we are not that different from those who seek our help, and we can use that communality to understand their difficulties.

Before proceeding, you might find it helpful to go over your responses to the exercises provided in the beginning of this chapter to see whether these elements contributed to your successful or unsuccessful attempts to get help.

IV

Counselors' Expectations and the Surprising Challenge

Introduction

Even if we know that counseling is a method for helping people solve their own problems, and that clients cannot be equated with their problems nor fixed up like malfunctioning cars or televison sets, we still tend to think of the counselor as a technician, and of counseling as a mechanical process. Inexperienced counselors, when seeking advice for the difficulties they encounter, ask questions like, "What should I do to help Mrs. Brown talk more freely?" "How should I handle Mary's anger?" "How can I refer Richard to someone else without causing any bad feelings?" This type of query implies that there is a proper response or technique to employ at every given moment.

Rarely are there satisfactory answers to such questions. Problems like a client's reluctance to talk, a client's hostility, or the best way to introduce referral are not phenomena occurring in the abstract, but events developing in the context of a relationship. In different relationships, similar problems require different responses. Just as we cannot equate clients with their problems, we cannot think of counseling responses as automatic and interchangeable. Counselors must use themselves, their humanness, their understanding to respond effectively at crucial times. *Counseling is an interaction between people, not an assembly-line process with prescribed steps.* The appropriate response at a given moment is a result of the human needs and expectations of both participants.

The focus of the previous chapter was the ambivalence with which we become clients and seek help for our problems.

In contrast, we rarely feel ambivalence about becoming counselors. We may question our skills and effectiveness, but we are sure of our intentions; we want to help. Aware of the problems of others, we want to do something about them. Asked why or how we developed the interest, we may simply reply that we care.

When, in the last chapter, you were asked to recall instances in which you sought assistance, you may have had difficulty remembering specific examples. Many people do. It seems easier to recall the times we helped others or the times when we managed on our own. The discomfort most of us feel in such circumstances may cause us to forget instances of our needing help from others.

At least this seems true of the admission interviews of many who wish to be professional counselors. In their interviews, applicants frequently report that success at helping others has motivated their interest in counseling. Rarely do they report good experiences in receiving help from anyone, even from the professionals with the jobs and degrees they hope to obtain. Some applicants, openly critical of whatever help was available, vow to do better. Others seem to view their interest in helping others as incompatible with needing or getting help for themselves.

We could understand this perceived incompatibility between getting and giving help if all, or even many, would-be professionals were more fortunate and problem-free than others. But this is not so. Prospective counselors seem to experience the same kinds of problems as those of people they want to help. Moreover, their recognition of this similarity often makes them feel qualified to become helpers.

The incompatibility between giving and getting help is better understood psychologically if we view helping others as one way of dealing with our own troubles. *Helping others helps the helper*—to feel useful, needed, and appreciated, and to gain perspective on personal concerns.

Helping Others Is a Way of Helping Ourselves

This formulation may seem strange, even insulting, to

individuals generous enough to want to give to others, but it should not be dismissed. When down in the dumps, have you ever listened to another's problems and felt better about your own? Have you ever suggested that someone overwhelmed with self-pity take a look at the troubles besetting others? Have you ever reassured a disappointed friend by pointing out that things might be a lot worse? Most of us have. We seem to know intuitively that, when troubled, gaining perspective helps. Knowing that other people's burdens are as heavy as, or heavier than, ours makes us appreciate the good things we have. Trying to help others, and, in turn, helping ourselves does not invalidate our concern for others; in many ways it seems to enhance it.

If counseling required a constant sacrifice of personal needs and satisfactions, few of us would do it well for long. Like any other endeavor, helping others must provide some gratification and reward. If not, we would soon resent the role. Although they usually receive little financial or tangible compensation for helping others, nonprofessionals often feel personally enriched for the experience.

Finding reward in helping others is both a legitimate and necessary reason for undertaking the task with continuing enthusiasm, but we should examine the nature of the gratification we derive. We may feel good about helping others, but we are on dangerous ground if we lend a helping hand just to feel good. We are also on dangerous ground if we help others in order to avoid our personal problems. At times, we can be exploited in the role of helper, but we can also exploit those we try to help. If our personal needs come first, they will dominate and distort our relationships.

Much as we want to give our help freely and spontaneously, without too much self-analysis, we must consider which of our own needs can be gratified in counseling without doing a disservice to our clients. We must place ourselves under scrutiny and try to decide "what's in it for us" as individuals.

How can we do this? We can start by examining our interactions with others. Many professionals undergo therapy themselves to recognize the roots of their investment in the helping role and to identify problems which might limit their effectiveness. We are often a bit surprised to find a professional with problems just like other people; we seem to expect therapists to have no problems of their own. But this is impossible; all human beings have problems. Professionals have to discover and monitor those which can adversely affect their clients. Nonprofessionals may have fewer opportunities to identify what it is that goes into their desire to help others, but they must understand that their personal difficulties can undermine even the best intentions.

Self-Discovery through Experiences Helping Others

Think of instances in which you as a counselor, or a friend, or a colleague made efforts to help someone work out his or her personal problems. Choose one instance when you felt pleased with the relationship and/or the result. Try to answer the following questions as frankly as you can and use your answers to identify the satisfactions you obtained from the experience.

Exercise #1 Satisfying Experience

- How did you and the person you tried to help get together?
- What made you feel able to help this person?
- How much time did you spend together?
- What were your perceptions and feelings about the individual?
- What did you imagine the relationship could do for the other person?
- Were you comfortable in the relationship? What made you comfortable or uncomfortable?
- How did you handle difficulties that occurred in the relationship?
- What did you think was the cause of the problems which the person discussed with you?
- How did you use yourself in helping the individual?
- What did the individual gain as a result of your help?
- Did the relationship and outcome differ from your initial expectation?

• Did you feel as if you provided all the help that was required?
• Was the role you played a natural and comfortable one for you—a simple extension of the real you—or was an unusual effort demanded of you?
• Did the person have problems similar to yours?
• Did you learn anything about yourself that surprised you?
• What did you think the person felt about you and your help?
• What was most pleasing about the encounter to you?
• What happened to the relationship when your helping role was over?
• Did you find it difficult to end your role as a helper?
• And finally, how did your personal experience contribute to your wish to help this individual? How did it affect your role? What personal needs did the relationship and its outcome fulfill for you? How did it affect your self-esteem?

If you do this exercise again with others who not only give you feedback but share their own helping experiences, you will get more out of it. If that is not possible, you may want to contrast one of your experiences with one of mine.

A Satisfying Counseling Experience

Working as a psychologist in a college, I nearly stumbled over a young woman who was waiting in an obscure place after the office was officially closed for the day. She said she had come before at the same time but found no one there. We set up a time to meet and I asked her to fill out a preliminary form. One of the questions on the form asked what was bothering her. She wrote down one word, "anomie," which is a state of being unconnected, alienated, and adrift. When we met, she explained she had recently transferred to this college because she had been expelled from the religious order that heretofore had provided her education. She was expelled for dating a young man, who was himself committed to another ascetic religious order. Since her expulsion, she had moved to a new city, taken an apartment, enrolled in college, and handled school responsibilities well. The relationship with the young man continued. She was perplexed only by the way she felt, which she described as being "at loose ends." She was continually surprised and impressed by ordinary things like fruit stands displaying vegetables, friendly contacts with neighbors and strangers, the weather, and other everyday matters. We discussed the recent past events, her feelings of surprise, shock, and hurt at her dismissal, and her efforts to adjust to this abrupt shift in her life plan. She appeared to have everything well in hand considering all she had just been through. Finally, not far along in the second session, I gathered my courage and, with an unusual hesitancy, asked her whether she might be suffering, not from "anomie," but from happiness. Looking surprised she replied, "But I have always been told that we derive happiness only in the service of others!" Cautiously, I inquired whether she believed this was the only definition of happiness. With little encouragement she agreed that there might be other definitions besides the one offered in religious life, and she relaxed. We had a few subsequent sessions in which I said little (also unusual to my counseling style) as she reported the events in her life, especially her deepening relationship with the young man. I did not need to say much because despite the rude jolt in her life plans, despite her sudden independence, and despite her involvement in her first sexual relationship, she was not psychologically disturbed. She was instead experiencing feelings of disorientation at the unfamiliarity and pleasures of her new life. She discussed her doubts, the difficulties her family experienced with this change in her life, and her way of handling problems. We soon began to realize that she was managing well and was able to handle things on her own. Our relationship ended, and though she was free to come back if she later felt unsatisfied, she did not return.

I found counseling this young woman satisfying for several reasons. My years of training and experience had prepared me to work with disturbed individuals, and even in a college setting, I usually saw students who displayed serious emotional, educational, and psychological problems. I felt better trained to diagnose psychopathology than the emotion called "happiness." I was pleased to discover that I was able to recognize it when it appeared. Also, I was wary of interfering with this young woman's religious faith. Since we had different religious backgrounds, I wasn't sure if my feeling that she was better off out of the religious order was an accurate or biased perception. Also, her definition of happiness was a reflection based on religious beliefs, and I had difficulty offering her another that was contradictory.

The experience was gratifying because it appeared I was correct in my unusual "diagnosis" of happiness, and because I was able to recognize a resourceful and self-sufficient person when I saw one. I enjoyed my role in welcoming her to the real, or at least more typical, world. In spite of my minimal counseling role, I was delighted to see her negotiate a difficult life passage with relative ease and limited support, and I was pleased to be able to remain quiet when little help was required. My quietness reduced the chances of my biases influencing her choices and perceptions.

Now select another example of when you tried to help someone. This time choose an instance that was frustrating or unsatisfying. Again use the following questions to help you identify your personal dissatisfactions or disappointments.

Exercise #2 Frustrating Experience

- How did you and the help-seeker get together?
- What made you offer to help this individual?
- What made you feel you would be able to help?
- Did you have any initial doubts? What were they?
- How much time did you spend together?
- What were your perceptions and feelings about the individual?
- What did you hope the other could gain from the relationship?
- Were you comfortable with the relationship?
- What made you comfortable or uncomfortable?
- How did you handle difficulties that occurred in the relationship?
- In your opinion, what were the causes of the problems which the person discussed with you?
- Did you think that the person had other problems which he or she would not discuss with you?

• How did you help the individual?
• What did the individual gain as a result of your help?
• What did the person fail to achieve from the relationship?
• Were you surprised that your efforts were ineffective?
• Did you feel as if you provided the help that was required, and if so, why was it unsatisfactory?
• Was the role you played a natural and comfortable one for you? Was it a simple extension of yourself? Or did it require special effort?
• Were there demands which you felt unable to fulfill?
• Did the person have problems similar to yours?
• Did you learn anything about yourself that surprised you?
• How do you think the person felt about you and your help?
• What did you find most pleasing about the encounter? What was most difficult or frustrating?
• What happened to the relationship when your helping role was over?
• Did you find it difficult to end your role as helper?
• Did you discuss your frustration and disappointment with the help-seeker? With anyone else?
• And finally, how did your personal experience influence your decision to help this individual? How did it affect your approach? Did the relationship and its outcome satisfy any of your personal needs? Which personal needs remained unsatisfied? How did the encounter affect your self-esteem? Did the frustration which you experienced in this relationship have an effect on your desire to help others or on your way of handling subsequent encounters?

As with the previous exercise, discussing these issues with others can provide valuable feedback and contrast. It may be more uncomfortable to discuss an experience that did not go well than to discuss a successful one, but we learn more from our mistakes than we do from effortless encounters. If interchange with others is not possible, you can use one of my frustrating experiences as a contrast, but be sure to examine one of your own first.

Frustrating Counseling Experience

I had a frustrating and less rewarding time trying to help

another college student. This young woman demanded to be seen at once by a counselor, indicating immediate and pressing problems that could not wait. She was added to my full schedule on a busy day at midterm time, when the counseling office had many clients in distress. What she wanted was an answer to a question, "What makes somebody take a nervous breakdown?" Not understanding her concern, I asked her what she wanted to know and why. I explained there was no simple answer to the question as she stated it and that I needed to know more to be helpful to her. Although she insisted that all she wanted was *the* answer, she did explain that her boyfriend, Joey, also a student at the college, had "taken a nervous breakdown" following the last semester and had to be hospitalized. At this point, he had been in the hospital for a few weeks and was feeling better. She wanted to know how she could avoid the same thing happening to her. I sensed that she might think that the condition was transmittable from one person to another, so I assured her that a nervous breakdown was not contagious; that did not seem to calm her. Nor was she concerned over Joey, whom, she felt, was making excellent progress. She was not troubled by any immediate or long-term effect his condition could have on their relationship. She only wanted to know the cause of such a reaction so she could avoid it. She was difficult to work with because she insisted on getting *the* answer; nothing else interested her. Considering the various factors believed to contribute to "mental illness" frustrated her. Set on finding only one particular determinant, she was annoyed to hear that I thought there were more. I knew of no single explanation to give her and she was not able to name one she deemed sufficient. When I asked her about herself she seemed reluctant, as if such exploration were irrelevant. I did learn a little about her family, and I discovered that she had a twin. We were running out of time in the session, and the issue was far from settled. Because I entertained the notion that being one of a set of twins might be a clue to her uneasiness, I told her I thought her question might have something to do with her own psychological concerns. I suggested we talk more and she agreed. She did not mind coming back, but during each subsequent session, she began by reviewing all the answers which people in the ladies' room or on the subway had given her. Each time I encouraged her to talk about herself—the personal concerns, fears, or difficulties which she experienced in her relationship with Joey, school, her family, and so on. She complied, and often I thought she was becoming more attuned to herself, more aware of problems in her own life. Although she and her twin had been close while growing up, they had pursued different activities in the last year or two. Apparently she had been able to separate herself from, and be independent of (and, she thought, superior to) her sister. I speculated that because she was a twin, she might imagine she would also suffer the things that happened to others to whom she was close, and that because of this she feared she might suffer a breakdown similar to Joey's. While she found my hypothesis interesting, it did not succeed in easing her mind. She was still determined to find *the* answer to her question. We spent more productive time, it seemed, discussing her disappointment with Joey. She had been involved with another young man when she met Joey, and although the other fellow was a drug user (unreliable and not particularly desirable in any way she could name), she felt Joey's breakdown might imply that it was a mistake to choose him for her boyfriend. In her mind, his problems cast some doubt on the advisability of her choice. She talked freely on this issue, discussing the reasons for her decision. Eventually, she seemed satisfied with her choice, although it wasn't a "happily-ever-after" one. Yet, *the* answer to the question was still on her mind. I discovered that she tried to see another psychologist in the office (the college counselor who had helped Joey in his difficulties) and asked him what caused Joey's breakdown. The other psychologist saw her briefly, only to tell her that confidentiality would not permit him to discuss Joey's problems with her without Joey's permission. Finally, one day she came to her session triumphant! Someone in the ladies' room had told her that too much schoolwork caused a nervous breakdown. She was certain that this was the answer. Consequently she decided not to enroll in summer school as she had planned; she also decided to lighten her course load the following semester, even though she had not planned a particularly heavy schedule. She felt relieved to finally discover what caused someone to "take a nervous breakdown." This explanation did not seem adequate or accurate to me. By her own admission (or her transcript) she was not a very accomplished student. She did not display anxiety about her studies, and she had minimal job expectations and career plans. In contrast, Joey was very ambitious. Although school pressures can be overwhelming and disturbing to vulnerable students, it is unusual, and in her case, unlikely that they could cause a breakdown. She listened but showed little interest in my reservations. She was so elated with *the* answer obtained in the ladies' room that she could barely sit still. She saw no point to further discussion. She had silenced the nagging question, and, although *the* answer seemed more applicable to Joey than to herself, she now felt problem-free. That was our last meeting; she did not return to the office.

Many years later I still remember how frustrating this experience was for me. I am still not sure whether I understood her or her concern. I know I did not find the means to develop a working partnership with her. She did not report or complain of typical school-related symptoms of emotional distress, such as excessive worry, sleeping disturbances, concentration difficultes, or anxiety. But it is possible that college might have been inordinately stressful for her, perhaps even beyond her abilities. She was not in academic jeopardy or failing any courses, but her grades were just passing.

In sessions I felt annoyed with the endless reports from the ladies' room and the answers which seemed more accurate to her than those I had formed—this was a blow to my ego. I felt distressed when she sought another counselor at a point when I thought we were "getting somewhere." She seemed to me to be a demanding, self-centered person with no real concern for Joey or anyone else she discussed. She was so narrowly focused on her nagging question, I was unable to engage her or negotiate a satisfactory counseling contract.

We never developed trust or rapport. I was permitted to ask her questions, but I was really expected to answer hers. I never felt comfortable with her focus, or her eventual solution. I could empathize with her distress and I felt pleased when she finally seemed relieved, but I never felt satisfied nor gratified. Counseling had no visible useful impact, and she left tickled to death with both a plan and a solution that seemed unsuitable to me. I felt like the shoe salesman who shows a customer a full line of goods in her size only to have her walk out in a pair three sizes too small.

Answers to the questions presented earlier about your helping encounters can help identify some gratifications which you hope to obtain in counseling as well as some expectations of "clients" which relate to your personal needs. Comparing your reactions to those of others will allow you to see both commonalities and differences and help you to draw further conclusions about yourself. Whether or not you feel satisfied with helping others may depend on your goals and your standards of success.

What were the major differences between your satisfactory and frustrating experiences? What do these tell you about your expectations of clients, of yourself, and of counseling? Did it make a difference whether or not the client's problem was familiar so you could counsel from your own experience? Was the client's response to you—whether appreciative or critical—a major element in your feeling satisfied? Did your personal feelings about the client influence your efforts or affect your evaluation of the encounter? How were your personal needs satisfied in the first instance? How were they not satisfied in the second?

Your self-analysis will teach you more about yourself and your expectations as a counselor than my words. But it is important to be wary if the difference between feeling satisfied or frustrated when helping others depends heavily on your ability to direct others, or get positive feedback, or foster binding emotional involvements. These are rewards that may serve our needs, rather than our clients'.

Counselors' Feelings and the Human Helping Alliance

Warning counselors about their attitudes and feelings makes it seem as if counselors were free to choose how to feel at any given time. While it is easy to point out the dangers of being judgmental, controlling, or identifying with clients, and the advantages of showing concern, acceptance, and accountability, such guidelines are actually theoretical; attitudes and feelings do not remain constant in real counseling encounters.

Some beginners believe that, by natural inclination, they will always respond appropriately and remain in control of their feelings toward their clients; this belief is an illusion. Of course, we can express warmth, interest, and concern when we feel them, but what do we express when we are annoyed, bored, or offended? Trying to give the "right impression" and hide our real feelings seldom works; clients usually get the message anyway.

In the next several pages we will review a counseling relationship gone wrong and analyze it in detail. The purpose will be to consider how counselors can use even angry feelings in their clients' behalf. The session took place in a college's academic advising unit. Jane, who had been counseling for a few months, was typically kind, responsive, and accommodating to students who came to her for help. One day a neat, formally dressed, but unattractive and pudgy young man named Milton arrived for his first appointment. Brushing aside the usual introductions as a waste of precious time, he began to complain about the inefficiency of the counseling office, the delay in getting an appointment, and the general stupidity of college personnel. He let it be known that he was a very bright, very busy, very efficient young man who carried a heavy science course load that did not give him the luxury of waiting around to see someone about a simple problem. Intending to graduate at the end of the following semester, Milton wanted to be certain that he had fulfilled all the basic requirements. He did not want to be informed at the last minute that he had more "silly" courses to take. Jane, offended by his criticism of the office and college where she worked, tried to explain the impossibility of immediately seeing every student who needed help, but he was not interested. In fact, he got huffier and launched into a string of complaints about the registrar's office (another place where he could have obtained the information he wanted)—about its inefficient, self-indulgent staff who gossiped or ate on the job, misplaced records, and awarded erroneous items on transcripts. He explained that his view was shared by his esteemed professor so he was not alone in this opinion. Again Jane tried to defend the overworked, understaffed registrar's office and explain the computer errors on transcripts, but these attempts added more fuel to Milton's fire. He extended his critical attack to include everything connected with the school. He complained that the students wore bluejeans; they smoked and fooled around; the crowded elevators were run by rude operators; the atmosphere was unscholarly, and so on. Jane, who was herself wearing bluejeans and smoking, was responding curtly and impatiently. She listened as long as she could, and then abruptly turned the focus to his problems—not his academic concerns but his behavior. How dare he be so critical? What gave him the right to indict the whole college? How did he come to regard himself as superior to others?

Now it was his turn to be on the defensive! Although Milton had earlier expressed derogatory views of counseling (amateur "shrinks," and "couch questions"), he suddenly demanded that Jane spell out his problems and asked whether she thought he needed psychological help. Jane was dismayed—had she struck a nerve? Had she wounded the rude beast? She had difficulty dealing with his question and lamely tried to throw it back for him to answer. Suddenly the time was up. They still had not considered the problem which brought him there in the first place. Setting another meeting time caused him further anxiety about his busy schedule, and Milton muttered on his way out that, of course, it was hard to get an appointment with advisors who were unable to do their jobs efficiently.

We will review many aspects of this counseling session and the dynamics affecting Jane and Milton. But first, we need to ask, "What is the use of expecting counselors to show concern, acceptance, and warmth if such feelings fade away in difficult exchanges?" Why identify helpful and destructive counselor attitudes if we, like Jane, cannot show or hide them at will? Ironically, the standards are as useful in the breach as in the observance. They are valid as ideals and models and just as useful when indicating deviations from our original intentions. They are not behavioral expectations of counselors, but a baseline from which to measure the client's affect on the counselor, whose special responsibility is to use personal feelings in the service of clients. *A good counselor does not maintain a fixed demeanor, impervious to feelings provoked by clients; he or she recognizes and uses feelings and reactions in order to understand the meaning of the interpersonal process.*

Helping others is less a science than the constructive use of emotional responsiveness. However much we know intellectually, we all have feelings and emotions. We are affected, disturbed, and troubled by those we try to help. We are not just affected *for* them; we are affected *by* them. They "get to us" in our role as helpers, but more immediately, to us as individuals. They get to our sensitive areas, to our blind spots, to the parts of us we would prefer no one see, especially not someone seeking our help. We believe as counselors we should have no personal reactions; that as private persons, we should be totally removed. But it cannot be so.

Counseling is an intense and personal interaction. As helpers we are like the parent who intends to be understanding and patient with a child but who unexpectedly gets angry, impatient, or withdrawn. Our personal vulnerabilities make it difficult and demanding to help others with personal problems. Our task requires us to look at our reactions to clients and distinguish between our problems and theirs, to sort out our feelings and identify what client behavior has caused them. We may not be aware that self-scrutiny is necessary if a client triggers a personal response. We may go along with our feelings without recognizing their potential for harm. In the example, Jane was intimidated, insulted, and angry at the abrasive Milton. She felt it necessary to "put him in his place." Not only did she ignore his academic concern and fail to explore what was bothering him, she retaliated aggressively by challenging his mental health. This clearly disturbed him, and although it is likely that Milton did have personal problems, Jane raised the issue not as a psychological assessment or area of exploration but as an attack! Accurate or inaccurate, there was little chance for Milton to use the issue productively. Jane felt abused and provoked by him. Many of us would have felt the same way had we been in her place. However deviant from the positive reaction a "good" counselor is supposed to have, Jane's feelings provided useful information about Milton's impact on others. Instead of recognizing or discussing his effect on her, she acted on her hostile feelings as if she were dealing with a personal acquaintance.

In social situations, most of us react to attacks by defending ourselves and/or attacking in return, as Jane did. As counselors, however, we have to try to use our feelings about the client *for the client.* Almost simultaneously, we must feel, understand our feelings, and express our reactions in a way our clients can understand. We have to be ourselves and be detached from ourselves at the same time, so we can be attuned to the needs of the other person. We have to "objectify" subjective feelings so that others can recognize the impact they are having on us. To our clients we must be models of responsiveness and openness, not impassiveness, infallibility, or perfection. This is an ability that is hard to teach or practice, especially when clients behave in threatening ways. Luckily it is a natural gift for some people. Nonprofessionals can be as effective as professionals if they respond to the meaning, not the form, of behavior.

Parents, for instance, are often astute observers and natural helpers in child-rearing, especially when their children are young. Instead of responding angrily to the child who is suddenly provocative and quarrelsome, the mother or father senses a problem the child may be unaware of—illness, hunger, fatigue, or disappointment. Reading the reason behind the child's behavior, the parent responds to *it* rather than to the overt behavior. Rather than scold the child, the parent might put the child to bed, provide a bottle, or give medicine or comfort. Since children often cannot articulate their discomforts, parents learn to read behavioral signs.

Parenting a child and being able to read the cues provided do not make everyone a good diagnostician. Remember the strange Duchess in *Alice in Wonderland* who is nursing an infant in the kitchen where the cook has been too liberal with the pepper? While shaking the baby, she sings this familiar "sort of lullaby":

Speak roughly to your little boy,
And beat him when he sneezes

He only does it to annoy
Because he knows it teases.

Few parents would want to follow the Duchess's example, but it is still difficult to respond intuitively and effectively all the time. As children mature and develop more complex needs, many parents are confounded. When their children's behavior threatens their self-esteem and feelings of well-being, parents burdened by their own problems and expectations are not always able to understand, tolerate, and fulfill the needs underlying the behavior.

It may be misleading to describe intuitive responsiveness as a natural talent. None of us is intuitive and responsive at all times. Like the parent who speaks roughly to a sneezing child, we may misunderstand the cues. Or we may misinterpret our own feelings. Or we may be unwilling to admit our feelings to the client. It is a difficult and unexpected challenge, using our personal feelings on behalf of clients. It requires us to reveal ourselves. Jane had to recognize that Milton's arrogance upset her—and that it also worked against him. Sharing her reaction would have made him aware of himself.

Dealing effectively with the feelings clients arouse in us is not easy. Sometimes knowledgeable and well-trained therapists act on their personal feelings instead of articulating them for patients' benefit, their momentary needs subverting their judgment. We are all too familiar with horror stories of professional fallibility: psychiatrists who sleep with their patients, doctors who are more interested in money than in their patients' care, and other cases in which patients are exploited, abused, or hurt while receiving professional services. We deplore these actions. We maintain rigorous ethical standards for professionals and expel those who are flagrantly irresponsible from professional membership. But make no mistake. The responsibility of helping others often conflicts with and limits self-interest. It is not always comfortable to place the client's welfare first. Imagine the therapist's discomfort in terminating treatment with a private patient who makes gratifying progress and whose fee helps pay the bills. When the patient reaches the therapeutic goal, the therapist endures two losses at the same time. Nonprofessionals are less likely to suffer financial loss, but it is true nonetheless that decisions made in the best interest of the client may be difficult for any counselor.

We are not always aware of the subtle ways in which we are seduced, threatened, or provoked to action by the behavior and needs of people we try to help. Think of the lay person sought out and preferred to a professional for counseling. Such a request for help is flattering, ego-boosting, perhaps justified, almost irresistible, but is it in the client's best interest? Can the nonprofessional do the professional's task? Can the nonprofessional make a commitment equal to that of the professional? There are many difficult considerations. Sorting out what is for "us" and for our pride from what is for the client's good is arduous for professional and nonprofessional alike. Often we have to make decisions we would rather not make, and on occasion, deny our preferences. While nonprofessionals are frequently called upon to make judgments as sound as those of the trained helper, they are often handicapped by their inexperience, their wish to please, and their unfamiliarity with the risks and the ethical principles involved. Our impulses do not always lead us to the right choices or behavior. (Those who want to familiarize themselves with current, professional ethical standards will find them at the end of the book.)

Can nonprofessionals display sound judgment? Absolutely! There are many untrained, but thoughtful and scrupulous helpers. These individuals may be less able than professionals to explain what prompts them to make certain therapeutic decisions or name the cues they use. They are often unfamiliar with the language and methods of the specialist. Yet farsighted and aware of their responsibilities, they are as trustworthy and ethical as if they had memorized the book on professional standards. There are also nonprofessionals who have good intentions but may, through a lack of self-awareness and supervision, endanger clients.

The Importance of Self-Awareness

When do our efforts serve our clients' best interests? It's

not always easy to tell. At the time, Jane believed she was helping Milton when she defended the college offices which he criticized. She felt as if he needed to be told, in one way or another, that he was out of line. But Jane had to recognize that while she reached out and supported hesitant, troubled clients, she recoiled from those who were angry and troublesome like Milton. We have no way of knowing in advance if a client's behavior matches our preferences; instead we have to recognize and learn to use our personal sensitivities constructively.

How can we tell if a counselor uses personal feelings in the service of clients? One reliable way is to observe his or her counseling contacts with various clients over an extended period of time. A single observation is usually inadequate since different clients provoke different reactions, and many of us talk a better game than we perform. It is also difficult to be one's own judge. What distinguishes the consistently helpful from the potentially harmful counselor is self-awareness—the ability to recognize, admit, and keep one's vulnerabilities in perspective. The exercises provided earlier in this chapter are useful in this respect.

Self-awareness is as important to the counselor as life experience or technical training, but it is harder to learn and maintain. Since self-awareness is difficult to teach, most written materials focus on counseling techniques, as if skills were the key to helping. While professional training is partly academic and technique oriented, the most important learning experiences occur through individual and group supervision of helping relationships. Trainees are encouraged and even forced to look at themselves, as well as their patients, in order to understand and perform the helping role. Lacking skilled supervision, the nonprofessional is distinctly disadvantaged. Without feedback from others, it is difficult to appreciate alternative views and approaches or to see how personal needs intrude and distort relationships. When we label a client hostile, is it because the individual is angry at us or because we are intimidated by his assertiveness and frankness? Can the client be angry and hostile with reason—and not necessarily at us?

Let us return to the case of Jane and Milton. Milton was

brusque and irritable from the start. He walked in with a chip on his shoulder. Jane, intimidated, failed to explore what made him testy. It may have been a minor irritation—too long a wait for his appointment, a foul-up with the receptionist in the outer office, disappointment over a recent examination, or anxiety over missing a course required for graduation. (Administrative regulations can be infuriating to the student when rigid rules seem to deprive him or her of individual recognition.) Jane, offended by his criticism, did not ask what was bothering him. She acted as if he was attacking her personally. Her explanations of institution procedures and problems were really her form of self-defense. These statements must have intensified Milton's feelings of unimportance as an individual and as an accomplished student. So, in turn, Milton was provoked to tell Jane how superior he was and how offensive the college was to him.

Milton's views of college life probably troubled him. His clothes and attitudes suggested a formal and proper young man, and his appearance was unattractive and out of style. Seeing other students act and dress differently, he must have felt like an outsider rejected by his peers. Such discomfort might have been painful to admit, and Milton seemed to use bravado to cover up underlying concerns.

Jane also posed a threat to Milton. Her role was one of an authority who could "make" him take a "silly" course. Furthermore, she was an attractive, feminine young woman, informal in dress and manner, and only a year or two older than Milton. These features could not have failed to impress Milton, who clung to his rigorous academic program and esteemed professor as vital indications of his worth. Jane did not "hear" his need for respect and recognition nor recognize that she could be a threatening figure in his eyes. She struck back at Milton in a vulnerable area. Despite his previous scornful remarks, Milton showed concern over her opinion of his mental health. Jane was surprised by the impact of her exasperation. She became frightened and backed off. By her sudden evasiveness, she intensified Milton's questions about himself. At the very least, she failed to provide the practical academic information he was entitled to, whether he behaved in a rude or pleasant manner.

Do these remarks sound like an excuse or apology for Milton? He was arrogant and unpleasant, and perhaps deserved what he got! He had probably provoked many similar reactions in his other encounters with college personnel, which may have led him to indict school offices and officials. But the counselor's role is different from that of other institutional personnel; it is to recognize provocative behavior and *not* respond like everyone else. It was up to Jane to engage him in a collaboration in which his—and her—reactions could both be understood. Such an alliance does not absolve clients from responsibility; instead it seeks to make them aware of their impact on others.

Consider some alternative ways of responding to Milton. If Jane had managed to gain a little distance, she could have used her feelings productively many times during the session. She could have answered Milton's final question about her opinion of him by saying truthfully, "Hey, the way you've behaved makes me feel hurt and angry. I wonder if you want me to feel this way, and I wonder if it's in your best interest. After all, you did come here for help." Similar comments would have been useful earlier in the session as well. Hindsight gives us vision and allows us to put more appropriate words in place of ones we used, but Jane's script is rewritten here for a different purpose. It makes the point that the feelings clients evoke in us are not errors in themselves, however much they deviate from the positive regard we expect to feel. They are assets if recognized and used in the client's behalf. Ironically, more insight and awareness come from discomforts, misunderstanding, confusion, and confrontation than from smooth "polite" interaction in sessions. If Milton had been pleasant and polite, there would have been less opportunity to engage him and address the discomfort of his college days. And—from another viewpoint—if Milton were more comfortable in college, he would not have acted in such an abrasive way.

But therapeutic mistakes can often be productive. Once my analyst, who was sitting behind me, seemed to fall asleep during my session. That nap was painful but productive for me. My response to his dramatic disinterest put me directly in touch with previously concealed concerns about my unimportance to the important people in my early life, feelings I had never recognized or verbalized before. During the few minutes the therapist seemed to be asleep, I "heard" a melancholy song that had been haunting me for years, "Lost in the Stars." I began to understand what it meant to me. The analyst did not defend himself or apologize (although, had he done so, I might have "felt" immediately better), but he helped me explore its impact. Even though I doubt that insight could have come to me in any other way, I am not in favor of sleeping on the job.

A second example: As a college counselor, I was having a first interview with a young woman so tormented by self-doubt, about getting help and other aspects of her life, that she constantly wept. She cried so often and so much that she communicated very little. I found it difficult to gauge whether we were establishing a working relationship, if she was comfortable with me, or if I understood what was causing these painful doubts. A while into the session, she asked me a strange question. She said, "During a session do you ever feel as if you would rather not be here, that you don't care, or won't be able to help?" While I did not feel indifferent, I was at that moment interrupted by a call from my secretary about an important project that required my immediate attention. Instead of answering her question, I told the student that the phone message made it impossible to finish the session with her, and that we had to stop then and there. She was obviously distressed, and I was, at that moment, unwilling to help her. Had her fears come true? I urged her to make another appointment when she could talk more freely and cry a little less. I suggested she keep a diary and record her feelings and reactions so, the next time, we would have a written record of what she had experienced. She agreed and left.

I questioned whether she would ever return, but the next day she appeared. I was in my office working on the project and was not interviewing students. She interrupted me for a moment. She apologized for all her crying the day before, assured me that she was now more certain she did want my help, and gave me a sheath of notebook papers filled with all her recorded thoughts, ruminations, and concerns. Among her many jottings, many almost illegible because of the urgency of her thoughts, was a statement that she had found someone who would be able to help her.

That was the beginning of a successful counseling relationship which resulted in a profound diminution of tension, a remarkable degree of insight, and some behavioral change. That relationship seemed enhanced because her fear that a counselor might be uninterested in her was actually confirmed during the first appointment. In time I learned that she had undergone a previous experience with a counselor whom she believed indifferent. After our first meeting I suspect she felt that I would at least be honest with her.

So prescriptions for appropriate feelings and reactions in counselors are like the fair weather reading on a barometer: subject to wide variations. Deviations from our "fair weather" expectations of ourselves tell us what is happening in the human helping alliance. There are constant changes even in well-established relationships. If incongruities are ignored, they can undermine counseling.

It is almost never too late to use our reactions to help the client. In her next appointment with Milton, Jane could have admitted her difficulties with their first session. "You know I wasn't very happy with the way our last session went. You sounded as if you were dissatisfied with offices in this college, and I never asked you what your experiences were." Or, "Some of the things you said about the college made me angry and defensive, so I didn't give you the attention I would have liked. I'm sorry to say this, but I suspect others would react to you the same way I did." Or even, "I didn't like what happened in our first session. How did you feel about it?"

Counselor self-revelation serves many purposes. It lets clients know of their impact on us and probably on others; in showing the counselor's willingness to be honest and direct about feelings, it encourages clients to do the same; it indicates that counseling is a shared responsibility, not the work of a remote superior directing an inferior; it promotes trust and keeps the feelings which might undermine the relationship in plain view; and it makes clear that counseling is a meaningful human involvement with much in common with the most precious relationships of our lives.

The counselor concerned only with showing, saying, and doing the right thing, cannot succeed for long in the human helping relationship. Counseling is not a dramatic role or an exercise in choosing from multiple options. When we let clients know how and when their behavior affects us and interferes with our helpful intentions, we use ourselves and our feelings to show them a picture of themselves. The continuing challenge for all helpers is to increase this capacity for self-awareness—of using ourselves on behalf of others.

How to View and Deal with Counseling Failures

If you have done the self-discovery exercises earlier and reviewed some of your satisfactions and dissatisfactions in helping others, you have begun the important task of evaluating your counseling efforts. As you continue counseling, you are likely to have other disappointing and discouraging experiences. As long as there is continued contact with a client, errors and difficulties can be identified and discussed, but that opportunity is lost if the client breaks off the relationship. Most novices view such rejections as painful blows; but they are also opportunities for learning. Your development as a counselor depends on your understanding the reasons for your counseling errors and failures.

Many people who want to counsel make an assumption they are not aware of: If they are basically competent, counseling will be an easy, natural, and effortless task. The truth is that success in counseling is not only hard to achieve, it is almost a miracle. Helping someone overcome long-standing problems is arduous and trying, no matter how competent or well-trained the counselor is.

The difficulties and disappointments are many: when we do not know or understand enough; when we understand a lot but cannot use ourselves effectively; when we help a client with one serious problem only to find another even more devastating; and when we lose a client to illness, or even to suicide. Occasionally, a client recognizes the need for change but is unable or unwilling to effect it. Sometimes clients get in touch with us too late or when our personal difficulties or plans interfere; and sometimes we care too much or too little to be fully effective.

These words are offered, not to discourage, but to give you a more accurate picture of the odds. *Competency in counseling does not guarantee success; it can provide an understanding of what went wrong.*

Two points are important: the first is, *expect to make mistakes but use them to learn.* Accepting limitations while working to remove them is the mark of commitment and responsibility in a counselor. Errors often fit a pattern which, when recognized, can be changed. When Jane, in the earlier example, recognized that she had expected all her clients to be models of politeness and compliance, she grew more tolerant of those who were angry or assertive. She also recognized that part of the problem was her own lack of assertiveness. Once she developed this capacity in herself, she found it less threatening in clients. Changes such as these don't occur overnight, so counselors need to reserve some tolerance for themselves. But their development often begins with the discovery that certain client characteristics cause them to abandon the helping role.

The second point to remember: *if you are experiencing difficulties with a client, discuss them with someone competent before they become serious.* Describe them with as much openness about yourself and your feelings as you can manage, and be willing to get feedback about yourself as well as the client. Remember, though, that the person(s) with whom you consult must be carefully chosen so as not to jeopardize the client's right to privacy.

Most beginners are extremely self-critical—but unproductively so—because they cannot see themselves well enough to identify the underlying problems in their counseling relationships. They tend to explain things in situational or mechanical, rather than psychological, terms and compensate by trying to stifle behavior rather than understand it. Getting a different perspective from another person can help. The client can also give feedback. Jane might have said to Milton, "You know I'm usually pretty easy to get along with. You have only been here a few minutes, and I'm feeling pretty irritated. Let's stop for a minute and talk about what's going on here." This may seem risky, but there are times when the troublesome client, if given an honest opportunity, can play a part in the solution.

Chapter III analyzed the client's feelings about the counseling process, but this chapter considers the other side—that of the counselor's feelings. We counselors anticipate that in helping others we will feel constructive and successful and that we will always be understanding and accepting of our clients. What we find is a surprising challenge. Instead of having us play a role and bypassing our vulnerabilities, counseling requires us to be ourselves and to use our feelings, even our problems, in the service of others.

V

Clarifying the Helping Role

Previous chapters have described clients' misconceptions and misperceptions about counseling as well as the faulty expectations of would-be counselors. All these mistaken notions make it sound as if the whole world were deluded about the nature of the counseling relationship. There is some truth to this perplexing conclusion; and there are, also, reasons why each individual has a somewhat unique idea about counseling. This chapter focuses on two statements that may sound strange, but they explain why there are so many different interpretations of the therapeutic relationship: first, the helping relationship is unreal; second, the helping role is ambiguous.

The Helping Relationship Is Unreal

It may be hard to recognize at first that the counseling relationship is *not* a simple extension of common experience. In the normal course of our relationships we have certainly learned the rudiments and rewards of helping others. We have all been helped by many people, and these experiences are cherished aspects of our lives. But this help we have received and given has been an incidental feature of relationships which primarily served other needs and purposes. In the pressure of daily living, the people in our lives cannot often put aside their own concerns and personal preferences to focus exclusively and objectively on the problems besetting us. Such help extended by family, friends, teachers, and others is circumstantial, unpredictable, and rarely sustained for long. No matter how much they care for us, our intimate associates have vested interests in and powerful preferences concerning the direction of our lives because our behavior affects them personally. They also have their own concerns which often take precedence over ours.

While the help we receive incidentally and spontaneously during the course of our relationships is valued, it rarely suffices for persistent psychological problems. For these we need someone who can focus exclusively on us for the time it takes us to sort things out; who is not threatened personally by our feelings and thoughts; who sees us as we are and as we could be without preconceptions and distortions; whose welfare is not affected by our behavior; and who can attend to us, without distractions and extraneous pressures. In fulfilling these requirements, a counselor differs from other people in our lives. Unlike other relationships, counseling is unreal; it has no real-life equivalents except in brief accidental moments.

Therefore, it is not surprising that we find it uncomfortable to assume the counseling role. The methods used for helping friends and associates—giving advice, offering reassurance, warning of danger—do not automatically transfer into the helping relationship. Our efforts were successful because we knew the individuals who asked our help; they knew and trusted us. Our relationships made our help effective. Some counselors, eager to prove their usefulness, pattern their responses on such past experiences. They do not realize they must first establish a relationship—with a stranger—before they can judge what kind of help is needed.

Beginners have trouble seeing that they can be helpful by *not* trying to be helpful. There is a natural inclination to do something quickly for the person in pain or trouble, and the inexperienced are often unaware that they have anything else to give. Yet, if we can stifle our immediate impulse to make things better, we can offer clients what they can't find anywhere else—sanctuary, a place to discover who they are, how they feel, and what they can do. Most clients have been given more advice, direction, and sympathy than they can handle and have aroused the concern of many people. And yet, in counseling, they frequently say, "This is the only place I feel safe"; "This is the only time I can be myself"; or, to the counselor, "You're the only one who really knows what I'm going through." Though unreal in comparison to the relationships we are accustomed to, counseling has a power and authenticity of its own.

Effectiveness in counseling is less a matter of *doing* than of *being*. Many think of counseling as an active process of advising, informing, correcting, and directing; but more importantly, counseling is an active state of *being present*—of listening and being responsive to clients. Counselors' suggestions are more helpful in indicating their understanding and insight than in providing practical solutions to problems.

I remember becoming panic-stricken some years ago. I called my therapist hoping to talk it out. To my amazement, I felt my anxiety stop the moment I heard the therapist's voice on the phone. We discussed the situation but the talk seemed unnecessary. It was the simple greeting, the confirmation that the therapist was "there" for me, that provided the comfort. He did not, nor need to, give me any specific guidance.

We often think that helping involves specific acts—a loan at a crucial moment, inspiring words when one has lost hope, a good suggestion, or a new perspective. Important as these specific actions may be, in reality they show that we are not alone—that we are understood, and our needs are recognized. This is the important message, and it can be conveyed in many ways: with a facial expression, a question, or an attitude as well as with a simple favor or service. As counselors, we need to show that we are "there" for our clients and they are not alone.

Our achievement-oriented society makes it difficult to understand that counseling is a matter of being. Even the language fails; and "being there" is an awkward way to describe the way counselors use themselves to help others. But counseling is an "enabling" process, and doing things for clients undermines their ability to recognize and develop their own capacities. The receptive, facilitating role exposes us, as counselors, both to our clients' pain and to the dreadful awareness that there are no easy solutions to serious problems. At first, this makes us feel vulnerable and powerless.

The necessity to "be" rather than "do" is so uncomfortable and unsettling for some people that they find the emotional buffeting intolerable and gravitate toward an advisory role. Others, who quiet the impulse to suggest quick remedies, believe that their meetings with clients accomplish nothing at all at first! In training counselors, I have often heard tapes of sessions in which counselors have enabled their clients to share their feelings and articulate problems. But after listening to the tapes with me, the trainees invariably ask, "What should I have done?" Trainees find it hard to see that they have already encouraged trust and openness, in allowing the client to talk and feel without interfering. Initially they cannot see that counseling is different from our active interchange with friends, and that *to be* during a session is an achievement. *More is accomplished by "doing" less.* Willingness to know what the client feels, *being there* for the client, and starting a working collaboration in order to understand the obstacles to happiness and self-fulfillment is what counselors provide.

This kind of help takes time, effort, and selflessness not found in the course of everyday life. But while unreal and artificial in this sense, counseling arouses feelings and stresses that are real indeed. In order to understand the people we counsel, we do not divorce ourselves from our feelings. What differentiates the helping alliance from our personal attachments is not our degree of emotional involvement but our commitment to utilize our feelings in the service of clients' growth and awareness. We are detached in only one way: we are not participants in our clients' lives and their acts do not affect us personally. We use what we see and feel to help clients understand themselves and see their impact on others. Then we are both involved in and detached from our clients' lives. Simultaneously we can be in a relationship and be able to observe its nature and progress—we are "in" and "out" at the same time.

Counseling involves us in an emotional experience that rivals our closest personal relationships in intensity and intimacy, and yet, it demands that we use that same experience to illuminate the problems which disturb the client. It is as though we were on both sides of a looking glass—we see the client while at the same time we reflect the image we see. In the unfamiliar and unreal role of counselor it is hardly surprising to find ourselves confused about who we really are.

The Helping Role Is Ambiguous

We have examined some of the ways in which the helping relationship, a human construction designed to develop insight and awareness, is unreal. It follows that the role and the image of the helper from the clients' viewpoint is ambiguous and susceptible to multiple interpretations. The image of the counselor is often determined by the needs and expectations of the client. This will become clearer with a few superficial examples.

If the client cries, the counselor is inclined to be gentle and supportive; if the client lies, the counselor is likely to be on guard and suspicious; if the client brags, the counselor may challenge the exaggerated assertions. Is the counselor really gentle, suspicious, or challenging? Clients are rarely aware of their contributions to the counselor's reactions.In sessions, the counselor's real features are not truly apparent. The client knows little about the counselor's personality or how the counselor typically interacts with others. A client may experience me as understanding and accepting in one session, but confronting and challenging in the next. Often the way I am perceived has less to do with me and who I am than with how the client wants me to be.

This means that there are no automatic formulas, nor "correct ways" to respond to clients. We can play different roles with different clients or show varying reactions to the same client. On the one hand, the role we play at any given time has to be responsive to the needs and behavior of the client. On the other hand, we must also convey our feelings and observations. There are no general guidelines which apply to all situations. Despite the enormous variation in the methods, styles, and responses of counselors, they may all achieve the same goal. As counselors we are a bit like different musical instruments on which clients play their tunes. We sound different from each other and from time to time, but we all attempt to illuminate the client's themes.

Both participants find the ambiguity of the counseling role difficult. Counselors may look and sound like people engaged in everyday relationships, yet they use their human responsiveness, not for personal gratification, but to reflect the client's image. This ambiguity is baffling to both client and counselor. Let us look at the client's perspective first.

Clients find it hard to trust a relationship which promises an unconditional commitment from a total stranger. Life has taught us to be suspicious of strangers and to expect, at best, indifference. Researchers, studying suspiciousness toward strangers, have tried giving dollar bills away on city streets and found that many more people refuse than accept them. As children we are taught, as a safety precaution, to refuse generosity from people we don't know.

On the other hand, we think our parents and relatives are required to love us; we see it as part of their role. After an evening in which she had been particularly delightful, I asked my eight-year-old niece, "Why do you suppose I love you so much?" She replied without a second's hesitation, "Because you are my aunt," as if our kinship determined my feelings for her.

Yet, in growing up, there were many times when we doubted our parents' love for us. We did not always find them adoring and interested. They were not loving when: we misbehaved or failed to match some expectation; they went away and left us; they were preoccupied and busy with their own concerns; or they were demanding and hard to please. Whatever the reason, when they could not love us or show concern, we took the blame. From the egocentric vantage point of children, no other explanation makes sense. If our parents, who were obliged to love us, did not, we felt at fault. When they were indifferent or uncaring, we questioned our own worth. We thought parents, by definition, were loving, caring, ready and able to help us, and always concerned with our welfare. If they were not, we found reasons to explain why we were unworthy of their love.

But if our parents *had* to, and did not always show loving interest, how can an unrelated stranger without any personal stake in us be concerned with our welfare? How can the counselor's loyalty be trusted? How can we believe the attchment and the commitment are genuine? We are perplexed by someone who sets aside all personal matters to help us, who tolerates us when we are troublesome and resentful, who accepts us when we don't even like ourselves, and who helps us gain understanding and self-respect. Wary, we try to diminish our disbelief by assigning familiar motives to the counselor to assure ourselves of his or her continued interest.

One motive easily assigned to professional therapists is that of monetary reward. But, as the relationship progresses, even financial interest does not seem sufficient to account for the counselor's genuine personal concern and unconditional attachment. So, even with professionals, we look for other explanations.

As clients, we compare a counselor's commitment to those more familiar commitments we find in our everyday relationships. If the counselor is close in age or experience, we assume a common bond and perspective similar to those we share with our siblings or friends. To quell our suspicions, we look for signs of personal interest, affection, and commonality. If they are not immediately apparent (and they rarely are), we may question whether the helper's interest is genuine and dependable. Before committing herself, one patient insisted I promise to be her friend after treatment ended. Another, explaining the caution she showed toward me, was convinced that, if we were to meet for lunch, we would have nothing to say to one another. Clients find it easier to trust therapists with whom they feel they share something in common, so they attribute familiar and comforting characteristics to their counselors.

Clients also see counselors as parent figures, especially if the counselors are close to their parents' ages. A client may imagine the counselor's values and expectations match those of his parents and anticipate rejection if he does not conform to them. In one case, an otherwise open and trusting female client was hesitant to discuss her sexual activities in sessions. She was convinced that I, like her mother, would disapprove. Eventually, she volunteered more information and discovered not only that my response differed from what she would expect from her mother, but also that *her* discomfort with her own actions was the real issue. Clients' initial doubts and apprehensions about counseling give us our first impression of their perceptions of us; they less often let us know which of our attributes they view as acceptable and reassuring. Since their satisfactions with us are likely to facilitate, rather than block, counseling they rarely bother to mention them. Yet their positive perceptions of us are probably as inaccurate as the troubling ones, and we may learn about them as counseling progresses. ("Oh, I thought because you were a woman"— or married, or Jewish, or homosexual, or young—"I wouldn't have to explain to you why I feel that way about men!")

There are elements of transference in both the positive and negative features clients ascribe to their counselors. What they perceive is related, in part, to their concerns about themselves and their expectations about the reactions of others. For clients, the ambiguity of the helping role is a blank screen on which they project fears, fantasies, and wishes. Though reality plays some part, clients' perceptions of counselors and their interpretations of counselor responses have meanings derived from clients' past experiences and present needs. The same counselor characteristic, comment, or facial expression will convey different messages to different clients—and to the same client at different times. Clients are not aware that the counselor's role is ambiguous and that what they see is partly fashioned in their own minds. They are surprised if and when they discover that their expectations, demands, and perceptions of counselors more accurately reflect themselves. As discussed in the case above, the client who expected me to be judgmental about her sexual activities was beset by feelings of shame and attributed her own self-critical attitude to me. (My attitudes were not apparent to her, nor particularly relevant.)

The differences between the helping role and the roles more commonly played in our lives must be understood by counselors. Initially, counselors are more comfortable "being themselves" than they are playing an ambiguous helping role. They are often tempted to abandon ambiguity and act as they would in normal circumstances. They want to befriend the lonely client rather than explore the reasons for the loneliness. They try to defend themselves from client criticism instead of looking into what may have provoked it. They scold or admonish the uncooperative client rather than try to understand the reluctance. These are natural impulses, but they violate the counselor's unique means for understanding clients and helping them understand themselves. One check against these impulses is to articulate them to the client rather than to act on them ("You know I feel like scolding you right now because you are so close-mouthed, but I guess we'll both be better off trying to find out what makes you act this way here"). Even identifying and expressing our impulses, rather than acting on them, is difficult, but doing this reminds us and the client that the counselor's role is to understand, not just react.

I faced this challenge on the first occasion I was to administer a battery of psychological tests. Now the incident seems funny, but it didn't at the time. With my testing materials in hand, I was admitted into a locked room in a building of locked wards. The patient, a young and attractive man, was brought into the room and the door was locked behind him. He seemed very surprised that his examiner was a young woman and became flustered as we introduced ourselves. When I invited him to sit down to begin testing, he countered with another suggestion—that we have sexual intercourse right there on the floor. Although I wasn't interested in his proposal, I felt sorry for this young man who was locked away from any female companionship in a veterans' hospital. I was afraid to reject him and uncertain of what he might do to me if I refused. With an awkwardness I can still remember, I told him that, in the long run, it would be to his advantage to complete the tests since they were an important part of his treatment and could lead to his eventual release. He eyed me for an endless moment and then agreed. Without further mention or any other indication of his original request, he cooperated and completed the tests in a straightforward manner. Clients may not be as direct as this young man, in telling us what they want from us, but they frequently have wishes or expectations that can, if we let them, alter our role.

Uncertain of their abilities as counselors, beginners may find their intentions challenged, subverted, transformed, or undermined by their own impulses as well as client behavior.

It hardly seems possible that fulfilling a client's request or acting on a helpful impulse can be *non*therapeutic. Preserving the ambiguity of the counseling role and restraining our inclinations can be strenuous work, and the purpose may not be immediately apparent.

When counselors do respond to clients, not through their objectivity as counselors, but as they would in their own personal relationships, their responses are called countertransference. Here is a brief example. If I am resentful and short-tempered with senior citizens because I fear their possible helplessness and dependency, I may regard my seventy-year-old client's complaints about his heart condition as unfounded and quickly dismiss them. Were this the case, my personal reactions would interfere with my listening to the client and comprehending his concerns. Countertransference, like transference, is an expression of our unique responses to others. When unaware of countertransference, we do not perceive our clients accurately and cannot respond appropriately; we see threat where there is none, or encourage clients to take risks beyond their abilities, or become overprotective, or make other errors. Expressions of countertransference are as individual as we are and so much a part of us that we rarely see them unaided. Like someone whose eyesight has never been tested nor corrected, we may not know that some of our perceptions are distorted. Because of their potential harm to clients, countertransference reactions are an important focus in the supervision of trainees. No book can do more than warn counselors about countertransference reactions and emphasize the importance of self-examination and consultation.

There are, however, some misuses of the counseling role—usually provoked by disturbing or appealing client behavior—so common that they are almost predictable in the work of inexperienced counselors. These, called role confusions, are discussed in the next three chapters.

VI

Friend or Counselor?

Counseling and friendship have common dimensions. Both relationships involve close emotional attachment and concern for the other person's welfare. In both, shared experiences and personal disclosures are likely to increase mutual trust and regard.

These are such essential therapeutic elements that it is no surprise that we are sustained, enlightened, helped, and changed by our friendships. Perhaps with enough of the right kind of friends and enough time to nurture and enjoy our friendships, therapists would be unnecessary. This idea is so appealing that some, who believe that discussing one's problems freely with another interested person is the essence of counseling, have created a counseling system. In "co-counseling," two willing individuals reveal their problems to each other. There are regular meeting times and rules to ensure that the time for each to talk and to listen is fairly apportioned. The "counselor's" role is to help the other identify and articulate problems and to listen attentively and acceptingly; on the next occasion the roles are reversed, with counselor acting as client. The obvious rewards and gratifications in such an arrangement have proved satisfying for some people. This contract systematically provides what occurs naturally between close friends.

But in most situations requiring counseling, this method is either impossible or unsatisfactory. Counseling and friendship are essentially different. Friendship and co-counseling are based on reciprocity; counseling is asymetrical, with the primary focus on the client. Friendship often has no particular purpose or goal; counseling is based on the specific objective of ameliorating problems. While it is true that any confidant can be of some comfort, many clients require more. For example, people in crises, people who have problems relating to others, and people with physical, mental, or emotional disorders need undivided attention, special tolerance, and specific approaches. Such individuals have usually failed to develop or sustain friendships, and some are too burdened to maintain the discipline of co-counseling. Counseling is also different from friendship because it requires special concentration on the part of the counselor: to fully understand the client's experience, to observe one's own reactions, and to monitor the nature and course of the relationship. This strenuous and planned effort obviates the casual spontaneity typical of friendship; it turns social interaction into work.

Another important feature of counseling is the guarantee of confidentiality. Friends often promise to keep secrets, but when angry or pressured by others, they may not. Since public knowledge can endanger a client's career, reputation, and invaluable relationships, information revealed in counseling must be afforded confidentiality. Personal disclosure can be healthy and relieving for the individual but, if any details are revealed to others who might misuse or misunderstand them, it can prove dangerous. Despite good intentions, friends are often subject to different pressures than are counselors, who assume confidentiality as a fundamental responsibility. Information about third parties is a case in point. If a friend tells me a secret about someone I don't know or care for, I may feel less obligated to keep the secret than if a friend tells me something in confidence about another friend or esteemed colleague. Confidentiality in counseling is, for this reason, a blanket guarantee; without the expressed permission of the client, nothing the client reveals will be shared with anyone for any reason. Exceptions to this rule occur only when clients or others are in physical danger and some outside intervention is required. Laymen rarely understand confidentiality to be this all-encompassing. (See Chapter IX for a more complete discussion of confidentiality.)

Here is an example that may help. The husband of a

couple who are both my close friends told me in private one day that he was disturbed because he found himself, quite impulsively, kissing and embracing a business colleague—a woman he had never particularly liked—while on a business trip. Shocked and dismayed by his behavior, he wondered if I, as a professional, had any idea why he should act this way. If he had been my client, I might have asked questions about his marriage and his sexual satisfactions with his wife. But as a friend I had no right to these intimate details, especially those concerning his wife, who was not in the room and could not give or deny me permission. Instructing him to withhold any specifics, I asked if he thought there were any difficulties in his marriage that might bear on his behavior. He looked stunned momentarily, then nodded his head. I said that was all I felt free to ask, but I would recommend a professional colleague if he, or he and his wife, wanted help. This incident illustrates the privileges professionals have that friends do not, even when the friend is a professional.

The point is important. Psychological expertise has different consequences in personal relationships than in professional ones. In this instance, I could act as a consultant in a limited fashion, but if I went further, I would be prying. Possessing therapeutic skills, and then assuming inappropriate prerogatives, can harm friendships and friends. *Counseling works effectively in relationships established for that purpose; the methods applied out of context can be dangerous.* Intimate revelation should be encouraged only when one has the commitment and capacity to use the information constructively and there is no risk to others not present. Caution is required not to misuse counseling skills, in the belief we can help our friends.

When friends with serious, or potentially serious problems ask us, or when we are tempted, to counsel them, we have to decline. Perhaps having their esteem and trust, we can help them find a counselor or someone else outside the intimate circle of their (and our) lives. If friends are hesitant to seek counseling, we can explore their objections with them and clear up some issues, such as confidentiality, that may be troubling them. If there are practical problems standing in the way of counseling, we may be able to help find remedies. But neither our friends' insistence nor practical problems should convince us that we must assume or continue in the role of counselor.

Personal friends may be sought as counselors because, among other reasons, they are seen as equal, rather than superior, in position. Inequality inevitably causes problems for relationships. Authority is feared and resented. Our natural impulse is to eradicate it from the helping alliance as in co-counseling. But, however troublesome the issue of authority is, it is unrealistic to try to eliminate it from most helping relationships. Counselors are usually selected because they possess some special training, life experience, or personal characteristics which distinguish and make them appear qualified. (Some attributes which attract help-seekers are not always those required for counseling—for example, the expert who teaches women's history may not be interested in or capable of aiding female students with their personal problems but it is easy to understand why she may be consulted.) If the counselor is qualified to help, this expertise confers upon him or her the responsibility of encouraging a productive relationship, and avoiding a harmful one. It does not make the helper superior. When the issue of inequality intrudes, it needs to be examined and understood rather than swept under the rug. Since it often encourages transference reactions, it can, in fact, be used to advantage in understanding clients.

I remember once in the course of a session recounting an incident about myself—an incident in which I had done something stupid or acted in a foolish way. My client was stunned; he seemed to have assumed that because I was a therapist I was totally free from odd behavior. This permitted me to assure him that my expertise lay in my knowledge and training, not in the perfect state of my mental health. We were both human, both capable of making mistakes and of having "hangups." This small exchange pointed up a vital issue in his treatment because this young man attributed perfection to any person more skilled or experienced than he. Convinced he would be found out and humiliated, he suffered painfully from any lack of concentration or error in his work. He was also tortured if he discovered a superior to be careless or mistaken. In realizing that experience and competence did not imply absolute perfection, this client was able to establish more realistic standards.

Trainees have difficulty seeing differences between their counseling relationships and their friendships. Although they seldom seek informal personal contact with clients, and often do not seem to want it, they find it hard to resist their clients' invitations to parties and other social events. They feel they owe the same demonstration of interest to clients as to friends and think their refusal will be profoundly hurtful and damaging. They do not recognize the opportunity to use these wishes and invitations as another means of understanding clients. Clients' attachments to counselors are vital to the counseling process, but they need to be explored rather than simply reciprocated.

A case in point is that of a young man who was seen by a trainee for counseling. A rather obnoxious fellow with few friends at school, he attached himself to a group of peer counselors running a college telephone hot line. Initially, they were attentive, but when his self-centeredness monopolized their time, they sent him to their supervisor, a young female graduate student. He responded positively to the opportunity to talk to her but mistook her kind, reliable interest in him for a demonstration of friendship. He said that she displayed the behavior that a real friend would show but his peers did not. He resolved the perceived ambiguity of the counselor's feelings by imagining that she was personally attached to him and was helping him as an expression of her love. He shared fantasies and dreams in which he and the counselor were romantically involved, and he extended many invitations for lunch and other informal contacts. This was not a young man the counselor found attractive or appealing. At first she simply ignored his romantic overtures and hoped he would get the hint. But because she wanted him to feel good about himself, she had problems refusing all his invitations. Afraid of hurting him, she had trouble letting him know that the undivided attention she showed him was extended in the service of counseling, not friendship. What he needed to recognize was that his own insensitivity to others, his total self-involvement, deprived him of true companionship. In this example, the counselor knew that fulfilling the client's wish for personal contact would convey the wrong message, but she still found it difficult to refuse him. Disappointing a client who asks for some demonstration of personal regard may make counselors feel that they are aloof and hypocritical. They need to see that the counseling relationship in itself is a meaningful expression of caring.

There are many other reasons to avoid befriending or socializing with clients. We are not always aware of the special importance and significance our clients give us. Trusted with intimate matters which others may not know, revered for the promise and effort of helping, and invested with transferential capacities prompted by the ambiguity of the role, a counselor can seem an extraordinary figure. What that figure does and says can have enormous impact, exceeding that of a friend or a casual associate. Acting as an ordinary person in social situations, a counselor can, unknowingly, do things that hurt, threaten, embarrass, anger, or disappoint a client. The company of others limits immediate feedback and discussion. A client is apt to attach significance to anything the counselor does even unintentionally. For instance, a client may find the counselor's greeting of someone he hates a hurtful act. If we have difficulty understanding our client's expectations in the carefully scrutinized counseling session, it is far more difficult to do so under relaxed and distracting circumstances.

A moving example of a near disaster precipitated by a counselor's unknowing gesture occurred in the film *The Quiet One*. The movie was a reenactment of a case study of an abused youngster, Donald, who lived in a school for emotionally disturbed and delinquent boys. There, while awaiting his mother's visit with a gift for her, Donald learned that his mother had deserted him. After thinking hard and long about his loss, he decided to give the gift to the school counselor to whom he was deeply attached. This counselor had frequently allowed Donald the privilege of lighting his cigarette. Leaving his present in the counselor's room, Donald, unseen, glanced out the window at the counselor, who was supervising a group of boys during recess. Donald watched the counselor let another youngster light his cigarette. To Donald this act seemed like a betrayal and an intolerable blow following his mother's desertion. He ran away from school and came close to losing his life. The counselor (who eventually rescued and made peace with Donald) was not aware that his act would hurt Donald nor did he know the importance to Donald of tendering the cigarette lighter. Although perhaps less dramatically, this is the kind of risk we run when we cannot monitor our interaction with clients.

Clients rarely tell us directly how important we have become in their lives. They may be unaware of bestowing on us a special power or importance; or they may be embarrassed by their own feelings of attachment and dependency; or they may find it easier to voice complaints rather than express the devotion that makes them feel vulnerable. Counselors can underestimate signs such as regular attendance, trust in sharing intimate matters, wanting to refer friends for help. The willingness we see in our clients may be only the tip of the iceberg; their emotional investment may be profound, compelling, and hidden.

A trainee was amazed when the young man she had been working with started a session by asking her what she thought of him. This was a client who had been difficult to engage in counseling and had always acted reserved and diffident when in session. She tried to deal with the question before she had an idea of what prompted it, but as she was doing so, he grew increasingly irritable and angry. He accused her of being an unfit counselor on the grounds that she was "too short." At one point he told her she was too smart; at another, that she did not know anything. It took time for her to recognize that his extensive and contradictory attack was in reaction to a topic she had introduced at the end of their previous meeting—the topic of referral. In time she was to leave the center. His diffident manner made it difficult for her to see that the relationship meant a great deal to him, and that referral implied to him her wish to be free of him. His angry accusations were his attempts to explain away the hurt.

The last two examples have illustrated painful repercussions of clients' attachments to counselors. Nonetheless, this intense attachment is the medium through which progress takes place in counseling. In time, both Donald and the diffident young man were able to use these trying experiences to recognize their fears of abandonment and their acute sensitivity to acts resembling rejection. The safety and structure of counseling can encourage intense attachments; understanding these attachments may help clients establish more realistic expectations of others, and even a tolerance for rejection. Yet unfortunately, many inexperienced counselors question their own effectiveness and doubt their impact on clients. Responding as friends rather than retaining the ambiguity of the counseling role, beginners may confuse their clients. Instead of maintaining the distance which, in time, allows clients to use them as transference objects, they imagine their effectiveness is increased by becoming "real." Once "real," we cannot be counselors. Clients seek personal contact with us in the roles we've played rather than as we really are. Several times I have sought, or been sought out, to befriend former clients upon concluding my official role; all of such friendships have worked out poorly. As a friend, I was still expected to focus mainly on the (former) client's problems; I was not recognized as a person with needs of my own. In addition, my revelation of my personal concerns seemed to tarnish their images of me.

Sometimes there are unconscious or hidden reasons for mistaking counseling for friendship. The most obvious one is loneliness felt by either participant. The individual with few sustaining relationships may be tempted to fill that void with the intimacy, affection, and appreciation experienced in the helping alliance. Although occasionally two paired in a helping relationship find lasting love and permanent partnership from their association, this is rare. Usually such romances are short-lived. When subjected to the mundane pressures of everyday life, the safety and security inherent in the helping relationship can disappear. As counselors, we need to recognize and fulfill most of our personal needs outside of the helping relationship. Our commitment to our clients is to help them increase their involvement and effectiveness with others, not to deflect it toward us.

For some profoundly ill and withdrawn individuals, the initial and perhaps prolonged effort in therapy is to encourage an attachment to a counselor. One summer I worked in a day-care center for veterans, most of whom had been previously and extensively hospitalized. A middle-aged, overweight black man, who was assigned to me for therapy, was so withdrawn he was almost mute during our daily sessions and in other day-care activities. When asked a question, all he would answer was "Yes" or "No." Each evening he went home to a single room in a boardinghouse without speaking to anyone. Most of the summer went by before he gave any sign that showed that our sessions had any meaning for him. Then, one day during the crafts period, he decorated a black matchbox with a big red heart even though the other patients decorated their boxes with shells. When it was done, he gave the box to me. Again he said nothing, but I, along with the other staff members, celebrated this small expression of emotional attachment. Such clients, whose illnesses have "burnt" out their emotions, suffer most from emotional blunting. If they feel anything at all, they cannot show it. Whether this patient thought of me as a friend or a girlfriend on the basis of the hours I spent with him, I wasn't going to quibble with him or explain my role as therapist. His gift indicated therapeutic progress although it was only a first and tentative step toward becoming attached to others. Asking such clients to participate in as many "normal" activities as we can provide is an effort to stimulate a spark, and the wish to feel and risk emotional involvement again.

This example illustrates how a client's attachment to a counselor can be therapeutic, but this attachment is not the final goal for any client. It is the medium through which some clients may redevelop interest in other people and through which other clients can see how they fashion their interpersonal world. The trust and the insights they gain then have to be made applicable and operative in their other relationships. This is the point that eludes those counselors who befriend clients and directly minister to their wishes for greater contact. Such acts satisfy the client's immediate needs or quell his or her anxieties, but they do not help him or her develop insight or the capacity to function independently. Hard as it is to see clients struggle in an inhospitable world, we do not help them by acting as their friends—giving them money, taking them into our homes, or even boosting their egos, unless we can promise to do these things for as long as they need them. The important job is helping them become self-sufficient.

Counseling is a device to strengthen clients, not leave them dependent; if all they learn is that we can and will take care of them, we have done a disservice in the name of helping. We get clients to trust us so that they can learn to better trust themselves, and then, others. We develop their attachment to us so that they can learn to risk emotional involvement and develop affectionate relationships in the outside world.

At times it is difficult to differentiate personal from counselor involvement. When a counselor's private life provides few supports or is in a state of crisis, the client's devotion may be very gratifying. Personal distress in the counselor's life can lead to alarming repercussions in the helping alliance. Therapists who make sexual advances during sessions may think they are helping their patients, but they are more likely to be expressing sexual and other relationship problems of their own. To help clients understand their emotional attachments to us, our own emotional needs must be recognized and kept under control. Helping others sometimes helps us keep our troubles in perspective. But at other times our troubles not only overwhelm us but alter our perspective as well. When our own lives are in crisis, supervision of counseling through discussion with an objective individual may be badly needed. We then have to share not just the case material, but the strain of our own lives. We have to be doubly aware that during such times socializing with our clients places the counseling relationships in jeopardy.

Although it is better to avoid informal contact with clients, those that occur by chance need not cause panic. If we run into a client in a public place, we don't need to hide, ignore the person, or run away. We should keep our contact brief and explore its effect on the client later. Similarly we need not deny clients any and all information about our private lives. What we should question are the reasons behind their interest. If the client becomes evasive, the matter still needs to be pursued because their curiosity about us as private individuals has implications for counseling. Another point: Most clients are eager for their counselors to show interest in their achievements and endeavors outside the office—by attending their concert performances, reading their literary work, or viewing their art or other creations. Such "extracurricular" effort can be helpful to treatment. The counseling role is not a strait-jacket that restricts our every move. It does require understanding of the psychological implications of all "extracurricular" contacts.

In summary, since friendship and counseling do resemble each other in emotional involvement, counselors need to be wary of mistaking clients for friends or of being used by clients to fill social voids that should be addressed through counseling. Struggling with the unreal and ambiguous nature of the counseling role, participants may want to test the emotional attachment in ways suited to friendship. This will undermine rather than support counseling. The counselor may act as the proverbial "friend in need," but to continue to be effective in that role, counselors cannot become friends in the ordinary sense. Conversely, we can be confidants and help our friends in many ways, but we cannot counsel them without jeopardizing counseling, friendship, or perhaps both. Personal involvement is a hindrance in counseling. Recent research has demonstrated that the clients professionals like best as individuals are those who make the best progress in counseling.

Many of these points are likely to seem clear in principle and yet arbitrary and unreasonable in practice. Some examples follow.

Friend or Counselor: Case #1

Joe, a counselor-in-training, who interned at and also roomed in a rehabilitation institute, developed a close counseling relationship with Edward, a recent paraplegic. A victim of an automobile accident, Edward required physical treatment and training in living skills to resume life on his own. Joe had few friends and felt more attached to Edward than to most of his peers. When, in the course of counseling, Edward complained of difficulty washing laundry and making friends with others at the institute, it seemed natural for Joe to try to make things easier for Edward. So—by accident—Joe would show up to do his laundry when Edward did his, and when possible, he joined him at the cafeteria at mealtime.

Comment:

While Joe's efforts appear to be evidence of thoughtfulness, they actually undercut Edward's progress in rehabilitation. By doing things for Edward that he needed to do for himself, Joe interfered with his client's acquiring the living and social skills he needed to regain. Joe found it very hard to see a person he liked struggle. His close proximity to Edward and his own lack of friends made his relationship with Edward personally gratifying.

Friend or Counselor: Case #2

Mary was a college student, living in a dormitory where Susie spent two evenings a week as a counselor-in-training. Since it was difficult to establish regular counseling contacts with her limited schedule (and she was very eager to get some), Susie was outgoing, informal, and charming in her outreach to the dorm residents, engaging in friendly banter until one or another would confide a problem. Then Susie would set up regular appointments to discuss the issues in private sessions. Mary was one of the first to respond. Although she had a private therapist, she could afford to see him only once a week, and she was very grateful for Susie's engaging approach. Susie had Mary obtain the therapist's permission for their "supplemental" counseling, and the other therapist suggested the two women focus on current, ongoing problems while Mary and he reviewed Mary's history. Mary's current problem was that her boyfriend, a foreign student, when angry, would slap her around. Mary felt unable to end the relationship as both seemed to need each other, but when incidents happened, she felt cut off from her therapist who was available only at the scheduled time and not by telephone. Susie thought Mary's therapist was unresponsive so she gave Mary her home phone number. She soon had reason to regret the offer. Mary called often on Susie's nights off, sometimes more than once an evening. At times, the calls came late at night, sometimes lasting for hours. Having invited the calls, Susie felt trapped and unable to limit the number or duration of phone conversations. Having considered Mary's other therapist uncaring in the boundaries he had set, she came to understand their importance, but dared not set any of her own. But the worst part for Susie was that there was no beneficial outcome from all the time, effort, and inconvenience. Hungry for attention, Mary was delighted to have Susie as her tolerant friend rather than as a counselor. When she brought this problem to her supervisor, Susie thought her only recourse was to take the phone off the hook or to change her number.

Comment:

Here, circumstances, as well as personalities, contributed to unfortunate developments. Since counseling was relatively new at the dorm, the student counselors found it difficult to get started with clients. Susie's efforts "type-cast" her as the friendly confidante. But even when the counseling contract was set, she could not alter the ruse of being "one of the girls," even when Mary's calls made her angry. A kind and patient woman, Susie learned the hard way that effective counseling differs from the availability and support friends might offer in a crisis. Unlimited counselor availability can be misunderstood and even abused by clients. In counseling, assessment, setting limits, and helping clients examine their behavior and its effect on others are essential.

Friend or Counselor: Case #3

Several years earlier, with marginal achievements and with college officials unhappy with his behavior, Jim had dropped out of college. In the intervening years, he tried many jobs, many therapies, and many drugs, but lately he regained his confidence and felt that he could handle school. Bonnie, a college counselor, interviewed him for readmission and reviewed the administrative procedures applied earlier.

She thought he had been mishandled his first time around, and believed he could succeed with some support. She recommended readmission but asked him to return to see her if he had difficulty, or come to her at semester's end to plan his next step. He returned two semesters later, after having earned all A's. Having obtained only a B average his first semester, he postponed his return until he felt he had justified her faith in him. They continued the counseling relationship on an "as needed" basis, and although they had only a few sessions each year, the results were dramatic. Jim started as a hesitant, insecure, dilapidated-looking individual and became an attractive, directed, and successful student who, upon graduation, was admitted to a doctoral program in psychology.

The counseling was terminated, but both participants were so pleased with their accomplishments that when Jim got a part-time job back at the college where he had been an undergraduate, it seemed hard to leave well enough alone. Since they were now almost professional colleagues, they decided to write a paper together. Bonnie wanted to write about what had occurred session by session in counseling from two different vantage points—client and counselor. Jim was willing, yet hesitant. The project intrigued him but working on it made him uncomfortable. It forced him to see his counselor as an ordinary creature with feet of clay and faults he never noticed before. Though she was kind and concerned, he felt embarrassed by her imperfections, as if he now saw something he had no right to see. He had previously referred one of his good friends to Bonnie for private treatment, but now he became openly critical of the therapy which she was providing for his friend. In agreeing to the project, Jim had not realized that he wanted Bonnie to remain a therapeutic resource on whom he could depend in the future if necessary. Since she wouldn't stay on her pedestal, he felt abandoned. He could enjoy professional association with others but his one satisfactory therapist had disqualified herself.

Comment:

Ending therapeutic relationships, especially successful ones that are gratifying to both participants, is a painful loss to each party. The emotional investment, while not a personal one, is intense and does not disappear upon termination. It is easy to find rationales, excuses, and exceptional circumstances to support the relationship's continuation in some other form. Few of them work, and this collaboration, as plausible and professionally advantageous as it might have appeared, was as damaging as any other. The paper was finished and a lot was learned, but their friendship destroyed the relationship that had provided Jim with comfort.

VII

Authority, Advocate, or Counselor?

Few beginners want to assume a role of authority. Most are attuned to the difficulties people experience when dealing with life's harsh realities and are uncomfortable with an impersonal response to others' problems. Identifying with the underdog and harboring their own resentment of authority, many newcomers see counseling as a good alternative to rigid rules and coercive methods.

Yet despite such philosophical leanings, counselors-in-training are surprised to find that some clients provoke them to authoritarian behavior. Instead of collaborating with the client as they intended, they find themselves acting in controlling ways, defending the institution's or agency's rules and requirements, and becoming angry at their clients. In Chapter IV we examined such an episode at length—between the counselor, Jane, and her client, Milton. When such a shift occurs, counselors seem unaware of how or why they are deviating from the helping role. To them, it seems proper, unavoidable, and justified by the client's behavior.

Examination of such encounters often reveals that the counselor has been challenged, threatened, or irritated by the client. The client has been uncooperative, hard to reach, demanding, or, like Milton, outspoken and critical. Sometimes the client has expressed negative views of counseling or treated the counselor as a bureaucrat in an oppressive system. Occasionally, the provocation has been the client's indifference, reserve, or attempt to shift his or her responsibility onto the counselor.

Beginners do not expect clients to be uncooperative; lacking confidence themselves, they seem to need clients who appreciate their role and good intentions. When challenged, trainees may respond with admonitions, moralizations, and justifications; they may reply with sarcasm and veiled hostility. Sometimes they retreat into distant reserve as if the client were unworthy of any effort; or they may proceed arbitrarily, going through the motions automatically and ignoring client resistance. New counselors seem to believe that listening patiently to expressions of "negative" attitudes implies approval. They see no recourse but to take an opposing stance and to show clients that they are wrong.

Although few trainees would advocate an authoritarian approach, many adopt it when clients seem hostile to them. As counselors, they expect (and hope for) respect. They are shocked to have their role perceived as one of malevolent power or as one of authority to be challenged, tested, resisted, or ignored. Hurt and indignant (but afraid to say so), they resort to strong-arm tactics, as if they and their clients were adversaries at war.

The authority and status inherent in the helping role may not be apparent to the new counselor, but they are to those who come to them for help, especially clients who come unwillingly or with reservations. Even first-time counselors are seen as having special skills, knowledge, powers, or responsibilities that set them apart—and above—the help-seeker. Clients who feel threatened by these perceived characteristics are more prone to attack than to submit to them.

This was the case for one unfortunate trainee who had no previous counseling experience. On his first day as an academic advisor, he called out the name of the client assigned to him. A large imposing black man stood up, took one look at the graduate student, and shouted, "Oh damn, not another white honky!" As in this example, many clients come to their first appointment with feelings of anger and with doubts and preconceptions about what counselors will do to them.

Even on social occasions, such as cocktail parties, when professional matters are far from my mind, there are some individuals who, discovering that I am a psychologist, act as though they think they are in imminent danger. One person might say, "Oh, then I'd better watch what I say." Another may express concern about the observations or conclusions I might make. These persons are not responding to me as an individual. Instead they are responding to the power they associate with my professional role, and they seem to think that I will use it against them.

We must anticipate the sometimes unflattering notions and expectations new clients have about counselors. We cannot expect to form new and constructive relationships immediately when our clients come to us with ambivalence, fear, or anger from previous encounters. The counselor's face may be new to the client, but the role or the context may be familiar—another authority, another representative of a school, agency, group, or community, another threat. The counselor imagines that he or she is meeting the client for the first time, but the client often responds as if they had met before—and not necessarily under the best conditions. At times it seems analogous to the amusement park attraction in which one stands behind a painted screen and puts one's head through the hole, ready to be photographed or made a target for pies or balloons. We are seen by others in a totally different context from the way we see ourselves. Even before opening his or her mouth, the counselor may be viewed as a white racist, a prying judgmental "shrink," or a troublesome authority.

It is difficult for us to remain objective while observing our clients' reactions to us. When a client criticizes us, the setting, or the task, it feels like a personal attack. While our responsibility is to understand the threat felt by the client, our impulse is to defend ourselves. When challenged, novices are apt to use their position as their shield, often confirming clients' fears and escalating antagonism. They make the authoritarian threat a reality when defiance provokes them to a show of superior strength. This can be disastrous.

Ironically, the clients who are most likely to provoke authoritarian behavior in counselors are those who most fear authority. Rather than lend themselves willingly to a relationship in which they imagine they will feel inferior and humiliated, they challenge or resist it. Unfortunately, whatever powers the counselor holds can be used only on behalf of, and in collaboration with, clients. Our knowledge, skills, life experience, and commitment can work *for* clients, but not *against* them. Clients can be helped but they cannot usually be forced to engage in a helping alliance. (There are some exceptions which shall be described later.)

An authoritarian approach is not always provoked by clients. Some counselor personality traits and styles suggest an authoritarian attitude. A cold, distant, demanding, and "know-it-all" manner creates the impression that the "doctor" knows best. When the doctor seems intent on having the patient see things his way, the patient feels forced to conform or to retreat. An illustration occurred in Hannah Green's popular book *I Never Promised You a Rose Garden* (New York: Signet Books, pp. 159-60). Deborah, a young psychotic woman, is assigned a substitute therapist while her regular doctor is away on vacation. Deborah has a secret language with which she communicates with her imagined gods of the kingdom of Yr. Ignoring all her (indirectly expressed) distress at having her own therapist gone, Dr. Royson, the substitute, is fascinated by the strange words Deborah uses occasionally and sets out to analyze them. The text conveys the strained interchange between them and then continues:

> There followed a long silence between them, and though she tried at the next hour and the next and the next, his humorless and automatic responses brought down the muteness like a night. He worked hard to convince her that Yri was a language formulated by herself and not sent with the gods as a gift. He had taken the first words she gave him and shown her the roots of them from scraps of Latin, French, and German that a nine- or ten-year-old could pick up if she tried. He analyzed the structure of the sentences and demanded that she see that they were, with very few exceptions, patterned on the English structure by which she, herself, was bound. His work was clever and detailed and sometimes almost brilliant, and she had many times to agree with him, but the more profound he was the more profound was the silence which enveloped her. She could never get beyond the auster-

> ity of his manner nor the icy logic of what he had proven to tell him that his scalpels were intrusions into her mind just as long-ago doctors had intruded into her body, and that furthermore, his proofs were utterly and singularly irrelevant. At the end she marshaled all of her strength, and with as good a clarity as she could give him, she said, 'Please, Doctor, my difference is not my sickness.' It was a last cry and went unheard.

Deborah feels she is being treated like a textbook case or a laboratory animal rather than as a person. She admires the doctor's efforts, and even agrees with some of his formulations. Yet his brilliance at solving intellectual puzzles is "irrelevant"; she has not felt acknowledged or accepted as a human being in pain.

Royson's skills and capacities are not the problem for Deborah, nor is the role he plays. It is the way he uses the skills and role that creates emotional distance. The helping role is often authoritative, but if it is authoritarian, the best it can achieve is compliance. As in this excerpt, a counselor can be brilliant, insightful, and correct but still ineffective. Often being "right" and unyielding may be less tolerable than being "wrong" and willing to admit to human error. Eager to show how much they know and to earn client respect, beginners find this a disconcerting reality. Without rapport and trust to support collaboration, counseling can be a power struggle, a battle of wills, in which no one wins. (And if, for a moment, we consider counseling a power struggle, the client's ability to resist exceeds the counselor's power to compel.)

Initially the ambiguity of the counseling role shows us not as we really are but rather as what we represent—or what others like us have represented to the client in the past. Clients cannot see our intentions, however good they are, but they can observe our mannerisms, our facial expressions, and other elements of our style; and they can draw conclusions that seem to us unwarranted and unfair. Even though their impressons are limited, they will respond to them without waiting to have their suspicions confirmed or denied. The client who found himself assigned to "another white honky" was unwilling to see whether "this one" might be okay. *But we have to be on our clients' side even when they are against us.*

Perhaps clarification is required here. If some man at a cocktail party is convinced that my psychological training will cause him injury or exposure, I think of it as "his problem" and let it pass. But when my client displays anger or apprehension or complaint about me or my role, it is "my problem"; justified or not, it will affect counseling. I have to try to discover the source of the client's feelings and what has provoked them. While most of us prefer courtesy from others, we cannot—and should not—prefer it from clients. Directness and honesty may be surprising and, from a stranger, slightly jarring, but at least we know where we stand and what we are up against.

One way to deal with resistance (especially negativity) is not to oppose it, but join it. Instead of approaching clients expecting that we will be liked and respected immediately, we need to be more realistic. We need to assume that if the client comes with fear, anger, or reluctance, there is good reason for it. Rather than get uptight, we need to make it possible for clients to tell us why. Even the client who exclaimed "Oh damn, not another white honky!" might have responded to a counselor who said, "It sounds like you are dreading this meeting. Have 'white honkys' been giving you trouble lately?"

Whatever their reasons, clients always have *good* reasons for their attitudes toward counseling. However unfair their preconceptions are to us, they have grounds—sufficient to them—to be wary. They may have prior bad experiences in counseling or, from stories they have heard from others, imagine they will. They may come unwillingly at the request or demand of someone else. They may be worried about themselves and afraid of what we are going to tell them. However incorrect or misguided their expectations, their views must be acknowledged. We cannot deny or address their objections unless we know what they are, and although we can correct misconceptions about counseling, they may not believe us unless they have some reason to trust us. If they can tell us their negative views of counseling without making us angry or resort to authoritarian acts, we may give them some basis to trust us. And when later, their objections are directed, not at "counselors" or at "counseling," but at things we have said and done, we again have to enable them to tell us directly so we can know what has upset them. Are we "always late," "supercritical," "prejudiced," or "cold"? If we think we are not, did we do something to make clients think we are? However uncomfortable or unfair, we have to make ourselves listen so we can understand clients' perceptions of us, even when they vary from our own.

There are some exceptions to this approach with hostile clients. Most counseling methods are based on tolerance, acceptance, and understanding, but these qualities can be misperceived and misused. Antisocial individuals, most criminals, and many addicts are not responsive to conventional counseling. Just as they abuse other individuals who stand in their way, they abuse the unwary counselor who wants to help them change. The antisocial perceive those in positions of power as objects to be manipulated, deceived, or persuaded, and they are often very proficient at doing this. They see the accepting, tolerant, and understanding counselor as a patsy, a push-over, a chump—not only naive and gullible, but willing to work for peanuts in pursuit of impossible dreams. Such individuals will try any and all devices—"sob" stories, charm and flattery, clever arguments which establish the counselor's guilt and the client's innocence, plausible lies, and insincere promises—in order to avoid serious consideration of their own behavior and culpabilities. Some are so clever and convincing that experienced therapists are fooled, but they respect and respond best to counselors who can not only play the game but can use it against them. Apparently lacking both feelings of guilt and concern and empathy for others, most sociopaths are able to confound most counselors and ward off involvement. But even the rare therapist who can outfox the fox has little chance for therapeutic success in one or a few hours of weekly contact; too much time remains for the antisocial individual to work over the "suckers" and get satisfying rewards. In a confined environment with a consistent twenty-four-hour therapeutic regime, the odds are a little better, but the time, effort, and professional manpower required to help society's "undesirables" have proved too costly to sustain.

Disgusted with the minimal commitment of professional

resources, former drug addicts have recently set up peer counseling systems for themselves. Based on the assumption that the antisocial client misuses tolerance, acceptance, and understanding for self-indulgent and ultimately self-defeating purposes, these systems employ authoritarian methods wielded by peers who "know the score." Clients usually volunteer to enter residential treatment programs in which they are subjected to confrontation around the clock. They are attacked, criticized, and ridiculed; their every maneuver is exposed in order to force them to stop "conning" others and to look at themselves. In lengthy "encounter" group meetings, members' self-deluding behavior, statements, and attitudes are forcefully and brutally dissected. Members continue to attend these "encounter" sessions even after graduating from residential treatment. The message to the addict is: "Your behavior is unacceptable, no matter what its origins, no matter what provokes it, no matter what excuse you give. The group will not tolerate it for any reason!" This severity is tolerated because those who deliver it have undergone the same experience, and they have become models of successful rehabilitation.

These tactics are suited to antisocial clients and to those whose addictions have extinguished any genuine interpersonal involvement. They tyrannize the tyrant, and unmask the poseur, while supporting more genuine and productive achievement. The most successful treatments for addictions of almost every sort—drugs, gambling, overeating, alcohol—rely, in part, on authoritarian methods: those which enforce compliance with behavioral injunctions and prohibitions regardless of the client's immediate wishes. The program sets up the rules and tells clients what is good for them. Such methods seem to violate the basic tenets of counseling and psychotherapy which make clients responsible for their own choices. Yet these systems recognize that some destructive habits and appetites have a force of their own which are beyond a client's power to control. They use tactics aimed at the "target" behavior which, if not prohibited, makes other therapeutic progress and "normal" gratification impossible.

Employed strategically, authoritarian methods also work in other therapeutic contexts for a period of time and with specific objectives. For instance, in helping a student who is unable to complete a dissertation or term paper, it may be effective to require the client to meet a schedule of specific tasks on the assignment. If these chores are delayed until all work-inhibiting elements are uncovered, understood, and worked through, it may be too late. The consequences of failing to finish by a deadline may be so severe that therapy will either be terminated or complicated by a new set of problems. Using authoritarian tactics in a limited way is an example of the exception proving the rule. Even the most authoritarian treatment programs include many familiar counseling elements: voluntary compliance, agreement with basic therapeutic goals, and rewards provided by a network of concerned individuals. No one can force clients to alter harmful behavior, but clients may relinquish destructive habits with the conviction that the sacrifice of immediate gratification will bring lasting satisfaction.

Let us switch the focus back to more typical counseling situations. Like the provocative client who can elicit controlling forms of behavior from a counselor who is not usually judgmental or dogmatic, clients who act helpless and dependent can often seduce a counselor into taking command, interceding for them, giving them answers to questions they should answer themselves, and assuming other responsibilities. To avoid the anxiety of decision-making, some clients gladly relinquish personal responsibility in order to rely on an expert authority. This way they can absolve themselves. Should any action prove unwise, they can explain that they did it because their counselor told them to.

Dependent clients are deceptively appealing to the inexperienced counselor because they are agreeable, responsive, and appreciative. They are usually open about their problems, willing to admit their deficiencies, and enthused about the counseling process and their counselor's contributions. In counseling they behave the way naive counselors expect all clients to behave. Dependent clients make counselors feel important, effective, and needed. Furthermore, it is gratifying to do things for people who seem unable to manage on their own; it is difficult to resist requests for help at the risk of appearing uncaring.

Nowhere is this strain more evident or more painful for the uninitiated to observe than in a rehabilitation treatment center for patients who have suffered accidents or illnesses. Rehabilitation is demanding and strenuous work. Many of these clients, who feel they have already suffered and cannot endure more challenge, protest every step of the way. Physical therapists and rehabilitation counselors must turn deaf ears to some pleas, ignore tears of frustration, and demand all that the clients can do even in the face of accusations of being cruel and insensitive. If treatment personnel responded to clients' entreaties, they might be showered with gratitude and appreciation, but they would not help clients regain the self-sufficiency of which they are capable.

The excruciating process of physical rehabilitation is a dramatic example, but it clearly illustrates that fulfilling client requests is not always helpful. Most beginning counselors mistakenly regard pleasing their clients as the most important measure of their success. One experienced colleague, a therapist and a counseling supervisor, becomes suspicious if, at the end of a session, his clients or trainees say, "Thank you." He regards their expression of appreciation as a sign that he has demanded too little of them; that they have not worked hard enough; and—most important—that they feel that they have received rather than achieved something.

Appreciation may not always be a worrisome sign, but neither should it convince us that we have performed well as counselors. Our needs for gratitude and admiration tempt us to measure our counseling accomplishments by the thanks we receive rather than by the accomplishments of our clients. These needs also make us susceptible to the demands of dependent, manipulative, and provocative clients.

Advocacy counseling, which encourages specific client choices or behavior, is another brand of authoritarianism. Those who practice it are often not aware of their dogmatism. Some do not think that they are making decisions for their clients because they themselves see no alternatives; others insist that their approach is preferable to letting clients choose other options. This type of counseling is usually practiced by individuals who have struggled through experiences similar to those of the people they help. They believe they have found the only solutions or methods that others should follow. They may be advocating almost anything—special foods, diets, athletic regimes, therapies, sexual preferences, attitudes and actions crime victims should adopt, or religious belief systems.

Well-intentioned and often self-sacrificing, these counselors make decisions for their clients, without helping them to choose for themselves. They focus on solutions rather than on the clients. They may have some previous or on-the-job training, but most of it has been provided by their peers, not by professionals. If there is one threat posed by nonprofessional counseling, it comes from the huge number of advocate counselors. Consider a few current examples. Treatment centers, staffed largely by nonprofessionals who are also homosexuals, offer counseling to other homosexuals. These centers are really support and advocacy groups for the homosexual community. In such a setting, a client's decision to become heterosexual might be regarded as deviant. There are other counselors so enamored of health foods and vitamins that they recommend them, without medical evaluation, as remedies for most emotional or physical complaints. There are also the Moonies and other cults which promise guidance for life and a path to the hereafter. And there are many organizations, known by names which are abbreviations or euphemisms to avoid the explicit promise of therapy, which look upon counseling strictly as a business. In order to make money, such groups forego screening applicants and use nonprofessionals with marketing and advertising skills, rather than therapeutic training, as leaders. In addition to having an indeterminable rate of success, these groups periodically experience psychiatric casualties among their clients.

Though most of us would like to have clients adopt our preferences and viewpoints, counseling is no place to exert such influence. Clients are vulnerable, not only because they are eager to find quick solutions to their problems, but also because they grow emotionally attached to their helpers. Advocate counselors possess a zealousness and conviction that makes them persuasive, but their skills are more often aimed at converting others to their beliefs than at achieving more legitimate counseling objectives. Many, actively engaged in such counseling, are still struggling with their own unresolved problems; unintentionally, they use clients to confirm their own choices. The advocacy approach can be effective, and some individuals may be thankful for the single choice they are given, but such influence promotes allegiance and conformity rather than self-awareness and self-determination.

Finally there is another group of people who warp counseling into an authoritarian role: those who are rigid, dogmatic, and have set ideas about permissible attitudes, feelings, and behavioral expression. When their actions and opinions are admirable, these individuals are impressive figures who are frequently sought out for help. Often they have leadership capacity, persuasive abilities, and considerable strength of character—all admirable qualities. But these traits undermine them as counselors because their standards are too strict, and their expectations too high. Lacking tolerance and flexibility, they cannot permit others a range of choices nor the time necessary to explore various options. Concerned as they are with the welfare of others, they become tense and dissatisfied with the slow pace of counseling, often gravitating to activities which are more efficient and less frustrating, such as teaching and other modes of communication, administration, and management. Convinced of their views, they too focus on solutions rather than on clients, when counseling.

In this section we have examined personality traits which bring authoritarian overtones to the role of counselor, as well as several types of client behavior which may provoke directive and controlling counselor responses. An extensive description of a counseling exchange in which the counselor assumed an authoritarian stance is found in Chapter IV. Other illustrations of these role confusions follow.

Authority or Counselor: Case #1

Mr. R was a newly-appointed counselor in a high school where he had worked for many years as an English teacher. Jenny, a tenth-grader, was assigned to him for individual counseling because she had become so anxious during examinations that she could not perform. In junior high school, her grades had been good, but in senior high, where exams were not only more frequent but an important means of student evaluation, she panicked. Sometimes she would stick it out, attempting a few questions; but at other times, convinced of failure, she bolted out of the room. Her teachers, however, believed her to be prepared and capable. Although Jenny's parents' divorce linked family problems to her troubles at school, Mr. R only spent a short time investigating this. More certain of his skills as a teacher than as a counselor and going through a divorce himself, Mr. R decided that lessons in test-taking and in advanced reading would make her feel more confident in the classroom. Jenny worked hard and seemed to gain proficiency while in private session, but she continued to panic during examinations.

Comment:

New counselors, like former teacher Mr. R, may try to apply whatever special skills they have in counseling. Usually, counseling suffers. Teaching and counseling have similar goals, perhaps, but they are achieved by different methods and modes of interaction. The pedagogic role probably satisfied Mr. R's needs better than it did Jenny's, since her record did not indicate academic deficiencies. In situations like these, where counselors instruct their clients, the counseling role is eclipsed by that of the authority and clients' emotional problems are obscured. Jenny was kept so busy mastering her learning assignments, she had no chance to talk about the disturbing changes at home which made her feel overwhelmed and incompetent.

Authority or Counselor: Case #2

Mrs. K, a fifty-two-year-old divorced woman, is very open about herself although just starting therapy. In her sessions, she always tells her therapist the disturbing events of her week in exactly the same manner. She reports an incident with lots of detail about her reaction, and then she either stops and waits for a therapeutic pronouncement or, if none seems forthcoming, asks, "Why do you suppose I did that?" or "Why should I feel that way?" or "Why do I have those feelings?" Although she is attractive, well-educated, busy socially, and holds a responsible job, she sees herself as vulnerable, troubled, and easily hurt or upset. Should her therapist not rise to the bait, and she is forced to answer her own question, she does, but so quickly and with so much psychological jargon, she sounds like a college sophomore reciting from a textbook. Rarely do her explanations make sense. Sometimes she will quote an opinion someone else has supplied, but that also sounds confused. This behavior seems to prove that she is helpless and mystified by her feelings and relationships. She tries to force the counselor to play expert or oracle to reveal her true self and correct her faulty explanations. When the therapist points out this pattern, she feels criticized and reacts with hurt and confusion, making it easier for the counselor to answer her questions rather than upset her. She fashions therapy as a dependent relationship which provides important answers. Yet, though the answers she gets always fascinate her, they don't seem to do her any good.

Comment:

Those who are open about their experiences and eager to know the counselor's reactions seem ideal as clients. Compared to others who simply report facts, blame others, or resist psychological analysis, interaction with clients who seek the therapist's opinion is gratifying. Many of us enjoy speculating on the meaning of this behavior or that reaction, and like Dear Abby or Joyce Brothers, we may believe our answers provide the help the client needs. But Mrs. K's questions and many others posed by clients can make counselors into authorities and confirm clients' feelings of inadequacy and dependency. Though it may seem rude not to answer a direct question (and it is not always necessary to refuse), behaving like a psychological prophet transforms the counseling role.

Advocate or Counselor: Case #3

Sally is a counselor in a women's center offering counseling to rape victims. Aware of victims' problems from her own dreadful experience, she spends several hours a week trying to ensure that no other woman suffers alone as she was forced to do. One evening about a month ago, Anita, her twenty-year-old client, was pulled into a car, driven to a park, and raped by two men after she stopped to give them directions. Anita, recovered from the incident, is now physically well, but in sessions she frequently returns to the issue of why she was stupid or trusting enough to approach that car. Every time she does so, Sally assures her that while most rape victims feel as if they've done something wrong, she did nothing to feel guilty about. The center instructs its counselors to respond this way when clients express guilt and to make it clear to them that the rapist, not the victim, is to blame. But Anita, only momentarily relieved by Sally's words, just nods her head. In time she stops bringing up the subject, and feeling better but still unwilling to travel or be out alone after dark, she leaves counseling after a few more sessions. Sally wants Anita to continue, but Anita is convinced she must now learn how to manage on her own.

Comment:

In recent years the feminist movement and others active on behalf of rape victims have had great impact on public consciousness. They exposed the long-held belief that rape victims were responsible for the crimes committed against them—a belief reinforced by a legal system more protective of rapists than victims, degrading police practices and attitudes, and poor medical procedures and support services. Society seemed to respond by insinuating that rape victims wanted and deserved what they got. Advocates made it clear that this was an outrageous and damaging insult to women, and as a result, some beneficial social changes have been effected.

But influencing public opinion or policy and counseling individuals are two different functions. No act on the victim's part justifies rape, but victims do experience guilt about their actions and motives, however innocent or unintentional. When disaster befalls us, we tend to ask ourselves, "What have I done to deserve this?" and to try to find answers within our own character and behavior. While absolution and denial of our guilt by others is reassuring, it is not sufficient to stop us from questioning ourselves. Perhaps such self-analysis is unwarranted by reality, but on the other hand, if we played no part in our misfortunes, we must then conclude that we are helpless and vulnerable to tragedy, accident, or abuse at any time or any place. Anita needed the opportunity to explore her "stupidity" and to review her thoughts and feelings before, during, and after the incident. If Sally had supported her exploration instead of denying her that chance, Anita might have been able to recognize the real dangers, both within and outside her control. Rape counselors depart from sound counseling practice, when, in their efforts to hold the rapists responsible for the crime, they tell victims how to deal with their feelings. Social policy can be legislated, but victims' feelings cannot. Sally thought she was being supportive in declaring Anita blameless, but she failed to support her client's search for self-acceptance. Anita was forced to leave treatment because Sally, meaning well, told her that her feelings of shame and guilt were wrong. Anita concluded that her disturbing feelings could not be addressed in counseling. Research on counseling rape victims has shown better psychological recovery for those victims who have done something unwise (like Anita's approaching the car) than for those who were accosted without warning and who were denied any freedom of choice. The victim who has done "something" is able to examine her motives and actions and assure herself that, next time, she will be more guarded. The second group—those who have done "nothing"—continue to feel more vulnerable when they contemplate the future and find it difficult to regain a measure of security and safety.

VIII

Savior, Pawn, or Counselor?

Some people find that the counseling role does not match their idea of helping others. They find discussing problems more frustrating than gratifying, and prefer to take direct action. When told of another's personal difficulties, their typical response is to offer money, goods, or services, or to try to intercede directly for the other. They are convinced that they must either act themselves or persuade the client to act quickly to relieve distress. At times when they find no way to provide immediate relief, they begin to feel like failures and may become upset or wage war against any person or institution they see as responsible for the hurt or injustice. These individuals often make effective politicians, community and religious leaders, even revolutionaries, but they seldom make good counselors.

Direct action is called for in counseling only if the client is in dire straits, in danger of hurting himself or others, likely to be physically injured, or so distraught or disturbed that he or she cannot be left alone. These crises demand outside control, requiring the counselor, with or without the client's permission, to act and ensure the safety of all concerned. Notifying the police, initiating hospitalization, reporting evidence of child abuse or molestation, and other "saving" actions may damage confidentiality—perhaps irrevocably—but they are well worth the risk if they avoid possible life-threatening consequences. These circumstances are mercifully rare; we are seldom required to save clients from themselves or others. Only in such emergencies are we justified to think of clients as helpless and, therefore, dependent on our direct intervention.

Yet unintentionally, counselors often treat clients as if they were helpless. They make decisions clients should make for themselves, become protective, possessive, angered at those who hurt the client, and become a partisan member in the client's life. Although the client is not in immediate danger, the counselor acts as if direct intervention is the only way to reduce client pain and suffering. The counseling maneuver may be innocuous, like avoiding topics that might distress the client, or dramatic, like providing a false alibi for a client suspected of wrongdoing. But whatever the device, it is based on a premise that clients are fragile, weak, and unable to cope with reality or with the consequences of their actions.

In the few instances when this is the case, and we withhold disturbing news from someone who is gravely ill or has just lost a loved one, our protectiveness is warranted only until the person recovers the strength to be told the truth. However hateful it is to be the bearer of bad tidings, our responsibility is clear. As counselors, we must deal with reality, enable clients to face unpleasant truths, or help them cope with the challenges of their lives. It is hard for us to see them suffering, but in our efforts to protect them we may be only protecting ourselves.

The familiar view that the primary purpose of counseling is to make clients feel good (or at least better) places counselors in a trap—that of trying to save clients from discomfort and unpleasant realizations. In the role of savior, we alter clients' lives or their comprehension of their circumstances to make them feel more protected, comfortable, and assured. When we are deeply attached to them or can imagine how dreadful we might feel in their place, we can convince ourselves that we are helping by falsifying and manipulating their world. Counselors have, for instance, been known to hide illegal drugs for patients in a hospital to prevent patients from getting caught with them or going through the agony of detoxification. (This act relieves the patient of anxiety, makes the counselor feel benevolent, guarantees rapport between the two, and is totally destructive to treatment.) Or, if outraged that Old World parents arrange a marriage for their newly immigrated daughter with a man she does not know, the counselor might try to "educate the parents," rather than help the client make her own decision.

New counselors, believing themselves helpful, are actually overprotective. One trainee, assigned to help a college student with marginal grades achieve better scholastic results, never mentioned the client's academic problems during their first session. Asked why this topic was avoided, the trainee replied, "Oh, that topic would have been much too stressful!" For whom? For client or counselor? Feeling vulnerable themselves and confused about counseling objectives, novices may behave as if their clients cannot tolerate any frustration, discomfort, or unpleasantness. They see them as unfortunates, who are mistreated and misunderstood by others, and in need of constant reassurance and a totally safe haven. What they create for their clients is a "never-never" world which, while offering temporary tranquillity, forces clients to struggle with the real problems on their own.

Our concern for clients should not blind us to their strengths or lead us to lull them with false comforts. The counselor's obligation is, perhaps, best expressed by the psychiatrist (presumed to be the psychoanalyst Frieda Fromm-Reichman) in *I Never Promised You a Rose Garden.* When Deborah, the young psychotic girl, becomes distraught when another patient is brutally attacked by a sadistic aide, her therapist says to her:

> "Look here, . . . I never promised you a rose garden. I never promised you perfect justice . . . and I never promised you peace or happiness. My help is so that you can be free to fight for all those things. The only reality I offer is challenge, and well-being is being free to accept it or not at whatever level you are capable. I never promise lies, and the rose garden world of perfection is a lie . . . and a bore, too!"
> (*I Never Promised You A Rose Garden,* page 106)

Still, this principle is easier to read or say than to put into practice. At any given moment the counselor may not have an accurate view. Hearing only one side of the story, we often see clients as victims. While few clients lie deliberately, many do not give an accurate picture of the actual circumstances or the full range of their feelings when sharing their problems. In reporting arguments, for example, clients may report all the awful things said by the other person while leaving out or editing their own contributions. In describing someone with whom they are angry, clients will inevitably exaggerate or highlight troublesome features and omit compensating or explanatory factors. One client portrayed his father, with whom he lived alone, as unbelievably dependent and impossibly demanding. The client failed to mention until the third session that his father was permanently disabled and, at his son's insistence, denied any homemaker services. Was the father really the "bad guy" described? Was the client being victimized?

Clients often tell us what is bothering them at the moment without considering whether their report is accurate. Sometimes it is necessary to acquire (and to help clients gain) a clearer picture of the person they are describing; sometimes it is not. But it is always an error to accept a client's initial report as if it were the whole and only truth. We should regard it as a truth for *that* client at *that* moment. If we listen carefully, we can often hear the client attributing contradictory or incompatible qualities to the same individual and recognize that the impression given today may change tomorrow. Another, more troublesome issue comes up when clients report on other people whose behavior may strike the counselor as intolerable but may actually be desired or encouraged by the client.

Some clients need help to recognize a distortion of reality. One of my clients was a young woman whose mother had died after years of hospitalization precipitated by the client's birth. She remembered that as a young child she once visited her mother in the hospital and was convinced that her mother had, on that occasion, been disappointed and unhappy with her. Since this young woman had a poor self-image and seemed to absorb insult and disparagement the way blotting paper absorbs ink, I was suspicious and inquired how she knew this was true. She said she remembered it clearly and that she also had a letter which her mother sent to her after the visit indicating her disappointment. Not having been there or having known her mother, I replied I could be wrong but it seemed inconceivable that, after years of confinement, her mother would react to seeing her child for the first time with disappointment. Unimpressed, the client listened but remained convinced of her version of the story. Yet, in the next session, there was a joy in her I had not seen before. She had gone home and reread the letter and found no trace of disapproval. Since her mother's letter expressed only love and longing for her, she decided that she had somehow created this disapproval. This proved an accurate and important insight for her. I was thrilled with being intuitively on target, but it also made me uneasy. I saw how difficult it was to gauge reality from a client's report, and I wondered how often I had been misled by clients' distorted versions of events.

Clients' reports are colored and determined by their personal needs. Consciously or unconsciously, they provide us with biased information which is all they know at the moment or all they want us to know. Unintentionally, clients may try to elicit particular responses to their momentary needs and anxieties. In reporting events, they may be seeking sympathy or reassurance, expiating or reapportioning guilt, trying to make a certain impression, or gathering ammunition to use against troublemakers in their lives. In their descriptions of people and events, clients often provide a more accurate reflection of themselves and what they want from us than of the "real" world.

Counselors must be especially cautious when making conclusions drawn from the viewpoints of clients struggling to separate themselves from people and relationships on which they are dependent. Children, adolescents, young adults, and even adults try to enlist counselors in their battles against parents and partners. In their conflict and confusion they may fashion the truth so that the listener will sympathize with them and give them support. The quest for independence, we must remember, is an ambivalent one with no clear victories. Gaining the right to self-determination often means losing important advantages and protections; winning freedom can mean losing support. If *we* try fighting those whom *they* are battling, we'll be taking sides against essentially unknown adversaries—and their adversaries today may be their allies tomorrow. We need to see that the client's search for our support really signifies uncertainty and conflict. These are the issues with which the client needs counseling.

Few people, even counselors, have resolved their own dilemmas and conflicts with parents and other authority figures so thoroughly that they can view with total impartiality others' struggles for independence. To make it worse, adolescent clients seeking support for their side present open-and-shut cases; the parents are the "bad guys," and the children are innocent victims, pawns of parental power and prerogative. So when counselors have unsettled grudges against their own parents, it seems like second nature to identify with the "child" and sit in judgment on parental fallibility. Beware! The struggle for independence is as much an internal conflict as an external one, a complex transformation of external controls into internalized values, which affect the individual's capacity for discipline and responsibility.

Parents make easy scapegoats for any and all problems their children experience while growing up. Furthermore, parents are fallible, and there are few who have not made mistakes when understanding, assessing, and rearing their children. The only trouble is that once parental errors have been explored, identified, and established, the counseling task has just begun. Clients still have the final responsibility of rectifying the lingering effects of parental mistakes and of making the best of whatever their lives have to offer. There's little refuge for clients in the injuries inflicted during formative years. They may, however, prove a rich and liberating source of information for correcting clients' mistaken self-perceptions.

Clients may use counselors as authorities in parent-child disputes and march back home using the counselor's opinion as a weapon. This can result in full-scale war between the parents and the counselor as the new parental surrogate. It can prove destructive to both relationships, and the clients will gain nothing. Rather than learning to choose for themselves, they will, in this situation, leave the decision up to whoever wins the battle. Counselors can rarely rescue clients from parental power, no matter how destructive it appears; they must help their clients deal with it one way or another.

The task is to help clients sort out their feelings toward themselves and their parents, and to help them make decisions in their own best interests. In the process, clients often have to recognize that they have incorporated their parents' values.

This is the real problem—often disguised by clients' accusations about their parents—but soon apparent to any counselor who works with adolescents or young adults. These clients may seek counseling because they are outraged by parental criticism and restrictions precipitated by their engaging in certain activities like experimenting with illegal substances, hanging around with "bad" characters, or suddenly shifting goals and direction (as from college student to beach bum overnight). In sessions, after venting their hurt and anger, they begin to acknowledge their own doubts about the wisdom of their actions; in time, it becomes clear that the self-doubts are the real problem. Even in instances where their parents have overreacted and done things to provoke further rebellion, I am amazed by the response most of these clients give when asked the question "Tell me, what would you do if you were your parent and *your* child was doing the things you're doing?" With little hesitation, they reply, "I think I would act the same way my parents do." This response has three implications: they have never before considered their behavior from their parents' point of view; they actually understand and respect the parental reactions they first found so offensive; and while they know how to counter parental pressure, they are not confident enough to resist peer pressure, the influence which has often prompted the questionable activity. The most difficult challenge for young adults is to make responsible choices—to decide what *they* want or should do. When they can resolve their internal conflicts, dealing with others, even parents, becomes relatively simple. The problem with interfering in parent-child disputes is that adolescents struggle against dependency by doing the opposite of what they think their parents want them to do. While to them this appears to be an independent choice, it is really counterdependent, substituting "no" for "yes" or "will" for "won't." The adolescent's decision is still determined by the parent despite the fact that his or her behavior is counter to the parental demand. If the counselor takes sides, it makes the struggle one of right or wrong, which it is not; it is an internal conflict for the adolescent—how to learn to make choices which do not satisfy or counter parental authority, but which are sound in their own right and constructive for the future.

Whenever the counseling focus is on external events, such as parental behavior, the client cannot recognize or address internal conflicts. Yet young counselors, still not psychologically independent of their parents, find themselves at a disadvantage when grasping these issues. They have difficulties perceiving the client or the client's parents objectively. (On rare occasions, when young trainees come face-to-face with one of their client's adversaries—a parent or, perhaps, a disliked teacher—they are amazed to find neither ogre nor villian but usually a likable, sympathetic individual, who is as concerned about the client as the counselor. Having distorted an already biased perspective, trainees are shocked by this reality.)

If this discussion seems narrowly focused on parent-child disputes, the implications are far broader. In many different contexts, counselors are prompted to alter their role into one of savior, or defender, or champion. They do this because they often perceive clients' interpersonal difficulties as battles between the weak client and the strong—parent, spouse, boss, teacher—in which the client is the underdog. Counselors who hear elderly clients complain about thoughtless or neglectful children often see the parents as the aggrieved victims. The important point is that while there are *two* sides to every interpersonal dispute, the counselor may hear only one. It is often easier to hold others responsible than to confront clients' real difficulties.

No matter how sensitive we are to their misfortunes and suffering, we must remember that most clients are not simply passive victims of others' destructive acts; they also initiate, provoke, react, misinterpret, and contribute their share of trouble and good. Clients' relationships are determined to a large extent by their own actions. While responsibility for the outcome of a relationship may not be evenly divided between two people, our objectivity is lost if we regard our clients as innocent victims in their dealings with others. (This statement about personal responsibility does not, of course, apply to the effects of war, persecution, calamities of nature, massive unemployment, or other catastrophes which may indeed make our clients victims of circumstances beyond their control. Yet even in these cases we do our clients a disservice if we view them as bereft of any personal resources which would help them recover.)

Many people have a world view in which the "little guy" is pitted against the powerful—political, military, bureaucratic, economic, and natural forces. They identify with and support the "underdog." This view of the world may be as accurate as any, and I suspect I subscribe to it myself. But when this viewpoint is applied to the microcosm of counseling, it distorts interpersonal realities and does a disservice to clients.

I once interviewed an applicant to the graduate counseling program who had an extensive academic and work history, but none of his activities related to counseling. After having majored in political science, he had worked in construction and union work. He was from a South American country where most people, including those in his family, were poor and politically oppressed. When I asked why he wanted to become a counselor, he replied that his goal was to return to his country and convince others to stage a revolution; counseling skills would help him be more persuasive and effective in influencing others. Much as I admired his aspirations, I explained that they were incompatible with counselor training and performance—that counselors help clients make their own decisions, rather than determine their choices for them. It seemed to him that if this were true, counseling was useless—or worse—because in fostering individual choice, it worked to support the status quo and did not offer a solid front to fight oppression. In some measure, he was right; counseling is—or should be—apolitical. Evidently he believed the familiar rallying cry, "If you are not part of the solution, you are part of the problem!" But if and when counseling is used as a tool to further certain political ideas, it is a perversion. Although few intend to use counseling to overthrow a political regime, all of us are sometimes tempted to rescue clients by influencing or determining their decisions. With the best of intentions, we can do harm. Consider the possible consequences for clients who followed any of these suggestions, believing them to be well-considered and wise:Counselor to a thin, poorly coordinated, eleven-year-

old boy:

"That neighborhood tough is really picking on you, isn't he? Why don't you beat him up? He's about your age, isn't he?"

Counselor to a thirty-year-old woman living with her mother:

"You are enraged at your mother because her illness interferes with your life, but after all, it isn't her fault. Why don't you spend more time with her?"

Counselor to a patient on antidepressant medication:

"Your medication seems to be making you sleepy. Why don't you stop taking it?"

Of course, we want to see clients free of bullies, resentment, the side effects of medication (and even its necessity), but our job is not to choose for our clients but to help them explore their options. Counselors assume the "savior" role when they decide how clients should feel or act.

On one funny occasion, I was sorely tempted to deliver my personal bias as a professional opinion. A disturbed young man, whose regular therapy I supplemented by counseling him on college issues, had over many months made progress. While he still asked help in making some decisions, his confidence and logic had improved to the point where he could usually make sound academic choices. After a session in which he had repeatedly demonstrated this ability, he posed still one more question on his way out. He asked me (with the election fast approaching) whether I thought it was "sick" to vote for a particular presidential candidate. Detesting this public figure, I wanted to answer "Yes," not only to guide this uncertain young man but to deprive the candidate of a possible vote. But, of course, I had to bite my tongue. The client was just learning to trust his own judgment; my pronouncement would not help him do that. So, saying I thought it best he make his own decision as he had begun to do in many aspects of his college life, I declined to answer. On that occasion, good therapy for him did not feel therapeutic for me!

Professionals are also often asked to assess the actions and practices of other therapists. Since there are some incompetent therapists, and professionals know the qualifications and standards of ethical practice, seeking such professional opinion seems appropriate. Yet it is almost impossible for one professional to judge another therapist's work. Knowing the academic credentials, reputation, publications, or institutional affiliation of a therapist is no guarantee of his or her effectiveness with a particular client. When told a few comments or provided with other examples of a counselor's behavior, the professional still does not know the context in which they occurred, or the degree of objectivity and accuracy of the report. A breach of professional ethics is usually easily recognized, but sometimes even these violations of standard practice occur as a result of good intentions or in response to unusual provocation. Thus, in most cases, both professionals and nonprofessionals must be cautious not to offer their personal preferences or biases as "expert" assessments.

In this section we have reviewed the temptations to rescue, protect, influence, and control clients—to play a savior role which is incompatible with counseling objectives. In the next we'll examine a very different role that counselors choose or fail to refuse.

Pawn or Counselor?

Clients too can misuse counseling and the ambiguity of the helping role. Counselors can find their focus shifted or subverted by antisocial, demanding, or dependent individuals; in this way, they can have the "savior" role foisted upon them by clients who, though capable, refuse responsibility. If we let clients define our role in inappropriate ways, we serve as pawns rather than as agents of change. Although experienced counselors can sometimes be exploited by skillful manipulators, many well-intentioned beginners are "pushovers"; afraid of disappointing, angering or confronting clients, they are unable to set limits.

Determined to be understanding and accepting, novices feel compelled to display these characteristics automatically, whatever the client's behavior. Trainees will rush to do whatever clients ask of them without even waiting to learn the reasons prompting such requests. When clients are not outspoken about their wishes, some trainees wrack their brains trying to discover a chore they can perform; many seem to believe they will earn client trust by doing them favors and are relieved when they can provide some concrete service. Unfortunately, once the counseling role is shaped this way, clients get the wrong impression and rely on counselors to dispense information or run errands. The readiness of beginners to perform chores may mask their difficulties in being assertive and their fears of getting emotionally involved.

Busy "doing things" for clients, counselors can ignore the meaning and implications of clients' behavior. An example that frequently occurs in the college setting is that of the student with a poor academic record who comes for help in choosing a major or planning the next semester's schedule. In the session, the student shows no sign of preparation or thought about the impending decision, but the counselor eagerly reviews all the possible academic options as if they were attractive travel packages, trying desperately to find something to enthuse the client. The counselor imagines that the "right" major or schedule will improve the student's performance. But in ignoring the client's indifference, the counselor is missing the point. The student is likely to show the same apathy toward other school-related tasks, going through the motions, perhaps, but showing little involvement or responsibility. To help the student perform better, the counselor must address the client's attitude of disinterest in academic matters, not overlook it.

While some clients may need help with practical concerns, such a narrow focus in the beginning distracts us from getting an accurate grasp of their problems. Typically clients cannot tell us directly the nature or extent of their problems, so we must make our own evaluations. This is difficult for novices, who do not feel free to raise issues other than those the client mentions. (Supervising some trainees, I have a disturbing fantasy: if a client appeared, bleeding and injured, but only asking assistance in choosing a major, the trainees would unswervingly pursue the client's stated concern and never question the client's injuries.) By attending only to the clients' words, some trainees ignore all nonverbal behavior, facial expressions, and other impressions. Recently I read a transcript of a session in which a female trainee interviewed a young man. The client described his problem as an inability to tell whether a certain young woman found him attractive. From his innuendos and evasiveness, it was clear that he was teasing and that the "woman" whose responsiveness he questioned was really the counselor. She, however, was so literal-minded and dogged in pursuing his "problem" that she never picked up the cues. Instead, she asked question after question and proposed approach after approach by which he could test the sentiments of the "woman." Yet even when he tried out the approaches she suggested on the counselor herself, she never got the message.

While this example is humorous, naivete, single-minded determination to solve problems, and unwillingness to consider the meaning or impact of client behavior can result in counselors being gullible and easy to manipulate. In the guise of being kind and helpful, few would be naive enough to supply drugs to addicts, but counselors often try to satisfy clients by overlooking disagreeable or destructive client behavior.

There is widespread confusion in our society about judging the behavior of the mentally disturbed. In legal proceedings, mental illness is sometimes used as an acceptable excuse for inexcusable behavior; some convicted wrongdoers are judged not guilty by reason of insanity. Whatever merit the ruling has, it has no logic. Individuals are always responsible for their acts and guilty for their wrongdoings. Whether they are mentally ill, have been unfortunate, have genetic irregularities, or cannot distinguish between right and wrong, the wrongful acts have been committed, and no one else is responsible for them. Yet counselors often regard their clients as not guilty or responsible whenever they discover a psychological explanation for their behavior. They also excuse any acts that are unintentional. Understanding is not the same as excusing client behavior. Understanding does not imply approval, agreement, or justification. While psychological explanations for destructive acts can always be discovered, they never explain why others who come from the same environment, suffer the same illness, or experience the same hard knocks do not also behave destructively.

Counselors have to manage two almost incompatible tasks: understanding the reason behind clients' actions and still holding clients responsible for those acts. If we excuse the client—if we blame the environment, the system, the irrational impulse, the liquor, the background, or the childhood experience—then we are likely to be misused by clients. Rather than help our clients control their lives and behavior, we will be used by clients to justify their evading responsibilities, to find excuses for their behavior, and to support maladaptive patterns. These are important points to grasp because, as counselors, we can be pawns and dupes. Preventing this is our responsibility. Again some illustrations follow.

Savior or Counselor: Case #1

Sandra was a woman of delicate sensibilities—tactful, courteous, and gentle. Her client, Annie, a young black unmarried mother of an infant, was trying to finish college despite her new burdensome responsibilities. Although she had reduced her course load, she still found it difficult to study, mother, and find good care for her child. When, at the beginning of each session, Sandra would ask Annie how things were going, Annie would bring up her difficulties in coping with the baby and feeling comfortable as a new mother. To Sandra the topic of an illegitimate child was embarrassing, and she was convinced she would make Annie uncomfortable by discussing it. So recordings of sessions demonstrated long monologues by Annie with only occasional sounds of encouragement from her counselor. If Annie changed the subject to practical issues such as babysitting, school, or financial arrangements, Sandra's voice would be heard, but as soon as Annie turned the discussion to her new baby, her counselor, active only a minute before, would become silent. There were many awkward pauses while Annie waited for Sandra to comment, while indicating her openness and need for help.

Comment

It is very common for new counselors to be overprotective of clients and to avoid disturbing topics in interviews. Attributing to Annie the embarrassment that she, Sandra, would experience as an unmarried mother, Sandra shrank away from her discussion of the baby. The two women came from different class and ethnic backgrounds, and this discrepancy probably made Sandra more hesitant to appear insensitive. Intuitions about clients' underlying feelings can be helpful but they must be tested. Sandra's concern was an inappropriate projection and not an accurate impression. Because of it, Sandra failed to provide the support Annie needed.

Savior or Counselor: Case #2

Arthur was an outpatient at a hospital service which relied on neighborhood volunteers to assist with activities, recreation, and informal socialization. While attending college out of state, Arthur had suffered a serious depression and came home. Appearing suicidal, he was subsequently hospitalized for two months, until he showed improvement with medication and psychotherapy. Thereafter, he attended the hospital's after-care facility, where he became attached to Harry, a forty-two-year-old fireman who intended a second career as a counselor.

Harry, a warm-hearted man with no children of his own, was proud of Arthur's devotion and convinced that he had done as much to restore Arthur's confidence and optimism as any of the professional staff. When Arthur confided that he had stopped taking antidepressant medication, he made Harry promise not to tell because he believed the psychiatrist would not approve. While this promise made Harry uncomfortable, he felt he could "monitor" Arthur and would see any problems developing. Quite suddenly they did. Arthur, who had a girlfriend at college, received a letter in which she said that she still missed him but had started dating others. Despite a disturbing change in his mood and demeanor, Arthur adamantly opposed resuming his medication or going back in the hospital. He said if Harry "reported" him, he would lose Harry, who meant the most to him, and would have to stop the "after-care" program. Harry tried to discuss his other options, but Arthur got huffy and distant; he said that Harry's commitment was no more genuine than his girlfriend's and accused Harry of wanting to get rid of him. He said the thought of losing Harry made him feel like killing himself. Harry felt trapped. Since he was not always available, he gave Arthur the phone numbers at which he could be reached and made him promise to call him whenever he felt desperate. To himself, Harry prayed he would not be away from the phone too long. Two very tense weeks followed. Conversations with Arthur at the after-care center or on the phone did not lift his spirits. Harry also became worried every time he was away from the phone and frightened whenever he learned he had missed a call. Finally he decided to report his difficulties to his supervisor, but before he could, Arthur was discovered and rushed back to the hospital after an attempted suicide.

Comment

Depression with suicidal potential is one of the conditions that demands direct intervention, but Harry delayed reporting Arthur's discontinued medication and signs of relapse. He believed his special relationship with Arthur was effective therapy. Although the psychiatric methods had worked up to a point, Arthur now resisted them. Perhaps both believed Harry to be the curative agent. In addition, Harry feared any action that might seem like a rejection or add to Arthur's feelings of abandonment.

Although the details differ, this is a familiar predicament to many individuals who are the friends, neighbors, or relatives of someone who is severely depressed. How can one be "clinical" and resist the requests of someone teetering on the brink of suicide? To believe one holds the key to life or death for another individual is awesome; the responsibility is frightening and often seems inescapable.

Yet the demands of someone like Arthur are psychic blackmail. They make us feel needed and important but they also carry a concealed and hostile threat: "If you don't assume responsibility for me as I want you to, I'll kill myself, and it will be your fault!" As much as we may want to help we cannot take the responsibility for keeping someone from suicide or the blame if we do not comply with the demand. Although illness may make people temporarily dependent and unable to make rational choices, we cannot carry on our lives while they play Russian Roulette with our behavior. Can we be reached by phone? Have we the time to talk? Will we say the right thing or somehow be seen as rejecting? Suicidal individuals need hospitalization, attention around the clock, and services we cannot provide continuously. Such facilities are not always pleasant or attractive or agreeable; they are simply necessary, until some measure of self-sufficiency is regained. Accepting the responsibility of protecting someone from the wish to die and doing whatever they ask of us is more than a counseling error. It is dangerous.

Harry made another mistake common to counselors who grow too attached to clients: he became overprotective. He protected Arthur from the professional staff. On the basis of Arthur's professed dislike for his psychiatrist and, eventually, to cover his own mistakes, Harry did not consult others who could have helped him evaluate the situation. For similar reasons, trainees avoid reviewing cases with supervisors. They may conceal information about clients to avoid hearing the supervisor's opinion. They may fear having their own errors exposed or imagine they may get their clients into trouble. Or, they mistakenly believe that client confidentiality excludes professional supervision. None of these reasons is correct or sufficient to justify the resulting risk to clients.

Pawn or Counselor: Case #3

A nurse, Mrs. G, had developed a special interest and experienced success working with patients who had chronic illnesses. Her medical knowledge and the personal care she extended produced improvement in many individuals seen as hopeless or deteriorating. Gratified by her effectiveness in the institutional setting, Mrs. G took some counseling courses and began to see disabled clients privately. With Mrs. G's counseling assistance, Jane, a mature woman and mother of two teenagers, completed a masters degree in musicology despite her multiple sclerosis. Prior to that, Jane had been mostly home-bound, although she had suffered only occasional periods of acute distress. Attended by a homemaker when no family member was at home to care for her or to accompany her out, Jane began to require these services more and more as the children became independent and Fred, Jane's husband, stayed longer at his law office. A devoted husband, Fred had usually arranged to be home evenings. Now he often worked late hours and seemed short-tempered and distant. Fred agreed to accompany Jane to her counseling sessions with Mrs. G, to discuss the situation. At first, he promised to bring more work home to please Jane. In the next session, he was quiet despite Jane's expression of her appreciation that he worked at home two evenings. The following day Fred called Mrs. G and asked to see her by himself, and without Jane's knowledge. When Mrs. G questioned this arrangement, Fred began to sob over the phone. Mrs. G was touched and set an appointment for the next day. In the session Fred was very troubled—agitated some of the time, tearful and shaky at other moments. He explained that during the time Jane had been away or preoccupied with her studies, he had fallen in love with a colleague at work, and though he had tried many times to end this relationship, he found that impossible. Unable to balance the two relationships as he hoped he could, he had decided to leave Jane. He was convinced that if he told Jane directly, her medical condition would worsen, and he could not bear to cause her injury through the shock. He had tried to tell Jane before and during the joint sessions, but even Mrs. G's presence did not help. He insisted Mrs. G tell Jane his plans and provide the assistance she required, since she understood Jane's illness better than he did. When Mrs. G resisted his request, Fred was able to persuade her. It was she who broke the news to Jane.

Comment:

For several reasons, Mrs. G allowed herself to be used by Fred and assumed a responsibility that was his alone. She felt sorry for him in his distress; she felt as if she had special skills that could help chronically ill patients deal with difficulties; she knew her relationship with Jane was good; and she may have felt some guilt in supporting Jane's educational undertaking, which had undermined the marriage. But she did neither Fred nor Jane a service. Fred, now off the hook, could undertake an act which had troubled him so that he was unable to discuss it in person with Jane. Jane would resent him for his cruel kindness and Mrs. G for her complicity in helping her husband sever his marriage vows without even facing her. Mrs. G's kindness and sympathy for both spouses led her to act against her better judgment and be a pawn when she needed to help both partners deal directly with the crisis in their marriage.

IX

Personal Characteristics of Effective Counselors

All successful counselors share certain characteristics and skills, among which are:

A) Availability, reliability, and responsibility
B) Interest, warmth, enthusiasm, and respect
C) Openness and honesty
D) Objectivity
E) Empathy
F) Acceptance of clients and their efforts to help themselves
G) Accountability: monitoring the counseling process
H) Understanding confidentiality

This chapter will consider each of these categories separately, although some overlap. Readers may have to translate and adapt the principles to fit their own circumstances.

A. Availability, Reliability, and Responsibility

Although counseling objectives are occasionally reached in one meeting or a few, counseling is usually a prolonged effort. *Counselors have to be regularly and predictably available.* Trainees and volunteers who counsel only part-time while balancing other major responsibilities may try to sandwich in counseling when it suits their schedule, only to find that, when the time comes, there is little for them to do. Hours allotted for counseling should match the times clients are generally available and the requirements of the sponsoring agency or setting. It is smart to notify staff as well as others of the times you intend to be "on the job." Consistency is essential, so design a schedule you can hold to.

Often, new counselors are so eager to get started that they do not allow themselves time to become oriented to the setting in which they work: staff, co-workers, schedules, and policies. Ignorance can lead to embarrassment, so the time learning is well spent. Most agencies have an orientation program which gives all new members instructions and introductions at the same time. *Information-giving is not the crux of counseling, but it is often used by clients as the first criterion of counselor competence.* Counselors therefore try to be letter-perfect in dispensing information to clients; they investigate, rather than guess about information which they do not have.

In many settings, potential clients either do not know of counseling opportunities or need encouragement to use them. Therefore, in these situations, counselors have to engage in what professionals call "out reach"—making one's presence known by creating publicity, by contacting people who identify and refer clients, or by informal contact with potential clients. Too often trainees stay hidden away in offices. When counselors are not assigned to clients in an automatic or regular fashion, they should demonstrate their availability. They should beware of becoming inaccessible. An example of such inaccessibility occurred at a college drop-in center and telephone "hot line." Whenever things got slow there, the counselors would use the phones to make personal calls. In the process, they made it hard for anyone to phone in, and they appeared occupied when a client looked in to see if anyone was free to sit and talk. Since few people are comfortable approaching counselors, access needs to be as easy and inviting as possible.

Once a client indicates a wish for counseling, the counselor must be regularly available or should refer the client to someone who is. In some settings clients may show up unpredictably to be seen by any counselor who happens to be there.

This is not a good policy. Counselors are not interchangeable, and seeing someone different each time interferes with developing a relationship. Don't make yourself available to other counselors' clients, unless there is an emergency.

Reliability is closely related to availability. *Clients (and staff) will either count on you to be where you promised to be and to do your assigned tasks or they will count you out.* New counselors often start with a burst of energy but grow discouraged without immediate reward or result. In contrast, clients are often tentative and cautious in early contacts, testing to see whether they can trust the offer of help and guarding themselves against the disappointment they may have experienced with others. These two scenarios can work against each other. If the counselor frequently breaks or misses appointments, the relationship may never get off the ground. If a session must be canceled, try to let the client, not just the agency, know well in advance and personally reschedule the interview for another time.

Some of the tasks counselors must handle responsibly have been detailed above. Others are readily apparent: protecting the client's right to confidentiality, using supervision and consultation with superiors appropriately, and observing agency rules and ethical procedures. *Being responsible to and for others is an obvious aspect of counseling,* and few enter this field without some appetite for it, yet beginners should recognize that this appetite can get out of hand.

In recent years the helping professions have begun to notice the phenomenon of "burn out," the exhaustion of good will, enthusiasm, and dedication through overwork and self-neglect. Counselors can become demoralized by continuous exposure to the needs and demands of others as well as by seeing clients only in distress or crisis, never in "good times." They can feel that no effort is ever sufficient. In these situations, being responsible to others can overshadow personal ("selfish") needs.

While the syndrome of "burn out" does not develop overnight, new counselors should be aware of its eventual possibility. Preoccupation with the pain and suffering of others can distort our view of human nature and make us feel guilty about enjoying life. Yet, the capacity to give and keep on giving depends on a sense of well-being and a balanced perspective. Perhaps giving and getting will not always be in perfect harmony, but a healthy interest in the concerns of others is best sustained by sensible self-interest.

B. Interest, Warmth, Enthusiasm, and Respect

Interest in clients usually develops naturally because of our commitment to their welfare. But sometimes we fail to show or express it. Often, beginners who are afraid of prying stick too close to the problem originally presented. They fail to ask about broader issues and to pick up cues about other concerns. We may not need to get every last detail, but we do need to have a sense of our clients: what is going on in their lives, how they are feeling in general. Clients will follow our lead and provide relevant information if we indicate our interest in them.

As a psychologist in a college, I assisted some students who could not overcome particular learning problems. A young woman consulted me about her language learning block, and we discussed the issue for most of a session. Since time remained, I casually asked how things were going for her otherwise. To my surprise, she burst into tears and began describing her mother's recent operation for cancer and her related concerns. We needed to spend a few sessions discussing this crisis. I might never have learned of the troubles besetting her had I not indicated that my interest in her went beyond the technical matter which she first came to see me about.

Sometimes, technical or administrative issues may take up most of the session, but one can still express interest in matters clients may reveal along the way and extend an invitation, or arrange another appointment, to discuss them in detail. If paperwork can be postponed for a while, or done after the meeting, it is better to use the time to establish personal contact. A counselor's comment on little things, such as an unfamiliar accent, an attractive piece of clothing or jewelry, an unusual name, or something else that distinguishes the individual, shows interest and sometimes serves to break the ice. When seeing someone a second time, remember what was shared on the first occasion or take a moment with the client to refresh your memory. If necessary, keep notes, records, or other reminders, but be sure they are not left around for others to see.

Personal attributes in counselors such as *warmth and enthusiasm* are matters of style which differ from person to person. Since it is probable that one client could receive effective help from different counselors with widely varying styles, it is pointless to prescribe specific behavior for all. (One element frequently mentioned in books on counseling skills is maintaining eye contact throughout the interview, but a constant stare may be more unnerving than reassuring to a client. As long as you are clearly attentive and not preoccupied with extraneous thoughts, papers, or distractions, you will maintain the eye contact that is comfortable for you, and probably for your client, without thinking about it.)

New counselors have an emotion which can interfere with their expression of warmth and enthusiasm—their own anxiety. Trying to say the "right" thing, formulating the next question while the client is answering the first, warding off silence, and devising methods to keep the discussion moving along are distractions which make beginners appear formal, distant, inattentive, and even uninterested in clients. One problem in training counselors, especially when sessions are tape recorded for later supervision, is the added self-consciousness the tape recorder induces. Some nervousness is probably unavoidable in initial stages of supervision or self-criticism. However, if too self-focused, one stops being primarily interested in the client and the interview becomes an empty exercise. *Although counseling may be a new challenge, try to bring the "old" you to the interview and show the natural warmth, spontaneity, and enthusiasm you bring to your typical conversations.* Counseling *is* a conversation with the focus on the client. Pauses and silences may be quite acceptable. Neither speed nor quantity of verbalization indicate counselor effectiveness.

No matter how nervous you are, try not to rehearse your questions or comments before—or during—a session. When you are only considering what you are going to say, you cannot really hear the client. If you cannot listen you cannot counsel. From moment to moment, take your cues from what the client says or shows—not from a prearranged agenda. Make a note for yourself if you want to go back to an item that gets skipped over.

Clients probably measure a helper's warmth and interest less from constant words of praise or support, than from the sense that they have been heard and understood. They will take clues from your appearance, your posture, your varying facial expressions as well as what you say. Beginners often mistake activity (asking lots of questions, trying to find quick solutions, showing off the information in their possession, "doing for" the client) with eagerness to help. Often such activity is just distracting. It does not allow either participant to sort out thoughts, respond to one another, or struggle with feelings and problems.

Respect for the client is shown in many ways. One of the most basic is seeing to the client's comfort. Is the client seated comfortably? Does a window need to be opened or shut? Does the client know who you are, the purpose of the meeting, how long it will last? Do you know the client's name and how he or she prefers to be called? These have been some of the elements missing from interviews conducted by overeager trainees working in college offices. They have interviewed student clients who were dressed in heavy overcoats, balancing books and belongings on their laps, and without adequate introductions or orientation to the session's purpose. Institutional settings may be short on creature comforts, but they can include an extra chair to stash belongings, a box of tissues, an ashtray, a wastebasket, and other signs of consideration. Rushed or fearful clients may resist an invitation to get settled comfortably, but they will still feel more welcomed and respected if it is offered.

Some clients require special consideration. You may have to adjust your way of speaking for someone with a language or hearing problem. With a client who has a speech hesitancy or stutter, you may have to slow your rate of exchange, allowing more time for the expression of thoughts. You may have to encourage someone to speak louder or rephrase statements, or even write things out if you are confused.

Paying attention to the communication process and the difficulties it presents for clients shows the counselor's desire to persist despite obstacles. It may seem easier, or more polite, to "pretend" understanding, but if the client's speech is often unclear, you are really avoiding a problem that needs to be dealt with.

Sometimes clients set up their own conditions for counseling, identifying problems or areas that they do *not* wish to discuss. One should ask the reasons why a particular area is "off limits," because the answer may help to identify and resolve some confusion about your role. For instance, the client may not understand your assurance of confidentiality and may be afraid others will be told what is shared. Or the client may be overwhelmed or frightened by certain topics or find them to be particularly difficult to talk about, like intimate details of a sexual relationship. Sometimes the "no trespassing" sign is a test of the counselor, a method to measure counselor intrusiveness and control. If reviewing the reasons behind the hesitancy does not resolve or alter it, it is best to respect the client's wishes. In time, the client may share the concern, and in other instances, the secret may remain but not impede progress. A student assigned to me for counseling told me initially that he would not discuss his relationship with his oldest sister. We worked together for two years, during which he greatly improved his academic performance and grew in many ways. We discussed many of his family members and younger siblings often, but never his oldest sister. I admit to this day, many years later, that I am still curious. While I cannot judge whether discussion of that sister would have been useful, I have the clear impression that it was more important to honor his wish for privacy and control. There is no need to push for total disclosure as long as there is enough room to work productively.

Respect may mean informing yourself about unfamiliar practices, beliefs, and values that are important features in the background and culture of the client. Clients themselves may have to explain certain aspects of an unusual heritage, but it is considerate and worthwhile to learn what you can from other sources. It can be a struggle to comprehend another's frame of reference and priorities, especially when they clash with your cultural standards. A conflict common to many Hispanic students, for example, is between fulfilling family obligations and, at the same time, academic commitments. Counseling can help an individual find a route between two contradictory value systems without requiring a sacrifice of either, provided both are understood and respected. Our own cultural experience is always limited, therefore we must stretch to appreciate perspectives of other traditions.

C. Openness and Honesty

A common stereotype of counselors is that they remain completely aloof in the helping relationship. Perhaps this image stems from—and is appropriate to—the psychoanalyst who works to uncover unconscious processes from patients' associations, a treatment method which minimizes face-to-face interaction between therapist and patient. Perhaps it is our picture of an expert: detached and objective. But these are not the goals or designs of counseling relationships conducted by peer, volunteer, mutual-help, or paraprofessional counselors. *As counselors, we try not to get personally involved, but openness and the willingness to share feelings and reactions are essential.*

Training counselors makes it clear that the most successful are in touch with their own feelings and aware that clients' reactions are understandable in light of their own. The study of academic psychology does not seem to be the key to comprehending the meaning of clients' communications. In fact, evidence shows that English majors (or those exposed to the lives of others through literature) are most proficient as college peer counselors and most able to articulate awareness in the service of clients. Another experience which augments natural talent is psychotherapy, having struggled to identify and comprehend one's own dynamics. These findings suggest that openness to and curiosity about emotional experience are more useful to novices than most "academic" learning.

Looking at the issue another way: what kind of a model is the counselor who is removed and detached? We often choose counselors with experience and background similar to our own, hoping to find understanding of our feelings and sensitivity to our distress. If the counselor is not open, communicative, and willing to share experiences, this potential asset is lost.

Openness is an asset to counseling, but more often, it serves as an instrument of receptivity rather than expression since the focus is on the client's, not the helper's, experience. As long as clients are sharing freely, there is little need for counselor revelation. In those situations, it is enough for counselors to listen, encourage exploration, and lend themselves to the clients' searching. A nod of recognition, a useful question, an indication of understanding are reassuring enough. But when the going gets tough and the client gets bogged down or discouraged, the counselor's experience or feelings may be very useful—not in the recounting of a final resolution to comparable problems, but of a similar struggle. When our difficulty has struck a resonant chord, it is comforting to know that we are not alone, but we hardly want to be regaled with stories of another's triumph and success. Clients usually need to sense the counselor's concern and empathy rather than to hear about a counselor's accomplishment.

Counselor openness demonstrates a willingness to be in touch with feelings and an ability to communicate awareness when useful to the client. Sometimes our own reaction offers a comparison, adds perspective, or opens a new avenue for exploration. But it should not shift attention away from the client or result in "showing off" our suffering or success. Examples that always show us in a favorable light may seem more like bragging than understanding. So, in order to serve the client's needs, care must be taken in recounting experiences; their real usefulness lies in enhancing rapport and togetherness.

Openness requires honesty about one's feelings, motives, and failings, and this can be difficult. Counselors want to be seen as competent and knowledgeable. Trainees do not want to admit they are new to the job or that they don't have immediate answers to problems. They are afraid that if their inexperience, ignorance, or anxiety shows, their help will be rejected. Rather than saying, "I don't know, I'll check for you," they often pretend to have an answer. The appearance of competence is not the real thing. We want the client to appreciate not that we are without problems, but that we are able to admit them.

Honesty is not restricted to the things we admit to clients. What we tell the client becomes a matter of discretion, based on an understanding of the situation at that particular time. *It is important that we be honest with ourselves.* Our feelings are the clues to understanding many complexities in the helping relationship, and we dare not falsify them. A counseling trainee once made a special, but nevertheless inconvenient, arrangement to arrive an hour early in order to see a client whose schedule kept her in class the rest of the day. On that day, the client was so late that only ten minutes remained. Instead of mentioning their agreement to meet an hour early or the problems which the shortened session presented (both issues which bothered the trainee), she rushed through everything in ten minutes, rattling off answers to complex questions as if they—and the client—were not worth more time. She tried to behave as if she was not angry, but what she really did was give the client and her concerns the brush-off. This kind of pretending helps no one. Our feelings will show indirectly anyway; but if we don't admit them, we don't give the client a chance to deal with them.

We may not like all the feelings which we experience in counseling, but rather than wish them away, we have to deal with them. (I counseled a student for several sessions without being able to diminish or relieve her distressing attacks of anxiety and depression. She was forthright and comfortable in our relationship, insightful about herself, and apparently able to deal with problems in her life. We enjoyed the sessions and each other. Yet her anxiety and depression continued. I, at first, postponed sharing my suspicion that we were not getting anywhere and that her symptoms required another approach. But when I did, I regretted my hesitancy. She had reached the same conclusion, but the realization made her feel discouraged and helpless. She thought nothing would help. Luckily, that was untrue. Consultation with a psychiatrist suggested that her symptoms could be treated with minute amounts of medication. I was able to refer her for a treatment that was effective almost immediately.) Evaluating progress requires scrupulous honesty, however hard it is to have our efforts questioned and sometimes exchanged for better alternatives. *Seeking and giving honest feedback is fundamental to the counseling process;* for that, we have to be honest with ourselves.

D. Objectivity: Keeping One's Self and the Client in Perspective

A real problem for counselors is both being in a relationship and remaining objective about it. It is like operating on two different wavelengths: involvement and understanding on one, evaluation on the other. When we care for people we are tempted to overlook their faults and our limitations. In understanding the basis of certain kinds of behavior, we may find it hard to hold clients responsible. Instead, we feel inclined to protect, excuse, indulge, and comfort, as we might do in personal relationships. Listen to Virginia Axline's report on her feelings about Dibs, the disturbed youngster from a demanding and rejecting home, at the end of their first play therapy session:

> He dabbed clumsily at his tear-streaked face. It would have been so easy to take him in my arms and console him, to extend the hour, to try overtly to give him a demonstration of affection and sympathy. But of what value would it have been to add additional emotional problems to this child's life? He *did* have to go back to his home no matter how he felt about it. To avoid facing this reality factor would not help him. He needed to develop strength to cope with his world, but that strength had to come from within him and he had to experience personally his ability to cope with his world as it was. Any meaningful changes for Dibs would have to come from within him. We could not hope to make over his external world.
> (Virginia M. Axline, *Dibs in Search of Self.* New York: Ballantine Books, pages 46-47.)

Axline's restraint and perspective are painful to accept; the reader aches to protect this extraordinary little boy from his cold home atmosphere. Clearly however, Axline's reactions are in Dib's best interest, since her therapy—any therapy—provides aid, not an alternative.

In the case of a child who lives with his parents, it is easier to see that the therapist has an obligation, not only to the client, but to others in the client's life. If counseling gives us a vision of the client's fears and feelings, we should not be blind to everything else. Rather than provide a false security, our task is to help the client meet the challenges and cope with the demands of the external world. We cannot replace the other people in the client's life. *Seeing the client in the context of his environment, and as he appears to others, is an important aspect of objectivity.* We must supplement what we are told (from the client's subjective viewpoint) with what we know about the real world, and help the client see the apparent incompatibilities between the two.

A student, failing college after two years of coursework, discusses her teachers with a counselor:

Client: You know, two of my teachers told me, "All you have to do is really get a high, high grade on your final and you will do all right." They should have told me, "Well, if you don't get a good high grade on your final, I'm going to have to fail you."
Counselor: Wait a minute. They tell you, "You really need a high, high grade on your final." What does that say to you? What does that mean?
Client: That I'm not doing too good. Okay, I can understand that. But they could have told me bluntly too. They didn't have to put it like that, either. They could have told me bluntly, you know, you can get a good grade on your final and I'll pass you, and if you don't get a good grade, I'm gonna have to fail you.
Counselor: But what I hear you saying is that the teachers let you down by not giving you adequate warning. That makes it sound like they are at fault, not you.

In this example, client and counselor both address the reality of the situation, sort out responsibility, and examine the ways in which the student misread the teachers' comments. Some counselors might be tempted to avoid any hint of confrontation by supporting the student's criticism of the teachers who optimistically told her that she might pass.

Another aspect of objectivity is the ability to see clients in the context of the group or developmental stage in which they belong. To pursue this example a bit further, the student quoted above is revealing a typical expectation of students from high schools which, in effect, do not fail anyone who makes an effort. Teachers may warn students they are not performing well, but if they attend class and complete the assignments, they will receive passing final grades. The same message from a high school teacher would really mean, "You will have to do very well on the final to earn a high grade, but you will still pass with lesser effort." The student has not learned that in college students are failed when their work does not meet a certain standard. If we can understand the unspoken expectations that guide clients' lives, we can help them see those that are inappropriate to current situations and challenges.

When clients' views or behavior disturb or threaten counselors, objectivity is difficult to maintain. For instance, the very organized, systematic individual may be shocked by a scattered and impulsive client. A forthright direct person may find a shy and timid client disconcerting. Facing a client who is uncooperative, a counselor may respond with anger, disbelief, or condemnation—varying expressions of subjective frustration. Counselors also lose objectivity when they so identify with clients that they join them to battle the rest of the world. *When counselors do not see clients accurately because of their own biases or because they believe a client's distorted report, they operate subjectively.* Subjective responses do not give clients freedom to be themselves or help clients understand what is going on in their interaction with others.

Nonprofessionals are handicapped because they lack some of the experience and concepts professionals use for objective evaluation of clients. They must use their subjective reactions as important sources of information—diagnostic cues of a sort—but these must be understood and separated from the counselors' preferences and values. They need objectivity and insight into the way they, as counselors, see the world. People who know their own peeves and preferences are better able to gauge their effect on relationships with others who conform with or deviate from them. Introspection and self-awareness allow us to use our feelings in the client's behalf. If counselors use only their biases to form the basis of their counseling, they may not help clients as much as try to mold them in the images they prefer. Since this is a real danger (and distortion) of counseling, every counselor must work at keeping personal values in perspective. If counselors fear their preferences are too strong to permit objectivity, they should share them openly with their clients; revealed in this way, they are less apt to be subversive.

E. Empathy: Putting One's Self in the Other's Shoes

Objectivity—keeping ourselves, as well as our clients and the world they live in, in perspective—may seem antithetical to empathy, seeing things from the client's point of view. Objectivity and empathy are not incompatible, but they require a constantly shifting focus and the integration of information from varying sources.

Since sensitivity to and awareness of personal problems often prompt the desire to counsel others, few anticipate having difficulty empathizing with clients. We imagine that our having experienced emotional distress guarantees our understanding of others. However, the appreciation of human suffering rarely sustains us in all our dealings with clients. For example, college counseling trainees are all college graduates familiar with "the college experience." Yet, when counseling undergraduates, they do not often see themselves or their personal problems in their clients. Usually they see differences. There *are* differences, but that is not the real issue. Differences and similarities always exist between counselors and clients. *Empathy—the ability to see the world from the client's perspective—does not come from identical experiences but from a common reservoir of human feelings.* One who has been successful at a task can still understand the frustration and disappointment of one doing poorly; the circumstances may differ but frustration and disappointment are familiar to all. Yet at first it rarely seems so.

The hard part is to recognize that the way we react, or reacted, to circumstances is not the only way. Trainees are distressed, even indignant, to find that a situation which triggered one response in them provokes another in a client. We can learn to accept the variety of human response, provided we do not require that others' actions conform with our own. If I respond to the possibility of failure by exerting extra effort, I can still understand the person who gives up, the person who cheats, and the person who runs away. No matter what I do in similar circumstances, I have felt each of those temptations and they are recognizable to me. Clients' responses are not wrong when they differ from our own, but they may require that we reach deep inside ourselves to understand. Empathy is based on the premise that no emotion is wrong, that each is a familiar and comprehensible human expression. No human response is beyond understanding.

Empathy does not imply approval; it does not mean that we would feel or do the same thing. It does not mean that we see no better alternatives or that we are trapped in the same perspective as the client. It does mean that we can understand what the client feels. If we cannot do this, we will find it hard to form a collaboration. *Without empathy, there is, inevitably, a sense of distance between counselor and client, a distance which implies superiority and disapproval on the part of the counselor.*

In counseling, empathy is directed at feelings, not action. Actions are subject to conscious control, while feelings are rarely a matter of choice. Initially it may seem foreign to the counselor to separate emotions from actions in understanding clients and to restrict their judgment to what clients do and not what they feel. (Religious injunctions often condemn both.) The freedom to identify feelings, fantasies, and impulses without incurring disapproval helps clients release tension, face problems, understand their experience, and explore behavioral alternatives. If they fear their clients will act out their feelings, counselors may then be threatened by them and force clients to suppress, banish, or hide them. This response deprives clients of the opportunity to exercise and develop inner controls. Counseling is a safe place for clients to get in touch with, examine, and understand their feelings, but such exploration may make counselors apprehensive and controlling. Clients, too, have to be helped to recognize that their feelings do not have the same moral weight or consequences as their acts and should not be condemned.

Human emotions are universal but different things make each of us laugh, cry, and feel fear. A pregnancy makes one woman joyful, another fearful, and a third desperately unhappy. We can understand and empathize with all three no matter how we would feel in a similar situation. *The focus in counseling is understanding the client's response using our own feelings to inform and connect us; it is not deciding whether the response is right or wrong or whether it conforms to our own.*

On many occasions, I have had to struggle to understand clients' feelings and perspectives. I worked, for instance, with an identical twin whose close tie to his sibling interfered with his capacity to form other satisfying and loving relationships. Few outsiders could provide the understanding, empathy, and encouragement this pair could offer each other with their lifelong history of mutual support. Having no twin of my own, I struggled to understand such intimacy, drawing from the closest of my associations some sense of the security afforded by this twinship. I had to make a leap from my psychic world to his by a kind of emotional approximation. I had to project myself into his struggle to become independent by first imagining the bonds that held him, bonds of a type I have never experienced.

Sympathy is not the same as empathy. Sympathy places a distance between us and the other person as if we were on the outside looking in. It conveys pity. Empathy allows us to assume the client's vantage point, connect with his feelings, and imagine walking in his shoes.

Liking someone makes empathy easier but also can contribute to losing perspective and objectivity. Empathy is not a permanent but a shifting focus, a source of information in counseling. It is effortless with some clients, more difficult with others. In graduate school, several of my Jewish peers and I used to imagine whether we could sustain empathy toward Hitler if he were our patient: could we be tolerant and understanding? Counselors learn much about themselves by observing which clients engender their empathy and which pose difficulty; the groups are different for each of us, alerting us to the part played by our own dynamics in our work as counselors.

F. Acceptance of Clients and Their Efforts to Help Themselves

Empathy is the key to acceptance. Empathy permits a real glimpse of clients and the predicaments facing them, so that we can understand reasons for troublesome behavior. Some forms of behavior pose problems just by outlasting the conditions in which they originated, like study habits suitable for high school but insufficient in college, or practices expected of us as children that do not fit our lives as adults. Clients tend to attribute their problems to pervasive and permanent personality characteristics rather than to learned responses that are no longer useful. They think of themselves as lazy, irresponsible, immature, or dependent. Therefore, they blame themselves, feel guilty, and doubt their ability to change. For clients to consider behavioral alternatives and improve their self-esteem, they need an atmosphere that encourages self-examination in a reasonable and reassuring way. *Acceptance and respect from a counselor allow clients to look at themselves and their choices in a more pragmatic, less pessimistic way.*

Virginia Axline's approach to Dibs in his first play-therapy session is a good example. (*Dibs in Search of Self,* p. 41-42):

> On entering the room, Dibs touched many of the items there, naming each one out loud. After he had completed the first circuit of the room, I said, "Yes. There are many different things in this room, aren't there? And you have touched and named most of them."

"That's right," he said, softly.

I didn't want to rush him. Give him time to look around and explore. Every child needs time to explore his world in his own way. He stopped in the middle of the room.

"I say, Dibs! Would you like to take off your hat and coat?" I asked him after a while.

"That's right," he said. "You take off your hat and coat, Dibs. You take off your hat. You take off your coat, Dibs." He made no motion to do anything about it.

"Then you would like to take off your coat and hat?" I asked. "All right, Dibs, go ahead. Take them off."

"Take off mittens and boots, too," he said.

"All right," I replied. "Take off your mittens and your boots, too, if you want to."

"That's right," he said, almost in a whisper. He stood there, plucking idly and restlessly at his coat sleeves. He began to whimper. He stood in front of me, hanging his head, whimpering.

"You would like to take them off, but you want me to help you? Is that it?" I asked.

"That's right," he said. There was a sob in his voice as he replied.

I sat down on a little chair and said, "All right, Dibs. If you want me to help you take off your coat and hat, come over here and I will help you." This too was done with a purpose in mind. I offered to help him, but sat down in such a location in the room that in order to get the help he would have to take a few steps of his own for it.

What Axline is communicating to Dibs even in these trivial matters is respect and acceptance. She does not correct him when he uses language incorrectly. She does not pressure him or direct him. She indicates a recognition of what he is doing without praise or criticism, and she communicates indirectly that whatever he does is all right, acceptable. To make certain she understands him when he is unclear or uncertain, she restates her understanding as a question. He is free to be himself, an experience he desperately needs. This is essentially what therapy provides for Dibs, a child who has been subject to inordinate demands at home. But this excerpt also conveys a sense of *what every client needs from his or her therapist—undivided attention, consideration, and the feeling of being accepted.*

The counselor's desire to be helpful can interfere with conveying interest in and accepting the client's own efforts. Responding immediately to a client's problem with solutions is actually a "put-down," since it seems to imply that the client has missed the obvious. Counselors can be embarrassed to find the client has already tried and rejected the things they facilely suggest. Initial interviews, unless they follow a schedule of questions or serve a specific, limited purpose, are opportunities to listen. Counselors need only ask for clarification or details, convey interest and acceptance, and encourage open communication. Unless the client seeks information of a simple and straightforward nature, the answers are not simple. Counseling is not a matter of solving problems for people, but a process to help people explore and solve their own. When the counselor takes over, the wrong message is given: the client is unable to help himself (or herself). It is equivalent to Axline's explaining each of the toys to Dibs, correcting his use of language, and showing him how to take off his coat.

Some clients may exert pressure on counselors to solve their problems. People approach counselors after all else fails, feeling desperate. Their urgency can encourage premature and superficial problem-solving. But longstanding psychological problems are not speedily resolved. The counselor who recognizes and accepts this fact is less likely to set unrealistic goals or encourage impossible expectations. Even when clients begin to see an undesirable pattern in their behavior, they may not be able to alter it easily or swiftly. Personality patterns are not faucets to be turned on and off at will.

One reason beginners find it hard to accept the slow pace of counseling is the understandable wish to prove themselves effective. Novices measure their success by the suggestions they make, the problems they solve. Professionals have diagnostic guidelines and experience to temper their expectations, but beginners have no yardstick to use. Afraid to take a more passive role or *not* to offer advice, they want their recommendations to be effective immediately. They suspect to have failed if discussion does not produce resolution or if their advice does not work.

Counseling is the wrong endeavor for one who demands quick transformation and dramatic results. Clients often need reassurance, when their insights do not produce sweeping and permanent results, that counseling is slow, painful, and difficult work. If we aim at understanding, not changing, the client, acceptance and respect more easily follow.

Accepting the client requires appraising the counseling task realistically and understanding the pace at which change occurs. In the initial stages, success must be measured not by dramatic transformation, but by the client's willingness to join in the work.

G. Accountability: Monitoring the Counseling Process

An important, and sometimes uncomfortable, feature of the counselor's role is accountability. It differentiates the help we offer clients from that we extend to friends and family. In personal relationships, the help we give is usually unplanned and spontaneous, an added dividend to a relationship not usually dependent on the effectiveness of our advice. Hesitant to anger or hurt a friend, we carefully choose and tailor our words to match what we think is desired, expected, or safe. Often what we want most is to preserve the relationship and ensure its continuation. Our friends know us reasonably well and can put our counsel into the context of our lives and our personal value system; they know "where we are coming from" and how to shape our advice to fit their needs. Only rarely do we feel at risk.

Counseling clients is obviously different. The relationship has a singular and acknowledged purpose—that of ameliorating problems. Client and counselor start as strangers to each other. The relationship precludes the kind of familiarity which permits our friends to judge our opinions in light of our personal background and biases. Greater weight is given to counselor opinion since we are presumed to have expertise. We are also presumed to be well-informed, aware, and constructive in responding to clients, not just reacting to momentary pressures or impulses. A greater responsibility is involved in this kind of relationship. While our friends are apt to overlook, dismiss, or forgive the errors we make in assisting them, *intervening in the lives of strangers to address their problems makes us accountable for what we do.*

Even when we have others to advise us on our work, clients are often our best supervisors. Without meaning to, they let us know how we are doing. If they don't come back a second time, we are left to wonder why. They object to things we say or do, sometimes directly and often indirectly—a look of annoyance, a deprecating remark, lack of cooperation, a missed appointment. It is difficult to know sometimes whether clients are resisting the counseling process or responding to something we have done to make them uncomfortable or uncertain, but it is necessary to find out. Few people like criticism and most of us go out of our way to avoid it. Report cards, critical supervisors, job evaluations, other forms of assessment, all make us apprehensive. Yet, as counselors, we have to expect it, encourage it, and seek to understand it in order to gauge and facilitate the helping process.

Friends might offend us if they questioned or criticized the help we offer. If they have asked for it, we feel they should be grateful for it. This, however, cannot be our attitude as counselors. Client discomfort and dissatisfaction are important messages. Though they may frighten or threaten us, we are pledged to use them to help clients articulate their objections to us and to the helping process as part of their dealing with other problems in their lives. Few clients are comfortable revealing their doubts about us. So we have to actively encourage their expressions of discontent and question their hesitation. If we don't acknowledge those signs when they occur, we may not get other opportunities.

A young woman came to see me when I was a college psychologist. Luckily, I knew from office records that she had seen another counselor previously and had not returned for a second visit. While the two of us were exploring her problems, she reacted to something I said to her with a fleeting look of irritation. I asked her about it, and she expressed discomfort with the idea I had conveyed—that it would take time to work out her problems. I mentioned her previous visit and asked whether she had had the same concern then. She affirmed the question and said that, both now and in the past, she had so many apprehensions and fears that she doubted if she could make the effort that was necessary. If there was no immediate solution, she believed there would never be one.

Once her concern was out in the open, we could both recognize her feelings of hopelessness. I assured her that I thought she could be helped in counseling, but warned that I could not make the process magical or instantaneous. I told her that unless she could temper her expectations, she would make it impossible for anyone to help her. After deciding to continue, she did well and gained insight which quickly reduced some of her tension. Had I not caught that small cue (or divined in some other way the unspoken test to which she was subjecting the counseling process), she would not have given the relationship a chance to succeed. Convinced when she started that her only hope was instant relief, she was ready to quit when that was not forthcoming.

Concerned with their performance and determined to prove themselves, beginners can miss important signs of client discomfort. They may be afraid to explore any negative expressions they see for fear of hearing something unflattering. They concentrate on *content,* the information clients report, when *process,* revealed in the momentary responses of client to counselor, is more essential. Content "keeps" and can be dealt with later, but indications of discomfort or anxiety, when neglected, can snowball into major resistance. Only the counselor can monitor the process; the client is wrapped up in whatever he or she is reporting, and is often unaware of nonverbal behavior. Although reservations about counseling (or the counselor) are uncomfortable topics, the counselor's questions must be genuine and inviting. Counselors should not "accuse" clients of resistance or allow the issues to be clouded by their own defensiveness. A counselor who has erred or engaged in behavior that needs explanation should fully understand the effect of this behavior on the client *before* trying to explain or rectify the error.

This awareness, this questioning, this seeking of honest evaluation is difficult to learn because it flies in the face of social conventions. To enable casual conversations to go smoothly and comfortably, we are apt either to ignore signs that a person is uncomfortable, tense, or upset, or change our behavior to smooth things out. Feelings are often concealed as though they were too private or embarrassing to discuss. In counseling, however, feelings are our business. Ignoring them may preserve superficial pleasantries but it prevents genuine engagement. Had I ignored the grimace on my client's face during our session, I would not have seen that face again.

Counselors need to make an assumption that is not often made in ordinary social interchange: *everything a client does during a session is significant in the counseling relationship.* In a business meeting if someone suddenly changed the topic and introduced a seemingly unrelated tangent, the switch might be regarded as an interruption to be dealt with speedily. In counseling, no agenda takes precedence over what the client is thinking, feeling, or saying. Although we may have to get back to unfinished topics later, our main task is to follow the client and understand thoughts, ideas, and feelings as they occur; if unspoken, we have to draw them out.

In polite conversation, we would change the topic of discussion if it seemed to make a person upset or anxious; in counseling we welcome emotional reactions and support the client in exploring them. Novices, determined to make clients feel better, worry that they are at fault if a client cries during a session. They often seem to expect clients to maintain a controlled facade rather than display uncomfortable or overwhelming emotions in their presence. Difficult as it is to observe someone in distress, we cannot expect, nor would we want, clients to contain their feelings in sessions. Some novices are also afraid that a client's tears will make them cry too. While crying may not be the most helpful response and may add another burden for the client, it probably will do no great harm either. If something the counselor says seems to trigger tears, the counselor is, most likely, not the cause of the client's distress; more likely, the counselor has tapped into or opened up a painful area. Rather than apologize or back away, we need to explore what has upset the client. My client reacted when I conveyed that time would be required to help her with her problems because she felt she had no time to give. Her feelings of hopelessness might have defeated our efforts had they not been identified and discussed. *Being accountable as a counselor is not the same as assuming the responsibility or blame for everything that occurs during a session, but it does entail trying to understand and account for the effect we have on our clients.*

If we are accountable for what happens in session, we are also accountable for what does not happen. Novices are apt to mask their feelings about clients in order to project what they feel is the "right" image. But if clients are not participating freely, are not forthcoming about problems, are silent or evasive, counselors experience frustration and resentment. Convinced that such feelings are "wrong," beginners play it "cool" and fail to ask clients about disturbing signals. The result is that, in such encounters, little of interpersonal significance occurs, no engagement takes place. *Whatever the client's attitude, the counselor is accountable for the process, for identifying and wrestling with the elements contributing to both success and the failure to connect.* If we are not involved with them, it is unlikely that we will get clients involved with us. Few clients come to counseling knowing what the relationship can offer and fully prepared to work; often they need our help to get involved. If they are doing things to keep us at a distance, we have to break the bonds of conventional reserve and ask them why. Obviously, we must show tact and concern, but we cannot avoid questioning or confronting behavior that interferes with the work.

The fear of making errors or causing harm often inhibits new counselors. But holding back and "role playing" are also errors. Although none of us is perfect, pretending perfection is worse than making honest mistakes. To be accountable, we have to deal with the errors we make; we have to learn their effects on clients, understand how they may have occurred, and be able to admit them to clients in a straightforward way. This approach sets an example of openness and honesty and encourages clients to be accountable for their behavior as well.

Counseling is neither an inquisition nor a search for significance in every cough or blink of an eye; it is a genuine and honest exploration of problems and of clients' willingness to address them. The client who starts off by resisting cannot be responding to the counselor (someone who is totally unfamiliar), but rather to what the client has experienced in the past, or imagines counseling to be. *Remembering that clients are responding to us in our role as counselors rather than to us as individuals makes it easier to shoulder the burden of accountability and question how clients view us and the counseling process.*

H. Understanding Confidentiality

Maintaining confidentiality is an important but different aspect of accountability and it demands much of counselors. It is an obligation to clients which, if ignored, can cause grave consequences. Nonprofessionals must be particularly careful to assess their capabilities of offering the protection and privacy required in counseling.

Without a guarantee of confidentiality, few of us would feel free to unburden ourselves to a counselor. We need this assurance to explore ourselves, our feelings, and our relationships openly and honestly. While others may eventually see how we have resolved certain issues in our lives, a breach of confidentiality occurring during or even after counseling can deprive us of control over our lives. Although there are rare circumstances which justify counselor violation of client autonomy and confidentiality (namely when clients intend to cause physical injury to themselves or others), counselors must protect clients from the scrutiny and interference of other parties. Confidentiality affords clients privacy and anonymity. Since, in many instances, even the fact that someone is receiving counseling can be damaging, this information should not be revealed by counselors without the client's expressed permission. (It is important to note that some employed individuals who could be compensated for the costs of therapy by company insurance policies prefer to pay their own medical bills rather than submit a monthly form. They are afraid that such disclosures may damage their careers.

Since insurance records are not always handled confidentially, this fear can be justifiable.)

Counselors must exercise considerable effort and self-control in order to protect their clients from the variety of adverse consequences that may result from any public knowledge of the details of their clients' lives. Who among us does not like knowing secrets and showing off "inside" information? Gossip columns are both popular and profitable because of our incessant curiosity about others. It is never easy to maintain confidentiality, but when clients reveal interesting details about people we know personally, the temptation to tell others is even greater. Even if we can protect our sources as counselors, divulging what they have told us can hurt them as well as the others in their lives. It can also hurt our relationships with those "exposed" in counseling.

Another threat to client confidentiality is the desire to help clients by allowing influential people to know of their problems. Although we may intend to relieve suffering or misunderstanding, meddling in the client's life is playing God, not counselor. Acting for them, we deprive clients of taking responsibility for themselves. Personal acquaintances are often used as confidants in order to achieve some effect, to get an ally in disputes or a defender in some cause. As friends we are willing to take sides, to take action, to intervene directly, but this is not a counseling function. As counselors, our goal is to help clients deal with their difficulties and disputes on their own.

Sometimes we are tempted to talk to others because our clients' disclosures make us uncomfortable. We want help in preparing a response or we may question the way we have reacted to a given situation. Ultimately, if the client's privacy is maintained, such discussions may help. This is not gossip, but consultation. Professionals consult each other for opinions with little danger to clients' privacy. Nonprofessionals, who do not anticipate them, often face a difficult dilemma when they experience problems in counseling: they can put clients at risk whether they do or do not discuss their concerns with others. If they do seek help without client approval from someone who might know the client personally they endanger the client's privacy. If they try to muddle through alone despite feeling uncomfortable, they may mishandle issues. Maintaining confidentiality can be a heavy and inappropriate burden for the nonprofessional, and one that ought to be recognized before establishing a counseling relationship in which it is explicitly or implicitly assumed. Who can the nonprofessional turn to when problems occur in counseling, as they inevitably do? Securing the client's permission and then finding a mutually acceptable consultant in the course of counseling can add further complications.

Another kind of personal involvement which may threaten confidentiality is the excitement and enthusiasm novices feel about their new role. It is often difficult for them to contain these reactions. Just as they would tell friends and associates about important events in their lives, beginners are tempted to discuss their clients' progress with their pals. But when their pals know who the clients are, anonymity and privacy cannot be preserved. Any discussion of clients, even for consultation purposes, has to be carefully considered and monitored. Trainees can appropriately use each other as consultants on cases, but if they do so in public places, like restaurants or elevators, they risk being overheard by someone who might be personally affected or involved. It is also important to realize that clients can also be identified from notes, tape recordings, and other materials; these too require special caution in handling. If they cannot be kept permanently and safely in one place they should not mention the full name of the client. Additional measures also may be necessary to disguise client identity.

For all these reasons, associates, neighbors, and personal acquaintances are likely to have more trouble maintaining confidentiality than the professional who is outside the intimate circle of clients' lives. Rather than hoping to succeed despite the risk, they should more often decline the counseling role. Friends, relatives, and relatives of friends should always be referred to others for counseling. It is wise to examine every proposed counseling arrangement for conflicting interests and threats to confidentiality. If discovered too late, they can undo whatever benefit counseling can offer.

There *is* reason to suspect "authorized" counselors in

some settings where counseling is not separate from administrative responsibility. If one's primary responsibility is seeing that an organization runs safely and effectively, it may not be possible to protect knowledge of deviant acts. Consider the dilemma of an understanding supervisor trying to help an employee out of difficult financial straits, who learns through counseling that the employee has been stealing and selling company equipment and materials. The supervisor is now in an untenable position where he must violate one or the other of his commitments. If he takes no administrative action toward the employee, he is derelict as a supervisor and places his own job in jeopardy. If he reports the client's action, he violates the client's privacy. If he fires the client, he abandons his commitment to help the individual with financial problems. This example illustrates a common problem; counseling and administration are incompatible roles which can directly conflict with one another. One serves the organization; the other, the individual.

If clients can incriminate themselves or others in the course of discussing their problems, if confidentiality is promised but cannot be delivered, then counseling can be entrapment. In circumstances where individuals are judged autonomous and responsible, we safeguard the individual's rights to privacy; we demand that guilt be proven in a courtroom, and we regard the information clients share with doctors, lawyers, priests, and counselors as "privileged." This protection of the individual is difficult to observe in circumstances where the individual's actions can jeopardize the rights of others within the institution or where the individual is not regarded as responsible or fully capable of independent judgment. In settings which have custodial responsibility for clients—such as elementary and high schools, jails and penitentiaries, psychiatric hospitals, and other residential treatment settings—client disclosures might not be held in confidence but shared with staff, administration, and perhaps other concerned individuals, like parents. The rationale is that confidentiality would endanger either the individual or others, or that the disclosure would be in the client's best interest. Certain client admissions which portend physical injury always require some disclosure to provide protective intervention. In hospitals and treatment centers where care is in the hands of professional teams, material revealed in counseling sessions may be vital to planning and institutional management, as well as to professional consultation and instruction.

Legitimate as these rationales and justifications are, their application has some negative consequences. When confidentiality is breached without clients' approval or permission, something essential to the nature of counseling is destroyed; the client is deprived of full responsibility for decisions and choices, since others, often not of the client's choosing, may act to protect, control, correct, or discipline. The client is no longer in charge of who knows what or how far the knowledge will travel. Not only the client, but others mentioned by the client in sessions may be affected. Imagine a youngster troubled by a parent's behavior, such as drinking, who discusses the problem with the school counselor, wanting help in understanding and dealing with this parent. A child may be regarded by many as incapable of dealing with such a serious issue without assistance. But if, instead of helping the child cope, the counselor takes the locus of responsibility away and informs school authorities, there may be more problems. If the school authorities try to intervene directly with the parent, he or she, infuriated, may go home and abuse the child. Alternately, the child's report of excessive drinking may have been inaccurate, but the word traveling from person to person may bring the family public disapproval. Still another possibility is that the counselor's report will call into question the parent's fitness, and become the catalyst in removing the child from the home. These are dramatic effects which can happen if a child seeking help plays the role, not of client, but of informer; the consequences can be worse than the original problem.

Counseling—or helping people to help themselves—is not the only way to effect behavioral change. Other ways are more predictable, quicker, and more suitable in some circumstances. Confidentiality to protect the self-determination of the individual in counseling often does not serve an institution's administrative needs. Those who counsel in prisons have a dual obligation: to help prisoners with personal problems and to keep officials informed, especially if their clients break rules or step out of line. Supplying information about prisoners is an administrative, not a counseling function, which destroys an essential feature of the counseling relationship. At best, such counselors can promise only limited confidentiality, and must spell out these limits to clients so they can weigh the risks involved.

Once, I counseled a very upset young woman who lived in a nearby residential treatment center while she attended college. She had been in therapy with a social worker at the residence for some time and was pleased with her treatment until the following event took place. She told the therapist of an argument between herself and another girl which had occurred during a drinking party held in one of the rooms. The therapist appeared to be understanding and helpful during the session, but the client later discovered that all those present at the party were going to be punished for having alcohol on the premises, an infraction of the house rules. The social worker reported the names to the administration—names supplied unwittingly by the client. The client had not been warned of the limits of confidentiality; she felt betrayed and duped. Not only did she have misgivings about her therapist, but she got herself in hot water with those students whom she had inadvertently squealed on.

Teachers, supervisors, employers, and administrators are frequently asked to provide personal counseling; however interested they are in the individual, it is unwise for them to comply. They will not be able to retain both an evaluative function and a counseling relationship without having their judgment affected by one or the other of their roles. In addition, it is not uncommon to have one's trust abused if the individual being counseled is not really looking for help but for a favorable judgment or a special privilege. *Generally, having any current relationship or association with clients other than that of counseling complicates, and often dooms, the counseling task.*

Peers and nonprofessionals are sometimes plunged into knowing "guilty" secrets before they are able to warn clients about issues of confidentiality or conflicting responsibilities. If they can, they should make every effort to respect the confidence. They may be able to encourage the individuals to report the misdeeds directly. (In counseling, people often ask for opportunities to sort things out and review their options before they make their "guilty secrets" public.) In this situation, the counselor may listen, then help find legal, medical, or therapeutic resources, and support the clients' efforts to work things out without having to expose them.

If that is not the case, and it is too late to warn the client not to tell us something because we feel obliged to report it, we can only share our reasons for breaching confidentiality with the client. We will need to warn clients of these intentions before carrying them out so that they can understand our decisions and still take the responsibility should they care to. Much as we may want to help, there may be occasions where confidentiality may seem to conflict with the obligations we feel as citizens, employees, members of a group, friends, or family members. Only professionals have some legal protection for maintaining confidentiality of wrongdoings; the consequences are different for nonprofessionals, and so are the issues and pressures.

It is important to recognize that confidentiality and the need for privacy are essential to counseling whether or not the client is concerned with punishable acts or guilt-provoking secrets. Although counselors may see clients' problems as "normal," devoid of shame or guilt, and not personally damaging in any way, privacy must still be safeguarded. It is up to the client, not the counselor, to decide what may be shared and with whom.

We are all private people. If we take the risk of sharing and exploring the truth about ourselves and our lives with a counselor, we still want to retain the right to control what others know about us. That right must be built in and maintained during counseling and after it is over. For counselors, this is no easy undertaking.

X

Skills Required Of Effective Counselors

The last chapter dealt with the personal characteristics of effective counselors. The helping role is also distinguished by counselors' skills in interacting with their clients. The most important of these are:

A. Observation
B. Listening and Checking Understanding
C. Exploring Content
D. Recognizing and Exploring Feelings
E. Facilitating Communication
F. Giving Feedback and Interpretation
G. Assessment

While we employ many of these skills in our interactions with others, we use them primarily to satisfy our own needs. Using them as reliable tools on behalf of clients requires practice.

A. Observation

As counselors, our perceptions need to be accurate. In order to understand our clients, we must notice their behavior, not just their spoken words.

Clients often tell us only what they think they ought to say, what they believe would make a good impression, or what amounts to only one theme out of the whole confusing cacophony of their lives. If we respond literally and ignore the other messages which they give us, then we are not being fully responsive. In their first appointment, clients often try to impress us with their casualness and ease. But we should note nonverbal signs of nervousness and apprehension: a cold and clammy handshake, a voice that seems a little tremulous, or a posture suggesting a readiness to flee. Appearances can contradict and obscure clients' underlying feelings.

Observation in counseling entails noting not only the client's physical bearing and mode of dress but its consistency with the client's role, age, and self-image. The mature, attractive woman who talks in a "little girl" voice strikes us in an incongruous way; so does the elegantly groomed man who speaks using crude language and poor grammar. We may not know what to make of these discrepancies initially but they are likely to prove useful later. We must also pay attention to the messages which the voice conveys: the sighs, the hesitation, the tone, and the difficulties in expressing certain words or thoughts. Facial expressions and postural cues also tell us more than the client articulates. To give an example: a young man I interviewed for the first time jumped around excitedly from one seat to another, gesturing with his hands and moving quickly from one topic to another with many half-finished thoughts. Along the way he complained that his wife was so scatterbrained that while he watched her making dinner, she put the pot in the refrigerator instead of on the stove. While he seemed unaware that his energetic enthusiasm might be unsettling to others, I was not.

Tape recording interviews is useful because it offers counselors opportunities to pick up messages they had missed, to hear themes instead of words, and to gauge the impressions they had made on clients. However, sound recordings are limited because they exclude body language, facial expressions, and other nonverbal forms of behavior. These must be observed at the time they occur because they quickly disappear.

Beginners are sometimes too distracted to notice nonverbal behavior. The anxiety of early encounters seems to affect some trainees; they are able to look, listen, or talk but not all at the same time. Others seem to notice nonverbal behavior but, constrained by social conventions, are afraid to comment or ask about them. For instance, sensing that the client is uncomfortable with a particular topic, they switch the subject rather than exploring what is bothering the client. Novices are apt to ignore a client's angry tone, furtive glances at the clock, a blinking away of tears, a sudden change in topic, or other signs that "something is going on" that may be important. Some beginners are so focused on words, and so unresponsive to interactional and nonverbal cues, that the process might just as well be conducted through the mail.

Nervousness also makes counselors afraid to stray from a set agenda, but human emotions are rarely predictable. To provide another example: a young woman comes to me to discuss her plans for a career change. She mentions that her father died recently. As we start to consider her options, she begins to recognize how closely her choices are connected to her father's views and opinions, and she begins to cry. Suddenly, she strongly states the wish to keep these two issues separate and get on with her career plans. While I understand her wish, I have to remind her that a career choice cannot be separated from personality and emotional processes. As the work continues, her grieving takes precedence, and it is some time before she can make her choice. Were this a more casual encounter at a party or on a street corner, I would honor her preference to compartmentalize her emotions. As a counselor, however, I cannot ignore feelings so obviously connected with important psychological issues and still be helpful. Clients' reactions reveal the real agenda at hand.

Being alert to nonverbal cues can point up important discrepancies between what clients say and mean, what they want and how they go about getting it, how they appear and how they want to appear, and which reactions they reveal and which ones we might expect. The content of their revelations is often not as important as the way in which the client deals with it. One of my clients follows every solemn statement with one that is upbeat and positive in outlook, thereby nullifying any troubling feelings by instantly transforming them. There are no sad or apprehensive moments for him! Another client is typically articulate and talkative, but in discussing one topic—looking for a new job—she becomes quiet and passive. She initiates the topic but then grows more silent until suddenly I am the only one talking. She is concerned about moving ahead in her career but is not yet willing to do much about it. The discrepancy between her characteristic style and the way she deals with this topic demonstrates her feeling of paralysis.

I notice that in this section on observing, I have used the present tense to lend immediacy to the case examples. Unlike statements and facts which can be recalled later, nonverbal cues are often fleeting: the juxtaposition of a bland facial expression and a disturbing topic, the smile which indicates disbelief, the sudden shifting in the chair suggesting discomfort. If not ignored, signs such as these have impact on counselors and can alert them to unspoken but meaningful themes and feelings. When counselors notice and share such observations, clients get a view of themselves that they cannot get alone. From there they often begin to observe themselves more closely and recognize patterns in their interactions and reactions. They learn to see what triggers their responses and begin to be able to consider alternative actions and perspectives.

Counselors must not only observe their clients' actions, they must also watch the reactions which clients provoke in them. When a client minimizes or denies a troubling issue, we may feel only a momentary pang of surprise or disbelief, but our reaction is important. Our clients have an emotional impact on us; our reactions can tell us something about them, perhaps even something about the effect they have on others. We need to be in touch with our feelings in order to learn how to use them on our clients' behalf.

B. Listening and Checking Understanding

Listening is a skill we take for granted, but hearing and comprehending what clients tell us can be demanding. Listening is not a passive activity but a strenuous effort to focus on the client, no matter how troubling or confusing the communication may be, no matter how much information has to be digested. New counselors have particular difficulty listening, because they are often distracted by their own self-consciousness, their need to structure and control sessions, and their desire to prove themselves immediately helpful. They can spend so much energy monitoring their own reactions that they bypass their clients' concerns. *It is impossible to listen to others when we are worried about ourselves.*

Listening involves not only remembering what our clients tell us, but acknowledging that we have heard. When we have trouble understanding garbled or contradictory messages, we should seek clarification from our clients. Since they may be as confused as we are about what they mean, our questions give them the opportunity to sort things out for themselves. Our responses help clients listen to themselves; this is the beginning of the process of self-discovery.

These interventions can make a major contribution to therapeutic rapport. A counselor who listens, remembers, and tries to clarify what a client says shows genuine interest. Counselors who can repeat, restate, summarize, and recall statements with accuracy give clients proof that they have been heard. Counselors who are afraid to appear inept or inattentive, or hesitate to ask for clarification, will lose the thread of the clients' narratives. Clients rarely object to repeating or amplifying statements along the way, but they are disheartened to find that their words have been missed, misinterpreted, or misunderstood by counselors. Since clients do not always speak clearly, especially about disturbing topics, such phrases as, "I'm sorry. I didn't hear what you said," or "Would you mind repeating that? I didn't get it the first time," are often necessary. If we become momentarily distracted, we should let the clients know that we missed the message and not pretend otherwise. By saying "I'm sorry but I missed what you said," or "Would you tell me that again? My mind wandered to another issue," we can get missing information as well as show our intention to be attentive.

Although we would prefer to be faultless as counselors, we may have to admit to a variety of failures when listening, like interrupting, talking too much, missing a point, losing the train of thought, and misunderstanding. We need to acknowledge these lapses openly. By doing so, we permit client and counselor to get back in touch and resume a meaningful interchange. This also demonstrates our honesty and the determination to keep our focus on the client. More important, by revealing our listening "lapses," we demonstrate the kind of self-awareness and openness we want to encourage in our clients.

Another type of listening feedback is one in which the counselor *"plays back"* something the client has said. The purpose of playback is not to parrot the client but to check for accuracy and focus attention on what the client has said. The tone of a playback response should be one of questioning rather than accusation. We might begin a playback this way: "You said you started to study nursing, but then members of your family objected?" Using the client's words and a tentative tone makes such an inquiry neutral and nonthreatening. In doing so, we ask the client "Have I heard you correctly?" Our clients are more likely to explain and explore with us events in their lives if they are asked about them in this nonjudgmental way.

Questions allow counselors the chance to get the facts straight before they jump to conclusions. Searching for ways to be helpful, counselors are apt to go off "half-cocked" without getting enough information; they stop listening and start to look for "answers." Well-directed questions keep the focus where it ought to be—on the client's view and explanation of the problems. "I understood what happened before you and Joe got to the party, but I don't think I heard what happened after." Or "Let me check out what I think you are saying. You believe you aren't being told the truth about your physical condition. Is that right?" Or "Which of your sisters are you referring to when you call her the family favorite?"

In sessions, clients concentrate on what to say and how to say it. Besides showing counselor attentiveness, a counselor's responses encourage clients to hear what they are saying. When the counselor "plays back" a half-finished thought, an odd or contradictory statement, or a significant issue quickly skipped over, both participants get a chance to confirm its accuracy and explore it further. For example: "You say you planned to discuss this matter with your boss, but when you got to the office, you decided to forget all about it?" Some questions, like this one, stop the action much like stopping the action in a film to examine a single frame. This intervention helps clients see things about themselves they hadn't noticed before.

Another helpful listening response is the counselor's summary. A summary retraces the route which the counselor and the client have traveled. The counselor may say, "Let's see. What have we discussed today?" and then identify the major topics covered. Although brief, such summaries allow clients to see their progress and direction. Like a road map, it imposes order on what may appear to be an aimless course of twists and turns. Clients rarely achieve this perspective without the help of a summary. Overwhelmed by immediate concerns, they may see the trees, perhaps, but not the forest. The counselor's response provides some orientation along with the assurance that the client is not traveling alone.

Just as clients may lose sight of the topics which they have discussed, they may also forget past feelings and things which they might have said previously. Another listening response recalls a client's previous statements, intentions, or attitudes. If the counselor's recall is reasonably accurate, clients may be astonished to remember how they used to feel. Psychological growth occurs in imperceptible increments, but when a counselor stops to say something like "Hey! I think I just heard you express something different from what you were saying about that earlier. What do you think?", clients may recognize that a change has taken place.

One of my clients repeatedly expressed apprehension over minor variations in his physical health and saw each ailment in life-threatening terms. After some time in counseling, working on many problems, he reported a worrisome physical ailment and without any apparent anxiety told me how he coped with it. I pointed out that I heard a difference and asked if he heard it too. He did, but not until I asked him about it. After consulting a doctor he experienced none of his previous difficulties in accepting the diagnostic conclusion that his complaint was minor, so he could report it to me in a relaxed fashion. Comparing his former and current reports of illness, we discovered happily that he was no longer a hypochondriac.

This example describes a change that took many counseling hours to achieve, but clients also express contradictory views on one subject in shorter time spans. For example, a college student may start by confronting a counselor with a plan to drop out of school immediately; then, after some discussion, he may express his intentions to "hit the books" again. This change in attitude may not be apparent to the student. The shift may indicate a positive change in motivation or self-image, or it can reveal continuing problems, such as insecurity, indecisiveness, or conflict. In either case, contrasting past and current statements may be helpful. This kind of response does not *tell* what has been previously said but *asks* if there is a difference between past and current communications.

Nonverbal forms of behavior such as responsive facial expressions and sounds, nodding the head, facing the client, also indicate that the counselor is listening. These signs are rarely absent in attentive counselors, but they can also be faked by those who are too anxious to concentrate. Trainees are often dismayed by hearing themselves on tape recordings. While they sound as if they are at ease with their clients, they repeat already answered questions or ask absurd ones in light of information which the client has provided. (A classic example is the trainee who, having been told that the client was an only child, then asked how many siblings he had.) As long as the counselor appears interested and concerned, clients usually tolerate some lapses in concentration. But the best antidote for beginners' anxiety is extensive use of listening responses to confirm understanding. They focus attention on the client and actually improve a counselor's comprehension.

Although listening responses add no new content, they are powerful therapeutic agents. There is nothing curative about playing back, recalling, or summarizing client messages, but each response gives clients an unfamiliar opportunity to hear their own thoughts and ideas. When counselors listen and respond, their clients feel as if their problems are being acknowledged.

C. Exploring Content

In initial interviews, counselors ask exploratory questions. These should be "open-ended" rather than "yes/no" or multiple choice queries, permitting the client the greatest latitude in replying. Exploratory questions ask the client to tell more, explain terms or phrases, give examples, provide chronological or historical facts, and fill in gaps in the narrative.

Counselors intent on finding immediate solutions to their clients' problems may start to work on them before recognizing how little they know about their clients. Instead of exploring what the son means when he refers to his father as "senile," they may offer him information on local nursing homes. Instead of finding out what a "lazy" college student does with her time, they may provide her with a study schedule. Without attempting to discover what makes a woman call herself a "failure," they may suggest a group of ego-enhancing activities. Focusing only on the problems, they still do not know what these terms or situations mean to their clients.

Many clients know the solutions to their problems as well as any counselor, but for one reason or another, they cannot act on them. "I know I should put him in a nursing home but . . ." "I should study more but . . ." "I should go back to school to get my college degree but . . ." These clients need opportunities to explore their feelings and circumstances. They need to understand why these conflicts make it impossible for them to take effective action. *Without exploration, counselors are working in the dark. When did the problem begin? What part do other people play in the client's life? How has the client dealt with the problem until now?* What does the client mean by "senile," "lazy," or "failure"?

Often, premature action is taken by a counselor who fears being overwhelmed. In this situation, the more the client reveals, the more inadequate the counselor feels. When a client's problem starts to seem serious, complex, or difficult to handle emotionally, novices start to pull back, simplify, minimize, or search for smaller concerns which they feel able to handle. The following is the beginning of a client's first session with an inexperienced counselor.

Counselor: Tell me, what's bothering you?
Client: Well, you see I had Hodgkin's disease. Do

you know what that is?

Counselor: Yes, I think so.

Client: Well, it's a form of cancer. I thought I was going to die. I had treatments for five years.

Counselor: Is it better now?

Client: The doctors say so, but I still think . . . It colors your whole life, you know . . .

Counselor: Yes, I know. I had a shoulder separation once, and I always expected it to come back. But you can overcome that . . .

Client: But it seems to affect my relationships, especially with men . . .

Here the client is trying to unburden herself and reveal her concerns but the counselor is backing away and minimizing. Unprepared to help the client with a life-threatening illness and the fear of death, he tries to reduce it to something he knows he can handle. Comparing cancer to a shoulder separation helps the counselor feel in control, but it may not help the client. Appropriate exploratory questions would be: "Tell me about your illness," or "How has being sick colored your life?" The counselor does not ask, because at that moment, he doesn't want to know. He is uncertain whether he can do anything about a problem that is so far beyond his personal experience; additional information will only make him feel inadequate.

New counselors often fail to ask exploratory questions because they cannot tolerate the answers or the emotions that may be induced. Exploring the client's concerns, asking for details, and listening to them are all challenging and difficult. It tests our strength and our willingness to know the burdens of our clients.

If the counselor is willing to listen, the questions are easy: "When?" "Where?" "How come?" "Tell me more." "Give me an example." "Who?" "What makes you draw that conclusion?" "What happened?" "What happened then?" Exploratory questions ask clients to elaborate on their experiences in their own words. Nervous counselors, afraid of pauses or inclined toward premature closure, ask multiple choice or either/or questions; their sessions sound like interrogations.

Example:

> Counselor: You said your brother had moved to Texas? (Yes/no question)
>
> Client: That's right.
>
> Counselor: Has he been there a long time or only a short time? (Either/or question)
>
> Client: Several years now, two or three.
>
> Counselor: How did he happen to go there?
>
> Client: He was stationed there in the service.
>
> Counselor: Oh, so he's been gone awhile? (Yes/no question)
>
> Client: Yes.
>
> Counselor: Too bad. If he were around, he could help with your mother. (Yes/no statement)
>
> Client: Not really. He doesn't get along very well with her.
>
> Counselor: Oh? But he would pitch in, wouldn't he? (Yes/no question)

Here, instead of encouraging her client to speak freely, the counselor uses the client to supply her with answers while she works on the solution. She has decided that the client's brother should help their mother, whose time-consuming medical problems have been a source of trouble for the client. Good exploratory responses follow the client's, not the counselor's, agenda. A lot of yes/no, either/or, or multiple choice questions can turn a potentially rich portrait into a lifeless questionnaire and a forthright client into a monosyllabic one.

Another unproductive approach is asking a lot of questions which begin with "why." Many times clients don't know *why* they do or feel something, so they answer with a shrug or an "I don't know." "What makes you hate your brother?" is somehow easier to respond to than "Why do you hate your brother?" Furthermore, questions that begin with "why" tend to sound disapproving ("Johnny, why is your room always such a mess?"). Clients can sense this and become defensively evasive. Most of us are so accustomed to starting questions with "why" that the word is out of our mouths before we can stop it. If that occurs, it is still possible to amend the question: "Why do you *think* you do that?" or "Why do you do that? . . . *Do you have any thoughts or ideas?"* These phrases encourage clients to speculate even if they don't have ready answers.

Listening and exploratory responses help clients learn about themselves. Given the freedom to describe the world as they see it, and encouraged to share their experiences and thoughts with someone, clients are able to see themselves anew. Often they need little more from us.

You can test this for yourself in an exercise familiar to many students of counseling. Ask someone to be a "client," to share a real concern with you for a few minutes. Restrict your responses to those that ask for clarification or amplification *and* to those that check your comprehension. Do nothing to lead or direct the "client"; just reflect what you hear and see. Your purpose is to receive the whole message, underlying feelings and all, and show your understanding to the "client." Afterward, spend a few minutes discussing the experience with your "client." Then trade roles. Share one of your concerns with a "counselor" who uses the same techniques and then review the experience. If the client presents a real issue and the counselor hears and plays it back accurately, then even these few moments are surprisingly productive. Many "clients" feel they have gained insight and awareness.

D. Recognizing and Exploring Feelings

Helping clients recognize, identify, and accept their own as well as other people's feelings is essential to the therapeutic process. Instead of honoring our inclinations at important points in our lives, most of us do what is right, what is polite, what is profitable, what is approved, or what is expected. Some of our social adaptations work and continue to satisfy us, but others do not. After a time, we find that some of our earlier choices don't match our basic attitudes, temperaments, long-term goals, or feelings of integrity. Some of these maladaptations impair our ability to function well. Our dissatisfactions often prompt us to seek counseling, not only to address immediate problems but to help us discover who we are and how we wish to be. Our underlying feelings often provide the essential clues.

Solution-happy counselors may find clients' feelings nuisances or obstacles to speedy problem-solving. If, for instance, a client seems unable to settle on a practical and conventional career choice, the counselor may be annoyed, rather than interested. The rush to find answers can force clients to fit established molds and submerge divergent emotions.

Perhaps because exploring feelings is unfamiliar and inappropriate in many social situations, inexperienced counselors sometimes show an awkward zealousness to uncover their clients' feelings. To give an example: listening to a client describe an incident, the counselor may suddenly say, "How did you feel?" The client will then stop, think for a second or two, and say, "Happy," or "Angry," or something else. Then the client will wait expectantly for the counselor to explain the inquiry, and the counselor will wait for the question to have an observable impact on the client. At other times, the inquiry will mystify the client who may respond with another question: "Feel about what?" Interrupting the client's discourse to ask about emotions is disconcerting and undesirable unless the client seems to be struggling at that moment with feelings that are not being articulated or acknowledged, perhaps by holding back tears or grimacing in pain. Otherwise it is better to wait until the client is finished reporting an event before asking "How did that make you feel?" or "Tell me what you were feeling during that incident." Some clients, unused to admitting or sharing feelings, may be hesitant to do so. In these situations, gentleness and patience are required; counselors should avoid acting like the F.B.I. on the trail of the elusive emotion.

In exploring feelings, it is helpful to ask for specifics or examples. Clients' reports are usually abbreviated summaries and studded with words that are subjectively defined. But when asked to give us the details of events, they reactivate emotions and reexperience them. Feelings aroused in the retelling sometimes reveal the meaning of the event for the client. Counselors' questions should be specific. "How do you feel when your mother criticizes you that way?" is preferable to "How do you feel about your mother?" The richness and specificity of the client's revelations can depend on the questions we ask; vague questions get vague answers.

Occasionally, when exploring their own feelings, clients are overcome by them. Witnessing another's pain is difficult, but counselors need tolerance for emotional display. People rarely remain cool and collected when discussing disturbing issues. Although the counselor's temptation is to back away from upsetting subjects, more is to be gained from supportive exploration. Helping clients articulate emotions and identify their sources, sharing their moments of pain, are, in themselves, beneficial. Exploring anger is often very productive, even at times when we seem to have provoked it, but it may not feel "comfortable."

Another way of helping clients explore their feelings is to share our own. If all we do is probe and poke into the client's experiences, never revealing how we might feel in the client's place, we may appear to be inquisitors. Clients often regard their problem and emotion as proof of weakness, and read counselor aloofness as judgmental. Our concern may show in our facial expression, posture, and other nonverbal forms of behavior, but clients often miss these signs. Often we need to say, "I know what you mean," or "That would bother me, too," or "I think I would have felt angry. How did you feel?" Sometimes it is helpful to share—briefly—a relevant personal experience. Willingness to share our feelings and admit our vulnerabilities, including our misunderstandings, distractions, and mistakes in sessions, does not invalidate our capacity to help; it makes us human too. Whatever else we do for our clients, we also serve as models. If we are open as counselors, clients are encouraged to be open with us.

E. Facilitating Communication

Communication is a two-way street, and there are no automatic formulas for facilitating it. What clients tell us depends, in part, on what we ask and how we respond to their answers. And our response depends, in turn, on what the client says and shows. Communication is influenced by many factors, such as the purpose of the interview, how it was arranged, the willingness of the participants, and the conditions under which it is held. There are no specific rules for a counselor's behavior, but there are some common problems, which need to be considered and anticipated.

The counselor's attitude toward the client can facilitate communication or inhibit it. If we lose patience with clients who prove uncooperative, uncommunicative, or unwilling to change their behavior, we may be tempted to coerce change. Here are some counselor responses that depend on the power of authority, concealed or apparent, rather than the encouragement of free exchange:

—"That's a stupid thing to say. You don't mean that."

—"How could you feel that way? That's ridiculous."

—"I'm glad you have finally come to your senses."

—"We went over all that last week. You don't listen to a single thing I tell you."

—"You promised me that you would make that call. I'm disappointed in you."

—"That's silly. I know she doesn't feel that way about you."

All these statements imply that the client is (or has been) wrong while the counselor is right and has the answers. Many of us cannot imagine ourselves speaking that way as counselors, since we do not set out to put clients down or force them to agree with us; but, if the client provokes or threatens us, we have trouble holding to our good intentions. Consider what you would say (or be tempted to say) in response to this client assertion: "You think you're helping me, but you are not. I really hate your guts." Or to a client who said: "All my life I've gotten the short end of the stick. No more. Now I'm going all out for myself. People better just get out of my way or they're going to get hurt—you included." Or to a client who said: "I don't want to be here. Nothing you can do will make me talk."

Even out of context, these statements seem to deserve angry and coercive responses. They challenge the counselor's competence and control; they pit the client against the counselor. Hearing such statements, novices are likely to become judgmental.

"But," counseling trainees are apt to say, understanding their role up to a point, "suppose the client is wrong?" That's the way it seems at times—that clients are wrong in their attitudes or behavior; they *need* correcting. When clients do not assume responsibility for their problems or do not lend themselves to the therapeutic process, new counselors think they must force clients to see their errors. The humbling fact, known to the more experienced, is that we cannot judge whether a client's decision about or behavior in counseling is right or wrong. We cannot see the future or be one hundred percent certain that responsiveness to counseling will improve it. If a client's uncooperativeness leads to flunking out of school, getting fired or divorced, using drugs, going to jail, or some other occurrence we view as unfortunate and avoidable, we still cannot be sure that counseling would have produced a different outcome, or that, in the long run, the event might not have some benefit for the client. Even if there are no other advantages, such experiences may teach clients important lessons.

Clients hold their fates in their own hands. We can and should warn of possible consequences to their actions in the hope they will reconsider, but we cannot make their choices for them or force them to do what we think best. If we find ourselves altering our role to one of coercion or correction, we need to identify the attitudes or kinds of behavior which provoked us and discuss these directly with clients. If we hide rather than discuss the feelings they arouse in us, we will try to control rather than understand their behavior. There is no way to force what we need from clients to make counseling successful: cooperation, openness, and willingness to work on problems. If the counseling role seems weak in encouraging cooperation, force will not strengthen it; it will destroy it.

There is the flip side to this issue which also affects the communication process. We may see the limitations of counseling power and still be perceived by some clients as very powerful. We are seen as experts, as persons possessing knowledge and insight that is remarkable, and we are thought to be wise even in areas for which our training has not prepared us. This perception of us can work against free and open exchange. Our opinions may seem more valid than our clients' own opinions, and even if we do not speak with the voice of authority or tell clients what to do, our comments may be taken as advice and have greater impact than we intend.

My work with a client who was required to design and sell merchandise led to a result that both surprised and frightened me. Trying to help her develop confidence in her creative ability, I offered some ideas. I intended only to start her thinking, but in a few weeks I learned that she had adapted one of my ideas into a product. I was staggered. She was making a sizable and risky investment in a notion that came off the top of my head. Luckily her adaptation of the concept was a success, but how would I have felt if it had been a bust? My expertise as a counselor does not extend to the design and sale of umbrellas!

It is often hard for beginners to resist giving advice because this mode is satisfying to both counselor and client. *However satisfying it is to be right, to feel smart, to impress clients, our success is measured by the outcome for the client.* When our advice is sought, we need to know why we are being asked and how the client views the opinion offered. Clients may assign us the role of advisor, or we may assume it, but in either case, the consequences are undesirable. It restricts the communication process by limiting exploration and interaction.

Counselors can make suggestions without impeding communication if they offer them as options for consideration and not as directives. The purpose of making suggestions is to explore the client's reaction, not determine the course of action. The client should be encouraged to raise objections to any recommendation and disregard those that seem unsuitable.

To avoid discouraging or inhibiting dialogue, similar precautions are required in providing information. *In counseling, information is not an end in itself. The counselor must understand what prompts the client's need for information and explore whether or not the answer is usable within the client's framework.* If the information is extensive, difficult to follow, and/or available in print, it is better to discuss it after clients have a chance to become familiar with it on their own.

Otherwise, what could be a dialogue will be a lecture, of which probably little will be retained. It is tempting to instruct clients on familiar topics, and information can be helpful, but when monologue replaces dialogue, counseling stops.

Disturbing questions from clients present for beginners another obstacle in the communication process. Some seem to assume that clients, but not counselors, are under scrutiny. They don't know how to deal with clients who are curious about them. In one case, a young woman introduced herself to her new counselor, a young man, and asked, "How old are you?" The counselor replied with false casualness, "Old enough!" In doing so, he missed an opportunity to explore the client's concern; subsequently, he encountered covert resistance because the client thought him "young enough" to be a suitor.

This kind of query is not rare. New clients are curious about counseling, uncertain about its merits, unable to wait and see what develops. The many questions some clients have about us can tell us a lot about them. Some inquiries are challenging in the skepticism they reveal. The clients' doubts can be discussed without defensiveness on our part. If the client wants an older therapist but gets a young one, the counselor should explore the problems the client sees in the arrangement. No offense need be taken. The discrepancy may tell us about the dangers clients anticipate in counseling. While on rare occasions a referral may be necessary, most concerns fade away as counseling relationships develop. Stifled or ignored, client reservations can undermine the helping relationship; articulated for both participants to see, they may be helpful. Since many clients find it difficult to mention their apprehensions, we need to be sensitive to the appearance of minor signs of hesitancy. If clients voice no doubts at all, we can assure them that, at first, every client has some. When asked direct questions about ourselves, we can explore underlying issues by briefly postponing the answer in the following manner: "Sure I'll be glad to tell you how old I am, but first what makes my age an important issue for you?"

The discomfort beginners feel when clients turn the tables and ask them questions may relate to a larger issue. New counselors seem to expect their clients to be motivated for and knowledgeable about counseling before they enter the door. If, instead, clients come misinformed, doubtful, inquisitive, frightened, or angry, they are seen as "rotten apples" rather than "good clients." But in actuality, few clients are well informed, motivated, or eager for the openness and interchange of counseling. Trust is established gradually, if at all; resistance is inevitable when the counselor moves faster than the client is willing or able. *The initial stage of encouraging clients to express and explore their reservations is not a preliminary, but a predictable and necessary, part of counseling.* Beginners should not imagine that they are the only ones subject to their clients' reservations and doubts; experienced counselors encounter them just as frequently.

Some counselors wait for specific questions before telling clients anything about themselves or counseling. If no questions are raised, no explanations are given, and this silence lends a sense of mystery and unapproachability. *Counselors should start with the assumption that clients are curious about them and have questions concerning counseling, confidentiality, and other procedures. They should directly encourage their expression.* In providing answers, we need to check their effects on clients and see if there are related issues to explore. Some counselors, uncomfortable with the task of identifying themselves and their procedures, give brief explanations but rapidly change the subject before clients have a chance to react.

If clients' questions give beginners trouble, silence makes them even more uncomfortable. New counselors abhor silence and rush in to fill it. Sometimes they become so nervous while waiting for clients to respond to their questions that they try to provide the clients' answers for them. Thinking, feeling, remembering, and summoning up the courage to reveal oneself are not always quickly done. Clients who are quiet, shy, or nonverbal will display even greater reserve if someone takes over for them. Pressuring clients to talk may force them to reply glibly or resort to stubborn silence.

Perhaps novices are active to show they are "on the job," or to maintain contact with clients or to be reassuring and undo any threat they seem to pose. Another possibility is that they may feel hurt and slighted when the client does not share his or her experiences openly. Forcing our way into a client's introspection makes us intrusive. *Silence is the client's space and protection.* We would not barge into an office unless welcomed; we should not intrude into someone's thoughts.

Uncomfortable with silence from their clients, inexperienced counselors also seem afraid to remain silent, even for the time it takes to formulate a question or identify a fleeting impression. They immediately reply to each statement as though it did not merit a second's thought. No doubt novices feel pressured to perform well, but speed is no indicator of competence. More is lost than gained in rushing through an interview, for it takes time for nonverbal forms of behavior, nuances of tone, complex ideas, and emotional consequences to register on both the client and counselor. If the counselor is slow in responding to a client's statements, the client is likely to go on unaided, elaborating thoughts and adding useful associations. A momentary pause does not always mean that the client is finished with the thought.

There is also a tendency to attempt too much in early sessions. Beginners are so focused on *content,* on covering as much ground as they can, that they lose sight of the *process,* such as small signs of client restiveness or discontent, indications that something is going wrong. Overlooking clients' reactions, they may lose the chance to engage them in meaningful collaboration. Pauses allow the counselor to think, formulate, see connections, and attend to all that a client conveys. *Effective communication allows time to evaluate the process.* There is no rule that says talking must be evenly divided between counselor and client, or that every client statement requires a counselor response. Some sessions are quite lopsided. There are good sessions during which the counselor says little; and some, especially with depressed clients, in which counselors do most of the talking. In early interviews, clients are usually active when describing themselves and their problems, but there are also some who refuse to talk. What then?

With uncooperative clients, the most important thing to remember is that counseling, not the counselor, is the object of resistance. From the view of some clients, resistance is justified. They may be there against their will. They may be afraid that if they talk, they will get in trouble. Some who come from authority-dominated cultures (or homes) are waiting for the counselor to tell them what to do or to ask them questions. Others are self-conscious about their manner of speech, their accents, their physical appearances, or other characteristics that make them feel ashamed. Individuals with good prior experiences in therapy may not want to grow attached to another counselor; those who have had unpleasant experiences may see no reason to start again.

Trying to force clients to talk is unproductive. If the reason behind the silence can be uncovered, reluctance sometimes yields. Many clients will talk about why they won't talk even if they intend to withhold other information about themselves. If the counselor can show acceptance of the client, exploring rather than challenging the resistance, there are sometimes surprising results. Still, there are some deeply mistrustful and frightened clients who require Job's patience to come out of their shells. Beginners are often more successful with such slow-moving clients than more experienced professionals. Sometimes, altering the form and method of interaction—taking the therapy out of the office—is useful in these instances.

Although counselors rarely intend to interrupt clients, it occurs frequently—especially with trainees, as shown by the tapes of their sessions. Interrupting conveys a message to the client that what the counselor is thinking is more important than what the client is saying. To stop clients from interrupting us communicates a similar message. Beginners can learn from their own interrupting. Often it occurs at times when counselors are disturbed by the topic or the clients' behavior. Instead of recognizing and dealing directly with the problem, counselors tend to conceal it by switching the focus and taking control.

When counselors develop tolerance for emotional display and can control their need to dominate sessions, preventing verbal collision is relatively easy: the counselor yields the right-of-way most of the time. Clients have different styles to which counselors have to adapt. There are some clients who rarely allow their counselors to get a word in. However frustrating, the counselor in this situation has to take a back seat until the pattern can be altered. Some clients, bursting to fill their counselors in on recent developments, permit counselors' participation only near the end. Reminder notes are useful in these instances and note-taking may help clients become aware of the way they are fashioning sessions.

There is, of course, one *necessary* interruption that gives beginners difficulty: ending the interview at the scheduled time. Although sessions work best within set time limits, new counselors sometimes want to extend them. Except in crisis situations, extending sessions is usually undesirable and presents problems later. It is best to warn clients, a few minutes before the end, that the time is drawing to a close, in order to permit opportunity for summarizing and feedback.

Another means of facilitating communication in counseling is the use of humor. Sessions need not be somber. The situations we get ourselves into are often laughable, and laughing can provide both a good perspective and a sense of relief. In their earnestness, new counselors seem to check their senses of humor at the door and react soberly even to clients' jokes. Perhaps the tension beginners feel precludes their having fun. Or perhaps a sense of humor seems unprofessional to them. Unfortunately, they often cast an air of disapproval on their clients' seeing the funny side of events. *Counseling is difficult enough without excluding laughter.* A counselor's sense of humor, provided it takes no hostile form—like ridicule or sarcasm toward clients—can be both appreciated and helpful.

One client, described by the friend who referred him as having a wonderful sense of humor, came for months of sessions without showing a glimmer of it. Finally, when I shared with him his friend's praise of his ability to joke, he regarded me soberly and said, "But I thought you only wanted to hear my problems and the things that bother me. My previous therapist disapproved of my sense of humor." I expressed amazement that his control was so complete that he could leave one of his personality features at home, and I said I would be more comfortable knowing "all of him." Subsequent meetings, which included lighthearted as well as sober thoughts, seemed easier and more productive.

Another kind of humor in counseling is caricature. One

client earned the name "the girl who can't say 'no' " from the popular song. In conflicts with others, she would agree to do things she didn't want to do rather than hurt another person's feelings. She could get so wrapped up in others' perspectives that she lost sight of her own. On one occasion outside of counseling she thought of the familiar refrain and worked out the situation in the way *she* wanted. In this context, the "name" given her was therapeutic. Caricatures or analogies like this one occur to me in response to material clients present. They often seem both apt and funny, and sometimes they have continuing usefulness.

Counseling is serious business, but those who use humor in other interactions should not judge it inappropriate here. It may be another variant of comfort and openness in the counseling role. Communication is facilitated by counselors who are at ease with the process and with themselves, warts and all. They show clients there is little to fear in self-disclosure. Professional training and experience can reduce the apparent commonality between counselor and client, but nonprofessionals who try to mask their reactions in order to appear "expert" conceal the human dimension that disarms clients and contributes to rapport. Openness is intrinsically therapeutic.

F. Giving Feedback and Interpretation

Giving feedback and interpretation causes beginners the most concern. However, in many sessions, it is unnecessary. When a client talks freely in an introspective manner, counselors need only ask occasional questions, explore feelings, reflect important themes, and display attentiveness and encouragement in various ways. Clients can make meaningful connections and gain insight without significant direction from the counselor.

Not all clients, however, are adept at understanding their own behavior, and many need help in looking at themselves, especially in the early stages of counseling. Some clients simply report events of their lives without examining how they have reacted to them. *Directional feedback* asks them to examine their experience to better understand themselves. It encourages clients to look further at what has caused events and feelings in their lives, and makes clients explore their internal frames of reference. This is an important part of counseling, the workhorse that carries most of the weight in helping clients understand their task in counseling.

Directional feedback tells clients where to look for answers, not what the answers are. Examining internal processes, seeing psychological connections, is, for many clients, an undertaking in unfamiliar terrain. The purpose is not to produce startling revelations or magical resolutions but to introduce clients to themselves, to lay the groundwork for self-examination. As clients develop proficiency and comfort in looking at themselves with the help of directional feedback, they begin to recognize psychological patterns common to many situations. This is groundwork for the development of insight into the self.

A second kind of counselor feedback is *evaluative* rather than directional. It is the voice of the observer who continuously monitors counseling progress and problems. While the monitoring of progress is often performed silently, it is also shared with the client at important points. Evaluative feedback serves many functions. A counselor may use it to do the following:

> *Underscore a direction or topic:* "This seems an important issue for you. Let's try to get back to it next session.";
>
> *Evaluate the nature of the session, topic, or interchange:* "This felt like a very productive session. I think we made some headway." Or: "This was a tough session for you today; it's not easy for you to discuss your feelings about him.";
>
> *Summarize and provide perspective:* "We got a sense today that school is going well for you. What should we focus on next?";
>
> *Identify changes in the client:* "I think that indicates an important development. You spoke up for yourself in that exchange. You used to think you couldn't do that."; and

> *Identify communication problems:* "I'm feeling uncomfortable now—as if we are arguing rather than discussing what you should do about this. Do you feel I'm telling you what you should do?" Or: "I hear myself interrupting you a lot today. I don't think I usually do that. I think I'm doing it because I keep hearing you put yourself down, and I keep wanting to stop you." Or: "It's hard for me to know what you mean when you discuss things in such general terms. Could you be more specific?".

Evaluative feedback is offered, not as a pronouncement by an authority, but as an invitation for the client to react and share observations. It lets clients know the counselor's point of view, not as the final word, but as a point for discussion.

Evaluative feedback may strike the novice as judgmental. Yet, the counselor is the "keeper" of the counseling process, attending to bottlenecks and roadblocks as well as to signs of satisfactory progress. To give evaluative feedback, counselors must be tuned into feelings and willing to share them, but they do not have to be absolutely certain about what is happening before expressing observations. The client's response is likely to provide additional feedback and a different perspective. Appearing uncertain may bother new counselors who need to feel in control, and giving clients the opportunity to evaluate counseling (and perhaps criticize their counselors) may pose too big a risk for them. Evaluative feedback is not accusatory: it is seldom countered by client attack. In effect, the counselor says, "Something's going on here—in me, or in you, or between us. This is what I see, or feel, or sense. What do you think?"

Experienced counselors have learned to trust the feelings and intuitions they get during sessions. Once they can be articulated, they are used like little searchlights in unfamiliar territory. Often, beginners have just as many valid impressions, but they consider them risky, trivial, or irrelevant and ignore or discard them. They have many reasons for hesitation: they hope the client will recognize the issue without their having to state it first; they are afraid of being wrong; they cannot tell which of their impressions they should share and which may be more personal concerns; they imagine the client will react negatively; and they can't distinguish an evaluative impression from disapproval. However, ignoring persistent feelings for any of these reasons seldom clarifies the tensions provoking them.

While there are some dangers in evaluative feedback, our impressions usually have some truth in them. If we present them out of context, at an inappropriate moment, or with the tone of authority, they can mystify, distract, or disturb a client. But the motto for evaluative feedback should read, "Nothing ventured, nothing gained." Even if clients stoutly disagree with an observation, their explanation or account may prove useful. If, on occasion, the client's version seems the more accurate of the two, it is all to the good and will also show that disagreement is acceptable. *The counselor's impression, offered to, rather than forced on, the client, indicates that the counselor is trying to understand not only the shape of the client's life but also the feelings engendered by counseling.*

Quick articulation is important in the presentation of evaluative feedback. Often it surprises clients, who are more focused on what they are saying than on the impression they are conveying. They may not always accept it even when the observation contains some truth; it may contradict the view they have of themselves, as in this example:

> Counselor: "You know, sometimes it sounds as if you were jealous of your sister."
>
> Client: "It does? I never thought so. My parents always seemed to prefer me. They gave me a lot of praise, and they always seemed disapproving of her. She was always in trouble."
>
> Counselor: "Well, I know that's what you've said, but I was just getting a different impression. She got all that attention and . . ."
>
> Client: "Well, that's interesting. I do remember feeling that I had to keep my troubles to myself because they were so worried about her. I'll have to think about that some more."

Evaluative feedback does not always produce agreement, remarkable insight, or immediate confirmation. Sometimes neither participant can assess the feedback's usefulness on the spot. A client's quick acceptance of the feedback may lead to eventual rejection, or to a variation of the counselor's first impression. *Counselors who are preoccupied with being "right" are likely to misuse evaluative feedback. It should be measured by its productivity rather than by its acceptance by clients.*

There are different kinds of evaluative feedback. Observations that summarize content, identify important topics, provide perspective, or relate positive impressions of clients seem relatively innocuous, or even unimportant, to beginners who sometimes neglect this feedback. But the second kind of evaluative feedback does not seem innocuous at all. Called "honest labeling" in the videotape series developed by Norman Kagan for counselor training (*Interpersonal Process Recall,* Norman J. Kagan, 1980), it is the means of addressing the undercurrent—the message felt but not directly articulated. The purpose is to get things out in the open, but to the novice this seems like confrontation. And confrontation seems frightening.

There is less risk in labeling ongoing but unspoken issues than we can imagine. Clients are usually relieved and encouraged, rather than distressed, at the opportunity to discuss disturbing feelings. But this intervention flies in the face of the rules observed in conversation and social exchange. There we downplay emotions and smooth over disturbing communications; in "honest labeling" we recognize and identify them. Here are some examples to differentiate responses to highly charged topics as they might occur in "polite" conversation and in the "honest labeling" mode of evaluative feedback.

Polite statement: "It's very difficult to be a step-parent."

Honest labeling: "You're really furious that your husband seems to take his children's side against you."

Polite statement: "Well, I guess you want to go and relax a little."

Honest labeling: "You seem pretty uncomfortable being here. I guess you doubt whether talking about these things can help you."

Polite statement: "Our next appointment is at 2:00 P.M. Tuesday next week."

Honest labeling: "You know, I'm getting the feeling today that you are not sure you want to come back next week."

Both the "polite" and the honest labeling response address the same topic, but the first minimizes emotions. In casual encounters, we do not always recognize emotional messages with accuracy; there is usually no time to "get involved." We ask acquaintances "How are you?" but we often feel annoyed if they actually tell us in any detail. As counselors we have to get involved beyond superficial exchange.

Honest labeling is difficult. It requires awareness, sensitivity, and openness. By directly addressing tensions and feelings, it invites direct and honest responses from clients. It is indispensable when emotional undercurrents are felt but not expressed. Identifying that which lies beneath the surface changes counseling from a polite and guarded acquaintanceship to a relationship of genuine intimacy, one in which emotions can be correctly identified, and resistance understood.

Finally, another type of counselor intervention—*interpretation*—identifies the largely unconscious motives and mechanisms that affect a client's behavior. Derived from psychoanalysis, interpretation identifies unresolved but active infantile drives as they appear in behavior, fantasies, dreams, and transference reactions.

Peer counseling, in fact most forms of face-to-face counseling, is less concerned with interpretation of the unconscious than is traditional psychoanalysis. It emphasizes, instead, a close and open relationship between client and counselor, a collaboration in setting and working toward specific goals, and a more focused, pragmatic approach to the resolution of psychological problems. Though exploration of childhood events and other past learning experiences is helpful, counselors in these forms of therapy focus on their clients' current problems and adjustments. While insight into psychodynamics or psychological patterns remains important, especially transference reactions, interpretation in the analytic sense is rarely attempted.

Sometimes when no "good" explanation can be found for

a client's undesirable behavior, counselors are tempted to blame it on unconscious factors. *However appealing it is to speculate about unconscious forces, these "interpretations" have little, if any, therapeutic value.* Identifying an unconscious motive does nothing to change the client's behavior. Presented with the view that some problem is rooted in the unconscious, the client often feels confounded and at the mercy of forces beyond rational control. Interpretation of unconscious determinants can also be dangerous. Even in psychoanalysis, where it is approached slowly and cautiously, illuminating the unconscious is not the goal, but the beginning of resolving underlying conflicts. Strong psychic forces are not eliminated or reduced by mere exposure to the light of day. Theories about unconscious factors, if necessary at all, should be used by the counselor to understand a client's behavior but not be actively introduced into the counseling work.

There are, however, cases in which, despite considerable time and effort, counseling does not result in behavioral change. In these instances, a client's successful adaptation seems to be subverted by habits that have an unquenchable life of their own or by apparent "accidents" that happen when a therapeutic goal is within reach. For example, a student may do all the work for courses but never complete the final assignments; a man may want desperately to leave his father's company but ruin each of his job interviews; or a young woman may suffer physical injury before each summer planned away and so stay home with her parents. These are instances in which the client's behavior might express unconscious conflicts. When repeated over years, these incidents point to some internal mechanism interfering with a client's rational decision-making.

Nonprofessionals will rarely face this dilemma. These symptoms are exhibited by relatively few clients and are usually identified through long-term treatment. Those clients who do manifest such symptoms will require referral. Interpretation of unconscious determinants is best left to professionals who have a thorough understanding of psychological development and personality functioning. In the brief, pragmatic, and focused effort of counseling, it is inappropriate and ineffective.

Lest nonprofessionals be miffed at being denied the use of an "important" intervention, however, let them take comfort in the fact that interpretation is now seen as having less curative power than was at first thought. The therapeutic alliance is believed to be the important catalyst for insight and change in counseling and psychotherapy. Evaluative feedback and honest labeling are both appropriate and effective forms of interpretation that fall well within the competence of students and nonprofessionals.

G. Assessment

Another skill all counselors need is assessment, the ability to identify client strengths and weaknesses. Without it, counselors must proceed by trial and error, finding out the hard way what they could have anticipated. A counseling relationship is not like a friendship, where each participant has equal responsibility for what occurs; counselors have responsibility to fashion the relationship so it will be constructive, not harmful, for clients. This requires assessing their clients' capabilities.

Afraid of being judgmental, beginners often fail to make the distinction between passing judgment and objectively assessing a client. If I am *judgmental,* I view a client's behavior and persona in terms of my personal values and preferences. If I do not like men who wear their hair long, I will want the male client with long hair to view his appearance as wrong. I am not thinking of the client's best interest (although I might convince myself I am) but of my own values. In *assessing* a client, I consider the characteristic from the client's point of view. Long hair and other aspects of appearance say something about a client's identity and values. The long-haired client may be conveying the message, "I am not one of your conventional types. I like things natural, not contrived or prearranged. I'll make my own standards and not try to live up to those of anyone else." There is no problem with this self-portrayal, no matter what my personal preference, as long as it presents no hindrance to the client's goals.

However, should this client want to get a job in a setting where conventional appearance is required, he may have to consider modifying the statement made by his personal appearance—not to conform with my values, but to achieve what he wants.

Clients do not have to live up to my expectations (or anyone's for that matter), but they will suffer certain consequences if they offend people who are important to them. In assessing clients, I have to consider their impact on others. At times I may present the viewpoint of "others" to help clients anticipate and weigh possible outcomes of their choices. These viewpoints are not disguised versions of my own preferences, but as accurate a picture as I can give of what the client may expect from the real world. The right to choose is still the client's. *The counselor's responsibility is to anticipate probable consequences, not influence the client to conform.*

Some young counselors object to such reasoning and insist that in a more ideal world, people would not be judged on appearance but on the basis of ability, and that they, as counselors, should not be concerned with the expectations of others—like future employers—in the client's life. They would argue that the client's long hair should never be an issue in counseling. On one level, this argument is correct. There is a danger that counseling can be used in the service of conformity, forcing clients to honor the preferences of others while limiting their individuality and personal freedom. Counselors have to weigh this issue carefully because not all social pressures are in clients' best interests; some should be resisted. Total conformity to the will of others is, of course, undesirable. But on the other hand, social rules and expectations—whether right or wrong, just or unjust, to the counselor's liking or not—have to be acknowledged and dealt with. They are part of the client's reality. Clients cannot make satisfactory choices without considering the reactions of others to those decisions.

Clients who are not prepared to accept the negative feedback sometimes accorded nonconformity may suffer from it. If the young man who prepares himself for a business career finds himself excluded or rejected because of his long hair, he is paying a big price for a personal statement—maybe bigger than he wants to pay. Counselors cannot ignore probable consequences of clients' behavior because they believe them to be wrong or unfair; they have to deal with what is, not what should be.

Let us consider a real example in which the counselor's mistaken assessment of the client (and of others in the client's life) drastically affected not only the outcome of counseling but also the client's life. The client was a young woman who lived at home while attending college. Her parents, exceedingly strict, would not permit her to date or even be alone with a young man. Since her peers suffered no such restrictions, she was very unhappy. She wanted to leave home and be able to do what she pleased, but she was not financially independent. Never having held a job or assumed much responsibility for herself, she appeared immature in many ways. She seemed attached to her parents, and though resentful, she was nevertheless grateful for most aspects of their concern for her.

Her counselor considered the parents hopelessly out-of-date and urged the client to be assertive, by expressing her views and arguments as forcefully as she could. She tried, but the parents did not budge. Next, the counselor joined the client's friends in advising disobedience in the form of holding clandestine meetings with an interested young man. The client went ahead with her "secret" date but had no skill at deceiving her parents. One day she turned up unexpectedly at the counseling office, kicked out of her home and with no place to stay. Dismayed but convinced that the parents were hopeless anyway, the counselor believed the incident would launch the client into long-delayed independence. She even helped the client find a place to live. Once on her own, the client showed poor judgment in handling herself. She was forced to modify her educational plans to take a job she hated. She got pregnant, she became depressed; and eventually she went home cowed and more dependent than ever on her outraged parents.

Someone hearing this story might be tempted to say, "You put an unhappy ending on the story. None of this is the counselor's fault or responsibility. The situation could have worked out well." We cannot ignore the potential for the negative consequences of our counseling. If we intend to avoid disasters like this, we have to use our role differently. Rather than encouraging clients to act in ways that might suit our lives, we have to assess and address their options and capabilities. In this instance, the counselor supported steps the client was not mature nor self-sufficient enough to take, although others her age might have managed them. Even though her parents' strict control contributed to her immaturity, opposing that control was actually worse for the client.

This case, demonstrating the danger of allying ourselves with clients in their disputes with others, also shows the necessity to recognize clients' strengths and weaknesses. The counselor could and should have anticipated the risks posed by the client's dependence. While it is more difficult to weigh clients' limitations with them than to champion their causes, we cannot address the real issues unless we do so. Assessment is not easy, but if we hear and explore what clients tell us and then consider our impressions, we will learn more about them than if we confine ourselves to what they tell us. We will know how clients appear to affect others, including ourselves; we will get a sense of their skills and aptitudes in handling responsibility, both in counseling and outside; and we will see how clients view themselves and their place in the world. While the impressions we get of other people in their lives may be quite distorted by clients' momentary needs, we will nonetheless learn something about them and about the clients' relationships. Even though we may need biographical information to supplement the picture we get of clients from interviews alone, we should be able to assess clients by "everyday" criteria.

Faulty diagnostic conclusions can be drawn if we attend only to what the clients say and ignore everything else about them. Presenting their work for supervision, trainees will sometimes play tape recordings without providing any information about the client they interviewed, as if all that mattered were the words exchanged in session. What the client says has meaning only in comparison to the norms and expectations of the age, sex, cultural, and other peer groups to which the client belongs. The fact that a client is attending college has different implications if the client is eighteen years old or twenty-eight or sixty. Living on one's own is common for people in their twenties but quite unusual for a fifteen-year-old. A college education is a real possibility for many people but it is not likely for one who is mentally retarded. To evaluate the client's goals, achievements, and problems realistically, we must see the client as an individual, as a member of a family and a culture, and in comparison to his or her peers; only then can we begin to know what help clients require from us.

I learned the importance of basic assessment dramatically during my first internship on a psychiatric ward of a hospital for veterans. There I tested a thirty-eight-year-old assembly-line worker who displayed severe interpersonal problems, arguing with everyone on the job and in the hospital. The tests showed him to be severely retarded. Not apparent in casual contact, this disability had never been recognized, but it was the cause behind the fights. I was afraid to tell him that he was not as intelligent as others; but once it was clear to him, he was relieved and grateful. He always knew something was wrong with him, but he didn't know what it was or what to do about it. From that point on, it was easy to help him, and his emotional problems "disappeared." He began to handle his real problem in sensible and appropriate ways.

An accurate picture of a client's abilities is usually more helpful than injurious. It may be uncomfortable to acknowledge that clients are not all gifted, attractive, or mature, but the truth does not diminish their worth as individuals; it just enables them to be realistic in their efforts. Like the assembly-line worker, clients often know "something is wrong," but need help to identify, manage, or change it.

Beginners question whether they can be both supportive and encouraging and also assess and address a client's limitations. How can counselors give clients feedback that may hurt or disappoint them? If counselors are supposed to make clients feel "better," how can they make them feel bad? Surprisingly, if an evaluation is accurate and points out reasons for a client's difficulties, as in the example of the factory worker, a client is more appreciative than troubled. If the college student who returned home humiliated had been helped to understand her inexperience and her readiness to let everyone (her parents, her friends, her counselor) tell her what to do, she might have recognized her dependent needs before they caused her so much grief.

In giving clients feedback about themselves that may be disturbing, tact and support are required. If someone wants to go to medical school but barely earns C's in science courses, the indicators are not promising. But the client knows this too, whether or not he or she openly admits it. We have to help the student confront this discrepancy between goals and performance. It may be a relief to have it shared and out in the open. Clients cannot escape the consequences of their situations and deficiencies. The real issue is whether we will help them confront the issues in counseling, where we can aid and support them, or whether they will have to struggle with them on their own.

"But," trainees are apt to say, "diagnoses can be wrong. In some cases, the wrong label has been applied and caused suffering. It's better to avoid labels altogether." Most of the time we are helping clients assess situations such as inadequate academic progress rather than calling them names. Yet, the point about labels is an important one. Right or wrong, labels cause harm because they tag the client with a characteristic or problem that seems permanent and unmanageable. It would not have helped the factory worker to know that he was "mentally retarded"; he had to learn how the condition affected his life and interactions with others. The counselor must find ways of communicating a client's problems in terms that correspond with the client's language and experience and that have practical meaning and usefulness. We must also make sure that clients don't label themselves and conclude, for instance, that because their chances are not good for medical school they are "stupid"; or that because they feel depressed they are "crazy." *Assessment benefits clients when it identifies the individual's special needs, differences, and abilities, so that appropriate action can be taken by and for the client.*

Many people are awed and frightened by "diagnostic" terms and see menace in them that is not warranted. Some trainees feel comfortable in their helping relationships until they learn that their clients are schizophrenic or disturbed in some other way. Suddenly afraid, and having lost sight of the person, they see only the label. Psychiatric diagnoses are behavioral descriptions, often shorthand names for complex behavioral patterns. Accurately applied to certain clients, they enable counselors to anticipate problems and choose the most appropriate methods of intervention. But few clients, even those with some form of mental illness, are dangerous. Psychiatric terms are not insults or criticisms of clients or reasons to fear them; they are descriptions of personality styles and problems which affect clients' functioning. To professionals, they are tools of the trade—less precise and uniform than would be desirable—but helpful in understanding and responding to clients. Working in settings where such terms are used, nonprofessionals need help in understanding their meaning.

While nonprofessionals' understanding of psychiatric terms may be incomplete, they will nevertheless be called upon to make some diagnosis or assessment of client strengths and attributes in counseling. This is essential because clients' self-evaluations are often distorted by unrealistic self-images and misperceptions by others. A very bright woman may be convinced she is stupid because her parents regarded her older brother as "the smart one." The counselor, not blinded by such preconceptions, can evaluate the client by more objective criteria and use more appropriate comparisons. What clients say about themselves usually conveys the truth as they see it, but their statements may still not be accurate or valid. And often they behave in accordance with their beliefs about themselves. To give an example: A client I counseled was remarkably beautiful, but she considered herself hopelessly flawed. She spent endless hours on her dress and makeup, determined to conceal any imperfection. Though she had a boyfriend she loved, she could be swept off her feet by any attractive man who was persistent. Overweight as a youngster and convinced as a teenager that she lagged behind her peers in heterosexual conquest, she acted as if these conditions were still true. In fact, she had been slim and attractive for years and had garnered quite a bit of male attention. Objective assessment was simple in this case. She was beautiful; her self-image was ugly. Unfortunately, clients are not always brighter or more attractive than they imagine themselves; sometimes they overestimate their capacities and waste a lot of effort trying to achieve goals that are beyond them. In either case, the counseling goal is the same—to help the client acquire a more accurate and realistic self-image.

When counselors discover clients who are unrealistically self-critical, they may attempt to talk clients out of their convictions with simple reassurances. Rarely is this effective in itself. These deeply held opinions have the power of self-fulfilling prophecies. Clients can perceive whatever they look for in their world. The young woman who began counseling with the belief that she was unattractive could, in time, acknowledge her appeal and relax her vigilance about her appearance. Yet, in one session when she discussed the movie, *10,* it became clear that only her standards of comparison had changed. Since she had spent so much time rating herself, she was understandably fascinated with the movie's numerical ratings of feminine beauty, but the concern she now expressed was that she could never be a "10" and compete with fashion models and movie stars. More realistic than she had been, she was still focused on comparative failure. A distorted self-image is not quickly altered. Simple reassurances and efforts of persuasion often do not help. But learning how clients see themselves and comparing their self-images with more objective and realistic criteria are aspects of therapeutic assessment. The counselor's purpose is not to reassure clients or boost morale; the purpose is to understand the impact and consequences, as well as the origins, of misperceptions. Some important questions to consider are:

- What are the client's goals and aspirations?
- What skills and characteristics does the client have to meet those goals?
- How does the client handle stress, conflict, and disappointment?
- How does the client respond to success?
- Does the client make good use of assets and resources?
- Is the client aware of actual deficiencies and limitations? How are they dealt with?
- Are there any serious self-image distortions? On what events or experiences are they based?
- By whose or what yardstick does the client measure

personal achievement or success? To whom does the client compare him or herself? Is the comparison realistic?

These are practical measures by which to evaluate clients—questions to help us observe discrepancies between goals and performance, between performance and self-image, and between self-image and goals. To help us understand, we have a variety of contexts in which to view clients: the context in which they grew up, including childhood experiences, expectations of parents and significant others, and opportunities (or the lack of them); their current context, with its dimensions of productivity and satisfaction in work or school, love and other social relationships, pleasurable pursuits and activities, and of basic enjoyment and gratification; and finally, the context of the counseling relationship, with its opportunities for attachment, commitment, and development. We can see where clients are, where they want to be, and what stands in their way. It is this assessment that clients need from counselors because inaccurate self-images, unrealistic expectations of others, and inappropriate coping mechanisms are not likely to change unless clients are presented with more accurate views of the world and of themselves.

If we give clients pictures of themselves and others that are more realistic than the ones they bring to us, we help them to see how they are perceiving the world and using its feedback. Not introduced to contradict, expose, or diminish clients, a realistic evaluation serves as a useful counterpoint in exploring clients' experiences. Clients cannot assess themselves. It is not likely that a client will say to a counselor, "My parents are unfair in not letting me date, but I am also very immature and dependent." Nor is it likely that a client will tell the counselor that, due to an unidentified handicap of limited intellectual endowment, he or she always felt inferior and defensive. A client would probably not attribute failure in college to the erroneous assumption that it operated like high school. Clients cannot tell us these things because they do not know about them. They need us to help them find what stands between them and their goals. They have an important part of the puzzle: their feelings, their perceptions, and their expectations of others. And we have other pieces: our knowledge of them and how they function in the real world. Putting the pieces of the puzzle that come from the client together with the pieces that come from the broader perspective is the final challenge.

Once we understand its importance to counseling, assessment is still a difficult and demanding process. It requires thoughtful observation, consideration of many alternatives, an awareness of the variety of behavior, and a skill in communicating our understanding to clients. Assessment is a task at which some excel but which no one completely masters.

In the preceding pages, we have considered counseling skills under the headings of observing, listening and checking understanding, exploring context, recognizing and exploring feelings, facilitating communication, giving feedback and interpretation, and assessment. Although some of the terms may be unfamiliar, these are natural abilities which many display without special training. Yet they are so essential to the helping process that much of professional training in the mental health specialties is directed at developing them into dependable tools.

XI

The Course Of Counseling

Up to this point, our focus has been on the human components of counseling. Now we need to consider the process. The guidelines that follow are a kind of road map, a simplified view of the tasks, stages in counseling, and technical information counselors need to know. Whether or not the points are new or familiar from previous discussion, they will be summarized here to offer an overview.

With brief tangents along the way, we will consider five major tasks required in establishing a counseling relationship, methods for evaluating progress in ongoing relationships, and finally, the difficult issues of referral and/or termination.

Initial Stages

In the initial phase, the counselor's primary goals are:

A. Creating a trusting atmosphere
B. Getting the facts
C. Putting problems into manageable units
D. Understanding the client and the problems
E. Making a joint contract or commitment

Although these tasks will be discussed in sequence, they are undertaken almost simultaneously. While they remain important in later stages, they are most crucial in the initial stages.

A. Creating a Trusting Atmosphere

Beginning clients are apprehensive about their decision to engage in counseling. Until comfortable with the relationship, few are ready to commit themselves. Evident or not, anxiety is there, and both participants need to see whether they can work together. Just because a client comes for counseling, we cannot assume that the client will stay in counseling.

In initial exchanges, counselors should explore the "vibes" and the emotional tensions. Rather than respond with long explanations about counseling, they should, at this point, encourage clients to express specific concerns. Even if the client begins to present personal problems right away, a working relationship is not automatically assured. The client may be trying to get through the interview as soon as possible and avoiding emotional involvement. It must be stressed that rapport still needs to be established.

All clients are concerned with the conditions of counseling—the rules of confidentiality, the basic comfort and privacy of the setting, and the availability and qualifications of the counselor. Clients also have reactions to their counselors' personal features, such as age, sex, dress, and manner. The counselor should anticipate and explore clients' initial doubts and questions about counseling.

I'd like to introduce a brief tangent about tape recorders here: if the first session is to be taped—and it is often the most important to have on tape—the purpose of recording must be explained at the outset. Nothing should be recorded without the client's knowledge and permission. Counselors who are themselves comfortable with tape recording find few clients who object, but a client's refusal needs to be explored. It may mean the client does not understand the protections of confidentiality. If the client remains adamantly opposed, despite the counselor's assurance, no recording should be done; the counselor may, however, ask again at a later time.

Once these basic matters have been discussed and clients start to talk, introductions are not over. Before work can get underway, the counselor needs to know: How did the client get to the counselor? Was the client referred? How does the client feel about the referral? Is counseling the client's own idea or someone else's? Do client and counselor know anything in advance about each other? If so, how may it affect the relationship? What does the client know and expect of counseling? Has the client prior counseling experience? Was it successful and appreciated? Answers to these questions can alert counselors to potential problems.

If clients are suspicious, doubtful, or fearful of counseling—and many are—they may not volunteer these concerns without considerable encouragement. If they do express them, with or without prompting, counselors must demonstrate willingness to recognize and deal with them. One way to get these feelings out in the open is to ask toward the end of the first session (or at the beginning of the second) how the client felt about the interview, whether it conformed to or differed from expectation, whether it raised additional doubts or questions, and whether anything important was left out. Such questions ask the client to focus on the process to assess whether the relationship "feels" like a workable arrangement.

Counselors' openness and invitations to raise questions and share reservations indicate that counseling is different from other relationships. They show that the client's feelings and impressions matter and that it is safe to express them. They show clients that they have a choice to participate or not. Sometimes the trial does not work. The client may back away from help or feel that another kind of help is required. The counselor may also, for one reason or another, feel his or her skills insufficient or unsuitable.

Should referral or another alternative seem more appropriate, some discussion is required. Clients who are to be referred need to know the reason or they may not follow the recommendation. The clients who reject help need to explore their decisions. Do the reasons make sense, or are they really afraid? Is the choice in the client's best interest, or are there possible negative consequences?

Initially, clients often need help assessing and accepting the need for counseling. Their reservations may be unrealistic or perfectly justified. Sometimes counselors feel threatened or insulted by a client's hesitancy; but doubts are the rule, not the exception! Whether the client stays or leaves, it is important to understand the elements on which the decision is based.

B. Getting the Facts Straight Before Attempting to Help

Trying to fix things up too fast is a common counseling error. Even if only trying to help, the counselor is engaged in wasted effort. Immediately, setting out to "solve problems" demeans clients' efforts to help themselves. Moreover, suggestions off the top of the head are likely to be unrealistic or unworkable. A great deal of information—current status and biographical details, the client's concerns and expectations of counseling, and his or her mood, motivation, and energy level—is required to provide the appropriate help. As an example, let us imagine a widowed client having a tough time coping with her husband's death. It makes a great difference whether the loss occurred two weeks, two months, or two years ago; whether the death was sudden or prolonged; whether the marriage was a good or troubled relationship, and for how long; whether others are around for support; and whether the widow is self-supporting or in a dependent financial situation. It is also important to know the state of her health. Has her prior experience prepared her for this occurrence? What makes her seek counseling at this time? What is it about her situation that bothers her most? Probably many other questions are also relevant, but it will take time to get a glimpse of even this much of the picture. In addition, sharing this information may be extremely painful for the client. Listening may be painful too. Counselors are apt to forego information-gathering whenever they feel the client's distress or are touched by the material presented. It is essential, however, to get the facts and sufficient details before trying to help.

C. Establishing Priorities and Putting Problems into Manageable Units

Although counselors may be concerned for clients, they also maintain a distance, a separateness, that gives them perspective. They can look at the situation with more objectivity and dispassion than the client. Typically, the client in crisis is overwhelmed by many problems, all occurring simultaneously. The result is a sense of helplessness and hopelessness. The woman who has ended a long romantic involvement, for instance, is not only grieving the loss but also finding the rest of her world suddenly topsy-turvy. She may discover her relationships with her parents and friends drastically altered; she may experience difficulty meeting her responsibilities; she may need to make new living arrangements or readjust existing ones; she may be experiencing physical distress as well as psychological symptoms, such as diminished self-esteem and self-confidence. For the client, everything seems to be going wrong at once. The counselor, however, can distinguish those concerns that need most immediate attention. In this example, an obvious priority is a medical referral to relieve the physical discomfort. When the counselor can appreciate the whole picture and help to establish priorities, clients feel cared for and reassured. Just labeling and separating problems provides a measure of order and security. Priorities change as counseling continues, but it is always helpful to break big problems into smaller, more manageable units. This is one opportunity for the counselor to act as a problem-solver—not in solving clients' problems—but in suggesting practical steps. The counselor's objectivity and pragmatism help both participants keep their bearings.

D. Understanding the Client and the Problem

Once clients begin discussing their problems and revealing themselves, they are often apprehensive about the counselor's opinions. One way of responding to this anxiety is to offer feedback to the client as early as possible. Even if impressionistic and incomplete, some indication of the counselor's view of the problem, of the client, and of suitable counseling objectives is reassuring. Offering early feedback seems risky, and certainly, mistakes are possible. But not responding at all contributes additional stress. Unable to tell what the counselor thinks, a client may draw negative inferences. Giving feedback also helps counselors check the accuracy of their impressions.

Counselors need to look beyond the client's presentation of the problems in order to understand the reason why clients are seeking counseling. Some of the questions counselors need to ask themselves are:

- What circumstances prompted the client to seek help?
- Is this problem temporary and unusual for a person who has dealt well with typical life challenges, or is it the latest episode for one who has consistent difficulty?
- What is the client's approach to the problem? Is the client taking any constructive steps to deal with the crisis? Does the client's behavior compound the problem?
- What support system does the client have in terms of family, religion, friends, or other resources? How well does the client use them?
- What are the client's personal characteristics and assets—physical appearance and health; special talents; intellectual, emotional, and financial resources? Is the client aware of them and able to take advantage of them?
- What are the client's limitations, real or imagined; how are they dealt with?

These questions alert us to other dimensions and help us see beyond the client's immediate concerns.

While clients may present problems familiar to us, our task is to discern the meaning of the problem for the client. Getting fired is a terrible experience for almost everyone; but the impact on someone who has been fired before and has always found another job is different from what it is on the person who is nearing retirement age, on someone prone to depression, or on a client terribly burdened with major responsibilities. The "precipitating problem" is the same for each, but the impact of the event is different. Counselors need to see the whole picture to be effective; they need to understand both problem and client.

E. Making a Joint Contract or Commitment

When the relationship seems reasonably secure, it is useful to discuss a joint contract, a plan of action to alter the practical and psychological problems besetting the client. An agreement to undertake a specific action, a joint contract, is as relevant in counseling as it is in other work situations. It represents a commitment of both parties; it directs and orients participants to a common task; and it structures the work. Describing a counseling contract here makes it sound more formal than it actually is, but it does establish and articulate what participants hope to achieve and the rules by which they work. One client and I agreed our task was to help her recover a sustaining interest in life and to ensure that the early, painful, and traumatic death of her husband would not leave her emotionally crippled and unable to feel love again. Another client is using therapy to help her achieve independence, the ability to depend on herself without requiring extensive financial and emotional support from others. The rules of the contract are the practical arrangements—the number and times of meetings held each week or month and other details pertinent to payment, cancellations, and time limitations.

A contract is helpful for several reasons. The first is to make clear that counseling is a collaboration rather than some service performed for the client. Another is that it focuses on the objective to be reached. If the relationship has to end prematurely, the client is more likely to accept referral to complete the process. And finally, clients need to see counseling as a commitment—to the counselor and to themselves—to stay for the amount of time it takes to work through problems. Otherwise, it is easy to quit when things get tough or when counseling achieves some quick but superficial results. Initial joint contracts may have to be reworked, but when clients help establish their own objectives, they are more responsible and motivated. Few of us neglect assignments we have chosen for ourselves.

The word "contract" connotes a legal business agreement. While counseling contracts are not legally binding, they imply commitment, mutuality, and purpose. Without those features, counseling endeavors have a hit-or-miss quality and amorphous boundaries, which make it impossible to evaluate progress. Some clients like the idea of a contract because they are afraid that, without limits, counseling could continue forever. But other clients resist them, showing a wariness toward commitment that manifests itself in their other behavior as well. Though clients may leave before reaching the contract's objective, it still provides criteria for evaluation, a way to measure progress.

The contract is, in some ways, a diagnostic statement, endorsed by both participants, about the nature of a client's difficulties and the counseling focus required to help. It is a statement of strategy to correct the distress in the client's life and relationships. With more experience, counselors may propose more sophisticated contracts, but a simple statement—"Let's meet regularly to figure out what is causing you to have so many fights with your colleagues at work"—can be effective enough. Beginners must be certain that the contract states their clients' views and intentions as well as their own, if the collaboration is to be genuine.

Middle Phase

F. Evaluating Progress toward Fulfilling the Contract

The importance of the contract becomes evident as work progresses or runs into snags. If a client begins to back away from the plan—by missing sessions, coming late, becoming withdrawn, or in other ways avoiding issues—the initial contract needs to be discussed. Often this can expose or resolve problems. The more often clients have excuses or reasons (even good ones) for canceling or coming late, the more reason to suspect alteration in priorities and in their commitment. The earlier their intentions are explored, the easier it is to identify problems that may sabotage counseling. Counselors who ignore the signals and view them as accidents unrelated to the counseling process may be unpleasantly surprised.

The contract makes it easier to note progress. Beset by many problems, clients are apt to overlook signs of improvement. Since we often forget formerly held attitudes, counselors may have to point out how and when clients have changed. Clients need reminders when they pass a test they fully expected to fail or when the invitation they were hesitant to extend is enthusiastically accepted. When a client, used to depending entirely on others' opinions, begins to make his or her own choices, the counselor should both notice and applaud. Clients need help in comparing their expectations with reality and in recognizing their gains. Recognition of a client's progress, required and implied by the counseling contract, is also an important form of encouragement and support, but it needs to be genuine, not gratuitous or manufactured, in order to be effective.

Helping clients identify shifts in their attitudes, expectations, and feelings is just as important as noting behavioral change. Alterations that occur in clients' internal frames of reference, even if not apparent in their behavior, are a kind of prelude to change. Clients also need help in becoming aware of these shifts. Very seldom does dramatic transformation take place in counseling, but if a client who once was terrified of her boss begins to imagine how she might handle a conference with him, she is taking a step in the right direction even if not yet ready to carry out the act. Effective counseling feedback helps clients appreciate such nuances of change within themselves.

Evaluating progress and providing feedback require accurate recall. It is important, therefore, to take notes on sessions and review them regularly. Since taking notes during appointments is likely to distract clients, it is best done immediately after, before the memory fades. Replaying earlier tape-recorded sessions also provides perspective; it can be productive for both counselors and clients.

When counseling is running smoothly, it may seem unnecessary to consider how the work is going, but much is gained in periodic review. Sometimes I use events, such as clients' birthdays, New Year's Day, or a certain number of sessions, as occasions to stop and share impressions of change and gains. Such reviews seem to provide new perspectives, a surprise or two, and sometimes a gratifying sense of accomplishment, as well as affirmation or reworking of the contract. Evaluating progress is an ongoing responsibility for the counselor, but the client's perspective is often the most elucidating. Counseling can be so problem-focused that clients have little opportunity to consider how far they have come.

G. Referral to Others When Their Help Is Required

During counseling, clients sometimes need to be referred to other helpers for separate, additional, or replacement services. When they are willing and merely lacking information, referral is a simple administrative chore. It consists of identifying (or helping the client identify) the appropriate agency, office, or person offering the needed service—whether it be tutoring, medical care, financial aid, or educational opportunity. There may be difficulty matching the service available to the client's needs, requirements, and resources, but usually clients can investigate options for themselves once they know what they are looking for.

When the client is ambivalent about a needed consultation, however, referral is a counseling task, not an administrative matter. For instance, if a young woman is afraid of having cancer because other family members have died of this disease, simply encouraging her to go to a hospital or providing the name of a specialist won't help. The terror of discovering the suspected truth, however unlikely, will interfere. Counseling will first have to address her fears and concerns, allow her to explore the dilemma inherent in going or not going for a consultation, and encourage her to reach an appropriate decision.

When referral is required because the present counselor is leaving or because the client needs a counselor with different skills, the task is more difficult yet. This is a termination of a relationship as well as a referral, and it demands special effort and advanced planning by the counselor. More frequently than professionals, nonprofessionals have to refer clients with whom they have established relationships. It is rarely an easy and painless matter. This kind of referral has frightening and disturbing effects, which have to be worked through before the transfer. To clients, referral may mean that their problems are more serious than they have imagined. Or it may mean they will have to pay for help which was formerly free. It always means starting over again—telling another stranger private and painful matters, forging a new relationship, risking another's scrutiny. It always means giving up the support and comfort of the present relationship with a special and unique person. In parting with clients, counselors too have disturbing feelings, which are more intense than they ever anticipate; how they handle these feelings affects the client, the referral, and the success of the new arrangements. Making a referral to another counselor is a complex and difficult emotional shift for clients who accept the need for continued or alternative treatment. The difficulties are only compounded for those who don't. A wrenching experience, transfer to another counselor cannot be speedily effected.

Leave-taking is painful and it reawakens all the desperate fears of being alone and rejected. If insufficient time is allotted to explore these emotions, they may overshadow therapeutic accomplishments and make clients unwilling to risk other attachments. Counselors rarely comprehend their importance to clients until the time comes when they have to part with them, and then they may feel overwhelmed and frightened by the clients' responses. Clients may react with anger or a furious rage because they feel as if they are being abandoned. They may act out their anger—missing sessions or being uncommunicative to show their independence—and they may need continued encouragement to articulate the turmoil they are in. They may pretend indifference and minimize the counselor's importance in an effort to conceal their attachment. Clients need time to understand this behavior, explore their fantasies and expectations, and grapple with the realistic implications of the referral.

When counselors realize the intensity of the client's attachment, they may begin to regard their plan for referral as an error that may be injurious to the client. They may believe the client who insists that the next counselor will not be as good or as helpful. The fact—a reassuring one for clients—is that those who have been able to establish a relationship with one counselor are likely to be able to form an attachment to another. The new relationship will be different, but given time, it is likely to work out. The fear of starting again is genuine, but it also reflects underlying concerns with separation, rejection, and dependency. It is not likely that one, and only one, counselor can help a client. Yet it is difficult to witness a client's reactions to referral without experiencing distress. If the client is angry and resentful, or fearful and clinging, or just grateful and complimentary, the counselor feels guilty. The thought occurs: "If this client regards me and my work so highly, why do I have to inflict this pain and carry out this transfer?" The original reason for the referral, which once seemed justified, may now seem hazy. Furthermore, the counselor, much like the client, feels pain at anticipating the moment of parting. It is hard to do something well that feels this bad. Our discomfort and our pride make us want to hold onto the relationship even when impractical, inappropriate, or destructive—sometimes even after the client has begun to work with another counselor.

If the referral is necessary and appropriate—a decision that has to be made before, not after, the referral process begins—then we have to do it so that the client can understand and accept it. We can let the client know we too find it tough going but necessary. Once referral is completed, we have to get out of the way and not interfere with the new relationship. Continuing the contact would be disruptive rather than therapeutic.

There are analogies between a parent's relinquishing of a child and a counselor's referring a client to another counselor. The thoughts and feelings are comparable to a mother's seeing her child go off to elementary school, to college, or to marriage. How will the child manage without her? Has she done a good job? How will her efforts be regarded by others? Who will be able to understand the one she has cared for as well as she does? The child's (or client's) fears and protests arouse sympathetic vibrations in mother (and counselor) and prompt the impulse to hold on. But like mothers, referring counselors must let go and encourage their charges to take steps without the familiar support. As counselors, we have to check our own conflicts so as not to increase client apprehension or encourage continued dependency. Without us, our clients can move on and progress. Despite our discomfort and uncertainty, we have to assure them of this and get out of their way.

Final Phase

H. Ending the Counseling Relationship

Since referral to another counselor is an ending (or termination) of the helping alliance, many of the problems inherent in termination have already been discussed. Although difficult to do, referring clients at least provides the assurance that someone else is taking over, that the client will be cared for. Ending counseling when no referral is planned or necessary removes that safety net and makes the risk seem greater.

Under ideal circumstances, participants begin discussing termination when the client's progress is significant and he or she is able to deal with the initial problems with minimal assistance. Clients at that stage seem to spend more time describing their effectiveness and insights in handling situations, and less time introducing new problems or concerns. When it appears that the client's gains are relatively secure and more or less permanent, the counselor should set a time for counseling to end. Since many sessions are required to anticipate and discuss termination and its consequences, it may take two or three months, and longer if the relationship has been long-lived or extremely rocky. Often, latent feelings, brought out by the anticipation of the relationship's end, induce backsliding, regression, and helplessness in dealing with problems clients have previously shown themselves competent to handle. Understanding these manifestations is the time-consuming work of termination. Just as counselors must be alert to hesitancy and resistance at the beginning of counseling, they have to carefully monitor client behavior when the termination date is set. Does the client start missing sessions and, thereby, avoid expressing feelings? Does the client ignore the impending event or treat it with indifference?

Does the client present a whole host of new problems as if to suggest that termination is unwise? Reactions to the stress of termination are varied, but clients will probably respond in ways that are similar to the ways they have responded to other stressful situations in their lives. Termination sometimes resembles a minirecapitulation of the whole therapy relationship. The manifestations of client distress—if subtle, indirect, or nonverbal—may be easily overlooked, so it is useful to adopt a mental framework after the termination date is set, viewing *all* client behavior as reflecting and related to feelings and fantasies about termination. Not all client responses will be "termination induced," but it is better not to overlook the many that are. The counseling task is to help the client articulate fears and doubts, explore conflicts and ambivalence, weigh losses and gains, and sort out probable realities from the improbable possibilities that termination may suggest. It is vital to examine and articulate the attachment client and counselor have developed for one another. When termination is appropriate and well handled by the counselor, many clients who believe they will founder and sink discover they can rely on themselves. They discover that the strength they attribute to the relationship or to the counselor has become their own; that they have incorporated, absorbed, or learned enough to feel confident of their own course. They will have moments of uncertainty and occasionally wish to return, but most will be able to hold their ground and advance on their own. The process of termination enhances this recognition, even in advance of its occurrence, when counselors can maintain a realistic and reassuring perspective. (The fees professionals charge for counseling are often an added incentive to end; in this regard, nonprofessionals may have greater difficulty helping clients terminate.) But the necessity for ending the relationship is the same for clients of all therapists. Continuing counseling past the point of its need is injurious and disabling. Clients need not be supported when they can walk on their own two feet, and counseling must end in order for them to see if they can.

Unfortunately, many counseling relationships end before they reach the point where all objectives have been achieved. Some relationships end at an arbitrary point, because either client or counselor has to leave or some other necessity intrudes. The more time to deal with leave-taking the better, but should time be short, participants not only have to deal with their feelings but also weigh whether another referral is required, or whether the client can go it alone at least temporarily. The latter choice may be advisable if the relationship is, in actuality, approaching the end. Otherwise referral is indicated. When counseling ends before the termination work is finished, the emotional consequences are disturbing for clients. Counselors should do all they can to prevent this occurrence, but sometimes it happens anyway; counselors may die or become too ill to continue with their clients. Though clients can understand such facts intellectually, they still feel abandoned, rejected, and bereft. Termination is stressful, but aborted termination can be unbearable.

Finally, termination is sometimes determined by the client despite the counselor's objections. The client may announce this decision in advance or just fail to appear for further appointments. The wish to quit or sudden absence may indicate a missed or slighted problem in the relationship that may be resolved if there is sufficient opportunity to explore it. Counselors may have to exert unusual effort and tolerate a lot of resistance in order to get recalcitrant clients to examine their feelings in session. The reason for sudden withdrawal from an effective counseling relationship is apt to be some profound distress accompanied by shame. Even if this distress has been triggered in some way by the counselor—and this cannot be known without discussion—counselors should not give up easily in trying to reestablish the relationship. Chances are the client is suffering and in need of the counselor's help, even while appearing to reject it. In unusual circumstances, involving physical danger or life-threatening consequences, or when the courts, institutions, or parents retain jurisdiction, other people may have to be notified of the client's unexpected absence or noncooperation. Otherwise, the counselor should try to reach the client without assistance from anyone else, and coax, rather than force, the client back into the relationship.

In those unfortunate cases where the client's decision is irreversible and no amount of effort is effective, there is relatively little that one can do. The counselor's only option—not a very satisfying one without the client's input—is to examine the whole relationship, especially the last few sessions, and search for the reasons which made the client quit. An outside opinion or a consultation may provide insight and a measure of comfort.

In this chapter we have traced the progress of counseling relationships from early stages to final ones and pinpointed counseling tasks required at each phase. The final chapter is an overview of the process and provides a means for evaluating its effectiveness.

XII

The Final Chapter and the Beginning

This chapter is both recapitulation and introduction. Presenting the basic framework and elements of counseling, it could be considered the starting point for counselors; but since the human factors make each principle easier to understand than to practice, these have to be reviewed as well.

Because it is often contrary to our natural impulses, counseling is a difficult undertaking. It is an abstraction, a distillation of human relatedness through which therapists use their personal resources to help clients see themselves. In our industrial age, we are used to accepting and mastering mechanical constructions, but the counseling role as a human construction is comprehensible only if one accepts its unique use of emotion and attachment.

While the mechanics of counseling are deceptively simple, its emotional implications are complex. What follows is an effort to put the methodological elements in their human context to provide guidelines to help counselors avoid some common pitfalls. Because our natural temptation is to help our neighbors, counselors have to learn to help our neighbors help themselves.

The last section of this chapter presents a series of questions, which will enable counselors to examine their helping relationships and measure them by professional standards.

Basic Elements of Counseling

Counseling is a working relationship focused on the

client, with specified goals.

It occurs within a regular and limited—but not rigid—time frame.

It is a relationship that occurs in the here-and-now, with boundaries that permit both help-giver and help-seeker to orient themselves to the task.

Counseling works best when based on a joint contract with goals that are feasible and mutually acceptable.

Counseling enables clients to deal with their problems when the helper faces reality squarely and honestly, understands life as the client sees it, and provides support during the process of change.

Many personal characteristics and qualities are useful to counselors but essential are: (1) an abiding concern; (2) acceptance of self and others; and (3) the courage and ability to deal with the risks and realities of the task.

The Counseling Framework

To begin with: *counseling is a working relationship.* It is not always pleasant or fun or relaxed; it can become a struggle in which participants may not always feel good about each other. Not necessarily somber, it is serious. Some counselors try to sugarcoat the effort with such comments as "Oh, it's not hard to pull your grades up, you just have to set your mind to it." Or, "You have such wonderful taste. I'm sure you'll have no problem attracting a boyfriend." They also may avoid discussing difficult issues to choose more comfortable ones. Clients may be disarmed by such approaches, but false assurance, charm, and avoidance are the stuff casual social encounters are made of, not counseling interventions.

Counseling is focused on the client. Without awareness, counselors can use clients' problems as vehicles for their own gratification. They are often tempted to misuse the helping alliance: to lecture, to talk about themselves, to avoid disturbing topics and feelings, to keep clients at a safe distance, to interrupt, to ignore client discomfort and to dominate sessions. In counseling, however, the spotlight is for the client, not the counselor.

Counseling has specified goals. Many view counseling interviews as rap sessions, casual and disorganized. They see the goal as one of getting clients to "open up" and talk freely. While encouraging openness and letting the client lead the way are important, participants can be swamped by a profusion of problems. Clients need a context in which to view their problems. The goals and purposes of counseling should be identified early, and sessions should be shaped and focused accordingly. If discussion seems to wander, participants can examine their original intent and decide to move back on course, enlarge the focus, or set new goals. It usually takes time for participants to explore the background and implications of the difficulties involved, but the purpose of the exploration is to establish specific and meaningful goals.

Counseling occurs within a regular and limited time frame. Counseling is often difficult work for both participants, so it is necessary to schedule and limit the duration of meetings. Although a productive session can occasionally be slightly extended, it will become tiring if it goes on for too long. Gains can be lost if too many issues are discussed in one meeting. At times extra sessions are called for when the help-seeker has a crisis or is anticipating some important event, or when the relationship is either in trouble or moving swiftly. Still, it is useful to have a baseline to which to return. If sessions occur spontaneously or unpredictably, participants cannot prepare, focus, or maintain perspective. With no set time to begin or end, clues to resistance and hesitancy are lost—like a client's introducing an important topic with no time left to talk about it, or arriving late to avoid addressing a disturbing problem. Eager to show concern and involvement, new counselors may extend meeting times only to find problems in sustaining their commitments and balancing their personal responsibilities. Although some initial counseling contacts do not lend themselves to prearranged or regular appointments, such as those resulting from chance encounters or emergency situations, subsequent sessions can be planned.

Obligations to clients sometimes conflict with personal plans and preferences that seem momentarily less important to counselors. But helpers must hold to their commitments if they expect to be seen as trustworthy. If an illness or a personal emergency interferes with a scheduled meeting, counselors need to provide clients with as much notice as possible and reschedule the canceled appointment. The circumstances and the goals of counseling determine how often meetings occur and for what length of time. Many options are possible, but the schedule must take the needs and availability of both participants into account. If either is resentful of the time committed, the relationship may suffer.

Counseling is a relationship that occurs in the here-and-now. What happens in counseling partially reflects the client's past and also relates to future events. The past, however, may serve as an excuse for our present actions—seeing ourselves as victims or spending time imagining what we would be like if this or that had not occurred. In their desire to understand, counselors may get trapped in this perspective and see present-day behavior as the inevitable sequel to past experience. Understanding behavioral origins can serve as a basis for change, but it can also provide a justification for continued maladaptive behavior. Softhearted counselors find it difficult to hold individuals responsible for behavior that has its origins in earlier misfortune. Since our clients live in the present and suffer the consequences of their daily conduct, their current behavior and our reactions to that behavior must be the primary focus of counseling. We can use the past to help clients understand themselves and to get them to recognize that what has occurred need *not* happen again, even when some scars and sensitivities remain. Our real usefulness lies in the exploration and establishment of new, and more adaptive, behavior.

Clients can also use sessions to imagine what circumstances the future will provide—such as a change of job or marital status. In the hypothetical state, current problems may disappear or become reduced in importance. But none of us lives in a hypothetical state. Although we can imagine that the future will provide solutions for our clients, we cannot depend on the future as a solution. Our energies are better spent addressing immediate issues, but we will understand clients better by investigating their current fantasies and expectations of the future. Tomorrow's possibilities can serve as incentives if our clients are held responsible for preparing for them today.

Another avoidance of the here-and-now occurs when clients focus on the disturbing behavior of others rather than on their own feelings and reactions. The young adult who complains constantly about restrictive parents, the worker who fills sessions with tales about insensitive bosses or co-workers, and the older woman who talks incessantly about her son's irresponsibility, all get some relief out of venting their resentments; but they make little progress if that is all they do. Others in the client's life may also be troubled and troubling, but they are not present in session. Clients learn to understand and deal with others more effectively through self-exploration. By considering their own options, by realizing how they are viewed by others, and by getting in touch with their feelings and fantasies, they can decide how to respond to those who upset them.

Counseling has boundaries that permit both help-giver and help-seeker to orient themselves to the task. There are many boundaries to the counseling relationship, and some have been named above. The goals of the relationship, its expected duration, and the times and locations of meetings give structure and boundaries to the work.

All rules, methods, and expectations must be discussed. Counselors may need to specify how, when, and where they can be reached only if they are needed at times other than scheduled meetings. Confidentiality, with its limits, also defines the relationship and its purposes and always needs to be received. Methods employed by the counselor (talking, other joint activities, testing, taping) and the counselor's expectations of the client should be identified. If participants are or were involved in another kind of relationship—administrative or personal—they must first decide on the advisability of their establishing a counseling relationship at all.

Finally, participants may be tempted to let their association develop into other kinds of relationships: friendship, romance, work of mutual interest, or some other arrangement. Some clients fear that counseling might develop into something else, and others want it to. When the issue arises, its consequences need to be considered and the boundaries clarified. Problems always arise when participants form other kinds of relationships and alter the dimensions of counseling.

Counseling works best when based on a joint contract—a partnership with goals that are feasible and mutually acceptable. Although we may help the very young, the very old, and the very ill with problems without first securing their agreement, helping people to help themselves requires their full cooperation. Establishing a counseling contract allows participants a degree of control, protects each one against unspecified and unrealistic expectations, and permits either to hold the other accountable.

There are important reasons for specificity. Clients may want results that counseling cannot guarantee—such as a promotion, marriage, new job, or a state of contentment. Nebulous emotional states, such as happiness and confidence, are rarely guaranteed. Moreover, obtaining a desired goal does not always produce the anticipated emotional consequence. While we imagine ourselves happier and more assured with a raise or a new title, we may find our feelings little changed once we do get what we want. Counseling can help people reach specific behavioral objectives, but it cannot guarantee how they will feel.

The model of counseling as a partnership based on a contract may seem strange. We often think that counseling follows the pattern of doctor and patient: the patient has something wrong, the doctor diagnoses the problem, then tells the patient what to do about it. The medical model is inappropriate to counseling. Personal and interpersonal problems do not follow predictable patterns; unlike diseases, they cannot be treated by medication or other technical procedures. People come to counseling with problems in living, coping, and accepting the limitations of their lives. In the last analysis, only they can do much about these problems. A counselor's perspective, support, and understanding can make an important difference; but the client is the determining force, not the passive recipient. The client, therefore, must choose, or help to choose, the goals and focus of counseling.

The contract between participants can be changed and renegotiated as required. Help must always focus on current needs and issues, which obviously change over a period of time. It can be helpful to review the progress, changes, and obstacles periodically to see how the partnership is working and to reevaluate objectives. One can either arrange a time to evaluate progress or use opportunities as they present themselves. The important thing is to make time for evaluation.

Finally, it is sometimes easier than it appears to establish a collaboration—even with the young, the old, and the sick. If we fail to get their cooperation and imagine instead that we know what they need and want, we may be disappointed. In making a contract with these "special" clients we have to make the language appropriate for them and be willing to take "no" for an answer.

For clients in some settings, counseling may be compulsory. Some are remanded by the court for counseling. Others, like students on probation or in high-risk academic programs, are required to take part in it. People confined in prisons or hospitals are also sometimes forced to accept treatment. There should be no surprise if such clients resist our efforts to involve them. When counseling is not freely chosen, counselors should expect resistance and create opportunities to explore it. Fear, ignorance, unfamiliarity, misinformation, and suspicion can be alleviated by frank discussion. A better understanding of counseling may take the curse off its compulsory nature. Freedom to choose the counselor, the time, or the nature of the contract can sometimes make these "compulsory" clients feel they are permitted some options. In these and other circumstances not ideal for promoting enthusiastic participation, counselors who recognize and address client resistance have a better chance to overcome it.

Counseling Skills

Counseling helps clients deal with problems when the helper faces reality squarely and honestly, understands life as the other sees it, and supports the client during the process of change. Facing reality can be surprisingly difficult for a counselor. Our desire to make clients feel better may inhibit our honesty and candor. Novices in particular are afraid to express "negative" views and feelings toward their clients. If we ourselves cannot face the realities confronting our clients, how can we expect them to face them?

We do not perform a service when we reassure a slovenly young man that he will get a job, tell a grieving widow that she will soon adjust, or stifle our irritation when provoked by an individual who has problems getting along with others. In these situations we have to ask ourselves: Who are we protecting? What are we protecting them from? These clients live with these problems and face their consequences every day. If we pretend the problems are trivial or don't exist, we make it harder for them to speak honestly, to share their feelings, and to deal with the difficulties.

In truth, we shy away from or distort some issues in order to protect ourselves. It is very difficult *for us* to face the fact that our client is sloppy, and therefore unlikely to impress an employer. It is painful *for us* to experience, even secondhand, the excruciating loss of a loved one, and we fear that *we* will suffer if we confront individuals with their unattractive behavior or let them know the disagreeable feelings they evoke in us.

Counselors should not falsify reality or confine their efforts to back-patting and ego-boosting. If the client is in trouble and the future looks bleak, or if a big disappointment has occurred, the counselor has to *be there* with the client, not off somewhere in search of the silver lining. More than making clients feel "good," counselors have to be able to accept how difficult life is for their clients. For many counselors this is the most trying task.

The helper's ability to understand life as the client sees it can help the client to deal with problems. Psychologists call this empathy, but the Indians used a more appealing image. Before judging someone, they said, one had to walk a few miles in his moccasins. Knowing the world in which another travels and sharing his or her perspective make it harder to sit in distant judgment or dictate facile solutions.

Peers, especially those sharing similar experiences, are rarely distant from clients. Except for the few who take a self-righteous stance by burying the memories of their own struggles ("I did it. Why can't you?"), the problem for most beginners is over-identification with the clients' problems. Empathy requires the ability to put ourselves in another's place but also to step back for a better perspective. Over-involved with clients, we tend to see them as victims, and we want to combat the hostile or indifferent forces in their lives. We tend to overlook their strengths instead of helping them recognize and use their own capacities.

Empathy is not sympathy either. When sympathetic, we feel *for* someone; when empathetic, we feel *with* someone. Sympathy makes us feel sorry for the individual, express pity, and offer condolences from a distance. Empathetic, we know what the other feels; but still separate, we can use our strength and resources to help them deal with their misfortunes. In offering sympathy we should recognize that the feelings a client's situation evokes in us are often *not* the client's feelings.

Clients need to know that we can tolerate and understand their feelings, however crazy, unconventional, or disturbing they are. We have to comprehend emotions that, in the same circumstances, we may not experience ourselves. We cannot reply, "Oh, you shouldn't feel that way!" or otherwise try to alter clients' reactions artificially. Our acceptance of their feelings can reduce their isolation and shame.

There is an important distinction between accepting the feelings and accepting all behavior of those we help. We can understand why a client is angry, but we cannot permit him or her to destroy the consultation room. We can understand depression and the wish to die, but we try to prevent suicidal behavior. We must place limits on certain behavioral expressions, while recognizing that feelings do not necessarily become transformed into action. We may sometimes try to suppress or alter a client's emotions when what we really fear is that they will be demonstrated in some dangerous or destructive way. Yet, behavioral expression is not altered or resolved when we deny, contradict, or prohibit the feelings clients experience.

One final comment on seeing life as the client sees it. If a client reports experiences similar to our own, empathy is not automatically guaranteed. We cannot assume we know how our clients are feeling or that the event has the same impact on them as it had on us. Empathy is a response to a person, not to an event or condition. We must still ask, listen to, and grasp what the experience means to the client without making assumptions based on our experiences.

We sometimes hear of "wonder" drugs or new therapeutic techniques that seem to promise quick transformations; we ourselves imagine that a new diet, outfit, skill, or degree will enable us to be all that we want, instantly. Counseling, however, rarely achieves immediate results. *The counselor's support during the process of change helps the client deal with his or her problems.*

As counselors, we imagine ourselves capable of making immediate impact—saying the right things that dramatically change the course of clients' lives. If we are not quickly effective, we assume other counselors are, and look for new approaches, new techniques. When the lack of progress does not seem to be our fault, we may blame the client for stubbornness, resistance, or poor motivation. And when there are still no quick or dramatic changes, we may become bored, frustrated, impatient, or angry.

We somehow expect that, once clients recognize their maladaptive behavior, they will change, even though we know our own bad habits do not vanish on command. It is frustrating for us to know (and have the client know) that some behavior is undesirable and find it occurring again and again. ("I know I always choose women who are unavailable, and you know, I did it again!" "I know I should have been assertive, but I just couldn't be!") Frustrating as it is, intellectual appreciation of maladaptive behavior does not eradicate it or its psychological underpinnings. Furthermore, conscious efforts *not* to engage in certain behavior rarely work. Change occurs—and, typically, it happens slowly and almost imperceptibly—when the individual begins to feel, see, and experience things differently. Then new behavior results naturally.

It is difficult but important to offer unconditional support to our clients even when improvement does not occur. Clients are often as frustrated as we are when they see the problem, its solution, and their failure to effect it. They may, perhaps, need to experience that frustration until, weary of things as they are, they become willing and able to break old patterns of behavior. We cannot be convinced by the clarity of our understanding that change is easy for clients. Though we can assist or harm the process, change will come only from within them.

My clients sometimes ask me what to do to speed up change. My answer, and it is none too comforting, is usually the same: "All you can do is be aware; watch yourself and your reactions to the people and events in your life, and learn what you can about them." Clients need our support and assurance that we know change is difficult. We have to be accepting of efforts that go nowhere, observant of small steps forward and new perspectives (of which the client is often unaware), sensitive to resistance and transference reactions which block collaboration, and careful to keep the client at the task. Oddly, progress seems to happen almost by itself when counselors stay attuned to the counseling process.

Essential Counselor Characteristics

An essential characteristic of counselors is *abiding concern*. In order to provide the support needed during counseling, helpers must possess and display genuine and unconditional involvement. Caring about clients and showing our interest in them is essential, because it is sometimes our concern which seems to allow them to care about themselves. Many clients have all but given up hope. A counselor's show of support and concern not only leads clients to believe that their current efforts will succeed even if they have failed in the past, it also encourages clients to reevaluate and reinvest in themselves.

Abiding concern implies interest, respect, consideration, and acceptance. It does not include the over-involvement that may cause us to panic along with our clients, be furious with those who hurt or disappoint them, become overprotective and possessive, or feel indifferent to our own personal needs. Over-involvement causes us to lose our perspective and objectivity and become partisan members of our clients' lives.

Contrary to popular belief, a counselor does not need to admire or even like a client in order to show caring and involvement. Concern for the client's welfare and progress is not contingent upon his or her personal appeal, our opinion of the person, or whether or not we would choose that person as a friend. We should depend on our personal feelings and reactions to infer how others react to our clients. In this way, we may be able to enjoy a client's playfulness and still see it as a nuisance to the client's teachers. While we may admire and even enjoy certain client characteristics, like generosity or self-sacrifice, we should not imagine that such characteristics are always in clients' best interests.

A second essential characteristic of counselors is *acceptance of one's self and others*. The counselor's basic tool is the ability to understand the relationship between feelings and behavior, between past and current experience, and between counselor and client. But this understanding is limited when counselors are not tolerant of feelings and behavior in themselves and in others.

Notions of morality, which start very early in our lives, are not easy to suspend. But if we judge others or ourselves too rigidly, these notions get in our way as counselors. Condemnation or approval is incompatible with curiosity, an important asset of a counselor, and will make it hard to understand and inquire about behavior of which we disapprove. If our real concern is whether our clients' behavior is right or wrong, we will not encourage their free expressions of feelings or fantasies. Passing moral judgment also reduces our ability to empathize with clients.

Counseling is not, however, amoral or antimoral. Understanding behavior is not the same as condoning it or excusing it. The methods of counseling—understanding psychological patterns, identifying disguised motives, articulating the underlying expectations—can be badly misused. These patterns, motives, and expectations are not facts in the same sense as observable actions. These are hypotheses which, in counseling, may help the client gain self-awareness and understanding and find more constructive expression. As counselors, we have to hold individuals responsible for their deeds. They have to live in the real world, where they will be judged by what they do, not by what they mean or feel. If we view psychological and emotional forces as dominant, overwhelming, and beyond control—as excuses for rather than explanations of behavior—we see clients as passive victims of their psyches, unable to be rational. Psychodynamic explanations of our actions do not relieve us from being morally responsible for them.

The counseling task primarily consists of understanding clients and communicating our understanding without disapproval or coercion. To do this, we must be able to see and accept what *is,* rather than what should or should not be, in ourselves as well as others. Acceptance of ourselves is the basis for our acceptance of others. Accepting ourselves enables us to use our feelings, reactions, limitations, and errors as tools in counseling others. Novices may try to undo or deny their human responsiveness to match some ideal or model. They believe that "good" counselors are never angered, frustrated, disturbed, or aroused by clients; therefore, they pretend to feel nothing. But counselors who recognize, admit, and accept their feelings are more genuinely in control. Suppressing a reaction because "it is not right to feel that way" leads to unexpected and undesirable results and may encourage clients to do the same.

In counseling, it is better to know and accept ourselves, including our limitations, than it is to act as if we were someone else. We do not need to be perfect to be good counselors; we need to be real. Of all the talents trainees bring to the role of counselor, self-acceptance seems to be the most important—and the most difficult to teach. That is one reason why psychotherapy facilitates learning therapeutic skills; for some people, it does more than any course or training experience.

Finally, the third essential in a counselor is *the courage to deal with the risks and realities of the task.* Based on our own personal experiences with helping friends, most of us start with an unrealistic view of the counseling role. We imagine that, as counselors, our efforts will earn us gratitude, praise, and a constant sense of accomplishment. We forget that, as friends, our help is an unexpected and appreciated bonus, but as counselors, it is the only measure of our worth—and our efforts may not match our clients' expectations. It takes courage to be a counselor.

Since clients are, initially, strangers, we have to get to know them. We have to begin as relatively passive listeners, which is more difficult than most of us can imagine. Listening exposes us to the painful and complex difficulties which clients experience. Clients' problems do not emerge in neat puzzles ready for us to "solve" on first hearing. Usually clients have exhausted many sources of support before they even get to us, so it is naive (and a bit insulting) to imagine that we have instant answers or remedies. Waiting for genuine understanding to emerge is demanding.

It also takes courage to face the fact that counselors are catalysts rather than initiators of change. When progress occurs, clients, more often than counselors, deserve the credit and applause. Rarely is there one counseling intervention or statement that in itself causes dramatic psychological change. To enable clients to take charge of their lives and destinies, our role should be more supportive and facilitative than commanding. Much of the control is not in our hands. Growth and development come from within the client; we are only midwives. We are also observers, the essential members of a special audience; but we are never the featured players. It takes courage to persist at a task that is so self-effacing.

It takes courage to undertake a task requiring honesty and frankness, continuous evaluation, and uncertain rewards. It is painful to face the fears and feelings of our clients, and instead of minimizing them, explore them. It takes courage to confront clients with their impact on others since they may respond with anger, hurt, or denial. While weathering the turbulence of one's own life, it is not always easy to immerse ourselves in the difficulties of others. Entering clients' lives, sharing our own personal and emotional resources, and helping them achieve their goals is risky and demanding; but leaving when the work is done is, perhaps, hardest of all.

A Method for Evaluating Counseling Relationships

The demands of the counseling role described in preceding pages are tough—both for beginners and for more experienced practitioners. Therefore, the standards must be applied with wisdom and common sense, not rigidity. Identifying many problems in the course of counseling does not mean that a counselor is inadequate; conversely, noticing very few does not mean a counselor is good. Seeing no danger at all is likely to be an illusion. Counselors are better off anticipating obstacles that don't materialize instead of missing those that may sink the ship.

In order to help you identify potentially troublesome areas, the questions that follow provide a means to examine your expectations and experiences in counseling relationships. Dangers may arise from many sources: from the circumstances in which you work; from the type of person you are; from your involvement and investment in the client; or from your expectations of how counseling should progress and clients respond. The criteria outlined above are important to consider even if your counseling is done according to strict rules prescribed by others, involves different methods, or is aimed at different goals than those presented here. These evaluation questions are offered for a special purpose.

Experienced counselors have an advantage over the inexperienced—they have a baseline for comparison. They know how they typically function in the counseling role and how they usually feel about and relate to clients. Therefore, they know when they are deviating from their own styles and standards. Their awareness helps them better understand particular clients, because they have an internal measure by which to gauge clients' impact on them and their impact on clients. Inexperienced counselors have no such baseline. So the questions that follow can be used as a means of comparison until you develop an awareness of your style and typical emotional investment. While not equivalent to case supervision by an expert, these questions are a useful means of self-examination and are also adaptable to group or individual supervision.

Counseling Is a Working Relationship

- How is your counseling relationship structured?

• Is it structured as a working relationship or is it more social, casual, or friendly?

• Are you and the client able to keep the focus serious and purposeful?

• Do you find it difficult to face issues directly?

• Are you apt to offer compliments or false assurances at difficult moments?

Counseling Is Focused on the Client

• Are you able to postpone irrelevant personal concerns and focus clearly on the client?

• Do you find yourself giving advice, expressing your opinion, lecturing, or avoiding emotional topics?

• Do you often interrupt?

• Do you always want to be right?

• Do you expect or seek appreciation for your contributions?

• Do you find your own needs incompatible with counseling at times? How do you handle these instances?

Counseling Has Specified Goals

• Do you and the client establish realistic and appropriate objectives?

• Do you try to encourage personal disclosure from the client for its own sake?

• Are your expectations for the relationship too ambitious, unspecified, or confused? Are you able to revise objectives when you learn more about the client?

• Do you try to evaluate progress toward the stated goals as counseling goes along?

Counseling Has a Regular and Limited Time Frame

• Do you decide on and then hold to a specified time schedule with the client?

• Are you able to end sessions on time?

• Do you observe how the client uses the time available?

• Do you overextend yourself?

• Do you tell the client if you are unable to meet as scheduled?

• Is there a date by which the relationship must end? Is it known to the client? Is it sufficient to reach your objectives?

Counseling Focuses on the Here-and-Now

• Is the relationship focused on problems in the present? On past experience? On future possibilities?

• Do you use the client's past experience as a basis for understanding, or does it serve as an excuse for current behavior?

• Is your work focused on the client's behavior or on others in the client's life?

• Are you able to use your current feelings, positive and negative, in the service of the client?

• Do you hold the client responsible for efforts which might make future expectations and objectives possible?

Counseling Has Boundaries

• Have you established boundaries that allow you and the client to define the task? Have you specified your methods, rules, availabilities, and limits?

• Are you clear about and observant of the rules of confidentiality?

• Do you have any other association with the client? How does it affect or interfere with counseling?

• Do you feel a personal involvement with the client that exceeds sensible and established boundaries? If so, how do you handle these feelings?

• Does the client ask or want to extend the boundaries? How do you deal with such requests?

Counseling Is Based on a Joint Contract

• Are you able to establish joint contracts and work in partnership with the client?

• Do you set goals independent of the client?

• Does the client have unrealistic expectations about what you are able to do as a counselor? How do you handle them?

• Are you realistic about the limitations of your role, your ability, or your time?

• Do you think of yourself as a partner, or as an advisor?

• Do you recognize and deal with signs of hesitancy, anger, or resistance?

• Do you hold the client responsible in terms of the contract?

• Do you examine how the partnership is working and identify relationship problems along the way?

Counseling Skills

Capacity to Face Reality

• How well can you confront and deal with the realities facing the client?

• Are you tempted to distort, minimize, deny, or avoid difficulties?

• Can you tolerate your client's distress?

• Do you offer reassurance, flattery, or encouragement at times when they are not warranted?

• Do you deny or disguise your feelings about client behavior and characteristics?

Ability to Empathize

• Do you experience problems in empathizing with clients?

• Are you able to see things the way clients see them and understand their feelings? Do you find this more difficult at some times than others?

• Does your empathy lead you to become overly involved or to lose perspective and objectivity at times?

• Do you sometimes see clients as victims without resources to act in their own behalf?

• Do you assume you know how the client feels without exploring the differences between you?

Willingness to Lend Support

• Are you impatient, discouraged, or annoyed with the pace of counseling? How do you handle these feelings?

• Do you resent the client who does not change readily, or do you attribute slow progress to your inadequacy?

• Do you expect that identifying psychological problems will eradicate them?

• Are you aware of small differences and changes in the client if and when they occur?

• Are you attentive to signs of resistance, transference, or other interferences in the relationship?

• Are you outcome- or client-oriented?

Abiding Concern

• Do you feel and are you able to show concern in ways that are apparent to the client?

• Are you able to pick up or intuit the client's feelings or unspoken concerns with accuracy? Do you test them out?

• Do your observations enable clients to see themselves better?

• Do you lose interest or sometimes withdraw from involvement?

• Does your concern become excessive and result in unnecessary or inappropriate action?

• Do you neglect yourself or your other commitments out of concern?

• Do you become overprotective or try to do things for clients that they can do themselves?

• Are you interested in clients you like, while indifferent to those you find less appealing?

- How do your personal preferences or prejudices affect your work with clients?

Acceptance of Self and Others

- Do you find it hard to accept clients and their behavior? What about yourself and your behavior?
- Do you experience feelings of disapproval or repugnance at times?
- Do you find it difficult to understand behavior or characteristics that offend you?
- Do you know what models or standards of comparison you use to assess yourself? Are they realistic? Are they useful?
- Can you recognize and admit to yourself feelings clients have evoked in you?
- Do you experience difficulties with clients whose values and behavior differ from yours?
- Do you condone destructive or self-destructive behavior in clients because you can understand the reasons behind it?
- Are you able to communicate your observations of clients without showing disapproval or condemnation?
- Are you patient and tolerant of yourself at difficult moments?

Courage in Dealing with the Risks and Realities of Counseling

- Does your experience differ from your expectations of yourself in the helping role?
- Do you back away from problems or meet them squarely?
- Do you encourage and permit clients to express whatever negative feelings they have toward you or toward the helping process?
- Do you expect appreciation and gratitude for your efforts?
- Are you able to persist when things do not go well?
- Are you able to honestly evaluate clients' progress? Can you do this with them?

• Are you able to end counseling relationships when it is necessary or time to do so?

Final Statement

If some of your answers or observations disappoint you and make you want to improve your counseling abilities, then you are beginning to think as professionals think. Their ultimate responsibility is to recognize their own errors, deviations, and problems in the helping relationship and work to understand and correct them. One definition of the word "professional" is an individual who upholds the standards and responsibilities of those belonging to a professional group; by this definition, nonprofessionals can equal professionals. To do so, they too must continually examine their management of counseling relationships, identify and address problems as they occur, and recognize and confront the obstacles and challenges which counseling presents.

APPENDIX

Ethical Standards of the American Association for Counseling and Development*

SECTION B: Counseling Relationship

This section refers to practices and procedures of individual and/or group counseling relationships.

The member must recognize the need for client freedom of choice. Under those circumstances where this is not possible, the member must apprise clients of restrictions that may limit their freedom of choice.

B.1. The member's *primary* obligation is to respect the integrity and promote the welfare of the client(s), whether the client(s) is (are) assisted individually or in a group relationship. In a group setting, the member is also responsible for taking reasonable precautions to protect individuals from physical and/or psychological trauma resulting from interaction within the group.

B.2. The counseling relationship and information resulting therefrom must be kept confidential, consistent with the obligations of the member as a professional person. In a group counseling setting the counselor must set a norm of confidentiality regarding all group participants' disclosures.

B.3. If an individual is already in a counseling relationship with another professional person, the member does not enter into a counseling relationship without first contacting and receiving the approval of that other professional. If the member discovers that the client is in another counseling relationship after the counseling relationship begins, the member must gain the consent of the other professional or terminate the relationship, unless the client elects to terminate the other relationship.

*Formerly the American Personnel and Guidance Association.

B.4. When the client's condition indicates that there is clear and imminent danger to the client or others, the member must take reasonable personal action or inform responsible authorities. Consultation with other professionals must be used where possible. The assumption of responsibility for the client(s) behavior must be taken only after careful deliberation. The client must be involved in the resumption of responsibility as quickly as possible.

B.5. Records of the counseling relationship, including interview notes, test data, correspondence, tape recordings, and other documents, are to be considered professional information for use in counseling, and they should not be considered a part of the records of the institution or agency in which the counselor is employed unless specified by state statute or regulation. Revelation to others of counseling material must occur only upon the expressed consent of the client.

B.6. Use of data derived from a counseling relationship for purposes of counselor training or research shall be confined to content that can be disguised to ensure full protection of the identity of the subject client.

B.7. The member must inform the client of the purposes, goals, techniques, rules of procedure and limitations that may affect the relationship at or before the time that the counseling relationship is entered.

B.8. The member must screen prospective group participants, especially when the emphasis is on self-understanding and growth through self-disclosure. The member must maintain an awareness of the group participants' compatibility throughout the life of the group.

B.9. The member may choose to consult with any other professionally competent person about a client. In choosing a consultant, the member must avoid placing the consultant in a conflict-of-interest situation that would preclude the consultant's being a proper party to the member's efforts to help the client.

B.10. If the member determines an inability to be of professional assistance to the client, the member must either avoid initiating the counseling relationship or immediately terminate that relationship. In either event, the member must suggest appropriate alternatives. (The member must be knowledgeable about referral resources so that a satisfactory referral can be initiated.) In the event the client declines the suggested referral, the member is not obligated to continue the relationship.

B.11. When the member has other relationships, particularly of an administrative, supervisory and/or evaluative nature with an individual seeking counseling services, the member must not serve as the counselor but should refer the individual to another professional. Only in instances where such an alternative is unavailable and where the individual's situation warrants counseling intervention should the member enter into and/or maintain a counseling relationship. Dual relationships with clients that might impair the member's objectivity and professional judgment (e.g., as with close friends or relatives, sexual intimacies with any client) must be avoided and/or the counseling relationship terminated through referral to another competent professional.

B.12. All experimental methods of treatment must be clearly indicated to prospective recipients and safety precautions are to be adhered to by the member.

B.13. When the member is engaged in short-term group treatment/training programs (e.g., marathons and other encounter-type or growth groups), the member ensures that there is professional assistance available during and following the group experience.

B.14. Should the member be engaged in a work setting that calls for any variation from the above statements, the member is obligated to consult with other professionals whenever possible to consider justifiable alternatives.

Selected Grove Press Paperbacks

E732 ALLEN, DONALD & BUTTERICK, GEORGE F., eds. / The Postmoderns: The New American Poetry Revised 1945-1960 / $9.95

B472 ANONYMOUS / Beatrice / $3.95

B445 ANONYMOUS / The Boudoir / $3.95

B334 ANONYMOUS / My Secret Life / $4.95

B415 ARDEN, JOHN / Plays: One (Serjeant Musgrave's Dance, The Workhouse Donkey, Armstrong's Last Goodnight) / $4.95

B422 AYCKBOURN, ALAN / The Norman Conquests: Table Manners; Living Together; Round and Round the Garden / $6.95

E835 BARASH, DAVID, and LIPTON, JUDITH / Stop Nuclear War! A Handbook / $7.95

B425 BARNES, JOHN / Evita — First Lady: A Biography of Eva Peron / $4.95

E781 BECKETT, SAMUEL / Ill Seen Ill Said / $4.95

E96 BECKETT, SAMUEL / Endgame / $4.95

B78 BECKETT, SAMUEL / Three Novels: Molloy, Malone Dies and The Unnamable / $4.95

E33 BECKETT, SAMUEL / Waiting for Godot / $3.50

B411 BEHAN, BRENDAN / The Complete Plays (The Hostage, The Quare Fellow, Richard's Cork Leg, Three One Act Plays for Radio) / $4.95

E417 BIRCH, CYRIL & KEENE, DONALD, eds. / Anthology of Chinese Literature, Vol. I: From Early Times to the 14th Century / $14.95

E368 BORGES, JORGE LUIS / Ficciones / $6.95

E472 BORGES, JORGE LUIS / A Personal Anthology / $6.95

B312 BRECHT, BERTOLT / The Caucasian Chalk Circle / $2.95

B117 BRECHT, BERTOLT / The Good Woman of Setzuan / $2.95

B120 BRECHT, BERTOLT / Galileo / $2.95

B108 BRECHT, BERTOLT / Mother Courage and Her Children / $2.45

B333 BRECHT, BERTOLT / Threepenny Opera / $2.45

E580 BRETON, ANDRE / Nadja / $5.95

B147 BULGAKOV, MIKHAIL / The Master and Margarita / $4.95

B115 BURROUGHS, WILLIAM S. / Naked Lunch / $3.95

B446 BURROUGHS, WILLIAM S. / The Soft Machine, Nova Express, The Wild Boys / $5.95

E793 COHN, RUBY / New American Dramatists: 1960-1980 / $7.95

E804 COOVER, ROBERT / Spanking the Maid / $4.95

E742 COWARD, NOEL / Three Plays (Private Lives, Hay Fever, Blithe Spirit) / $4.50

B442 CRAFTS, KATHY, & HAUTHER, BRENDA / How To Beat the System: The Student's Guide to Good Grades / $3.95
E869 CROCKETT, JIM, ed. / The Guitar Player Book (Revised and Updated Edition) / $11.95
E190 CUMMINGS, E.E. / 100 Selected Poems / $2.95
E808 DURAS, MARGUERITE / Four Novels: The Square; 10:30 on a Summer Night; The Afternoon of Mr. Andesmas; Moderato Cantabile / $9.95
E380 DURRENMATT, FRIEDRICH / The Physicists / $6.95
B342 FANON, FRANTZ / The Wretched of the Earth / $4.95
E47 FROMM, ERICH / The Forgotten Language / $4.95
B389 GENET, JEAN / Our Lady of the Flowers / $3.95
E760 GERVASI, TOM / Arsenal of Democracy II / $12.95
E792 GETTLEMAN, MARVIN, et. al., eds. / El Salvador: Central America in the New Cold War / $8.95
E830 GIBBS, LOIS MARIE / Love Canal: My Story / $6.95
E704 GINSBERG, ALLEN / Journals: Early Fifties Early Sixties / $6.95
B437 GIRODIAS, MAURICE, ed. / The Olympia Reader / $5.95
E720 GOMBROWICZ, WITOLD / Three Novels: Ferdydurke, Pornografia and Cosmos / $9.95
B448 GOVER, ROBERT / One Hundred Dollar Misunderstanding / $2.95
B376 GREENE, GERALD and CAROLINE / SM: The Last Taboo / $2.95
E769 HARWOOD, RONALD / The Dresser / $5.95
E446 HAVEL, VACLAV / The Memorandum / $5.95
B306 HERNTON, CALVIN / Sex and Racism in America / $2.95
B436 HODEIR, ANDRE / Jazz: Its Evolution and Essence / $3.95
B417 INGE, WILLIAM / Four Plays (Come Back, Little Sheba; Picnic; Bus Stop; The Dark at the Top of the Stairs) / $7.95
E259 IONESCO, EUGENE / Rhinoceros & Other Plays / $4.95
E496 JARRY, ALFRED / The Ubu Plays (Ubu Rex, Ubu Cuckolded, Ubu Enchained) / $9.95
E216 KEENE, DONALD, ed. / Anthology of Japanese Literature: Earliest Era to Mid-19th Century / $12.50
E552 KEROUAC, JACK / Mexico City Blues / $5.95
B394 KEROUAC, JACK / Dr. Sax / $3.95
B454 KEROUAC, JACK / The Subterraneans / $3.50
B479 LAWRENCE, D.H. / Lady Chatterley's Lover / $3.95
B262 LESTER, JULIUS / Black Folktales / $4.95
B351 MALCOLM X (Breitman, ed.) / Malcolm X Speaks / $3.95
E741 MALRAUX, ANDRE / Man's Hope / $12.50

E697 MAMET, DAVID / American Buffalo / $5.95
E709 MAMET, DAVID / A Life in the Theatre / $6.95
E712 MAMET, DAVID / Sexual Perversity in Chicago & The Duck Variations / $5.95
E801 MARIANI, PAUL / Crossing Cocytus / $5.95
B325 MILLER, HENRY / Sexus / $5.95
B10 MILLER, HENRY / Tropic of Cancer / $3.95
B59 MILLER, HENRY / Tropic of Capricorn / $3.95
E789 MROZEK, SLAWOMIR / Striptease, Tango, Vatzlav: Three Plays / $12.50
E636 NERUDA, PABLO / Five Decades Poems 1925-1970. Bilingual ed. / $8.95
E364 NERUDA, PABLO / Selected Poems. Bilingual ed. / $6.95
B429 ODETS, CLIFFORD / Six Plays (Waiting for Lefty; Awake and Sing; Golden Boy; Rocket to the Moon; Till the Day I Die; Paradise Lost) / $7.95
E807 OE, KENZABURO / A Personal Matter / $6.95
E687 OE, KENZABURO / Teach Us To Outgrow Our Madness / $4.95
E359 PAZ, OCTAVIO / The Labyrinth of Solitude. Life and Thought in Mexico / $7.95
E724 PINTER, HAROLD / Betrayal / $3.95
E315 PINTER, HAROLD / The Birthday Party & The Room / $6.95
E299 PINTER, HAROLD / The Caretaker The Dumb Waiter / $4.95
E411 PINTER, HAROLD / The Homecoming / $4.95
E606 PINTER, HAROLD / Old Times / $3.95
E641 RAHULA, WALPOLA / What The Buddha Taught / $6.95
B438 REAGE, PAULINE / Story of O, Part II: Return to the Chateau / $3.95
B504 RECHY, JOHN / City of Night / $5.95
E930 RECHY, JOHN / Numbers / $5.95
E806 ROBBE-GRILLET, ALAIN / Djinn / $4.95
B133 ROBBE-GRILLET, ALAIN / The Voyeur / $2.95
B207 RULFO, JUAN / Pedro Paramo / $3.95
B138 SADE, MARQUIS DE / The 120 Days of Sodom and Other Writings / $12.50
B313 SELBY, HUBERT / Last Exit to Brooklyn / $2.95
E763 SHAWN, WALLACE, and GREGORY, ANDRE / My Dinner with Andre / $5.95
SILKO, LESLIE / Storyteller / $9.95
B456 SINGH, KHUSHWANT / Train to Pakistan / $3.25
B618 SNOW, EDGAR / Red Star Over China / $8.95
E785 SRI NISARGADATTA MAHARAJ / Seeds of Consciousness / $9.95

E626 STOPPARD, TOM / Jumpers / $2.95

B319 STOPPARD, TOM / Rosencrantz and Guildenstern Are Dead / $3.95

E661 STOPPARD, TOM / Travesties / $3.95

B341 SUZUKI, D. T. / Introduction to Zen Buddhism / $2.95

E231 SUZUKI, D. T. / Manual of Zen Buddhism / $5.95

E749 THELWELL, MICHAEL / The Harder They Come / $7.95

B474 TOOLE, JOHN KENNEDY / A Confederacy of Dunces / $3.95

E559 TUTUOLA, AMOS / My Life in the Bush of Ghosts / $6.95

B506 TUTUOLA, AMOS / The Palm-Wine Drunkard / $4.50

E112 WALEY, ARTHUR / Monkey / $6.95

E84 WALEY, ARTHUR / The Way and Its Power: A Study of the Tao Te Ching and Its Place in Chinese Thought / $6.95

E219 WATTS, ALAN W. / The Spirit of Zen / $3.95

GROVE PRESS, INC., 196 West Houston St., New York, N.Y. 10014